Sing, Sing, Sing!

Published by Indies United Publishing House, LLC
First Edition published July 2025

Edited by Meredith Phillips

Cover art designed by Tatiana Villa

ISBN: 978-1-64456-835-4 [Hardcover]
ISBN: 978-1-64456-836-1 [Paperback]
ISBN: 978-1-64456-837-8 [Kindle]
ISBN: 978-1-64456-838-5 [ePub]

Library of Congress Control Number: 2025910384

INDIES UNITED PUBLISHING HOUSE, LLC
P.O. BOX 3071
QUINCY, IL 62305-3071
www.indiesunited.net

This book is dedicated to my mother. She rose from a long line of women who were fierce and determined survivors. I am grateful that the line continues.

PREFACE

Sing, Sing, Sing! was written by musician Louis Prima in 1935 and actually had words, although most of us have never heard them. It quickly became an instrumental, and in a 1938 Carnegie Hall performance, drummer Gene Krupa and the Benny Goodman Orchestra changed this anthem of the Jazz Age for all time.

That night, Krupa refused to quit playing at the end of the planned arrangement, and as he drove the tom-tom beat of the drums forward, various musicians stood up and took the spotlight, contributing their own solo to the twelve minute long extravaganza.

After that, whenever the band performed, the audience would demand that the closing musical piece be Sing, Sing, Sing! It became a living and changing expression of the era.

Use the QR code below to listen to this historical performance.

Sing, Sing, Sing!

Lexa M. Mack

INDIES UNITED
PUBLISHING HOUSE, LLC

CHAPTER ONE

April 1943

Wind blustered between the sturdy apartment buildings kicking up bits of paper and dust as Tilda dragged her suitcase down the steps of the front stoop. She'd hoped to purchase a less cumbersome bag, but the luggage manufacturers were now only making war supplies. The magazine ads even promised they'd be back after the war. For now, she'd had to settle for borrowing an unmatched set from her aunt.

Her father had pulled up directly in front of the building and her cosmetics case sat in the back seat of his cab. As he hefted the larger bag in and closed the trunk she turned to gaze up at the five-story apartment building. At Christmas most of the windows would have been strung with decorations, but now many of them boasted only white banners trimmed in red and carrying the blue stars that signified a family member in the military. The one in the window of her parents' apartment carried three blue stars for her two brothers and her brother-in-law. There were a few windows in the building adorned with the sad gold stars that signified the loss of a son, father, or sometimes a daughter.

"Well, that's it then. Are you ready?" Her father was not a patient man.

"Sure, Pop. I've got everything. Thanks so much for the ride."

"It's the least I could do."

"Yeah, but I had thought I might make the walk to Grand Central just to say good-bye to the city."

Her father snorted as he hefted his frame into the driver's seat. "I'd have liked to see you haul all this luggage down there on your own."

Tilda smiled. Her father wouldn't have understood how she could be happy to be going and yet so sad to be leaving.

She opened the cab door and slid into the front seat.

"Ain't you gonna sit in the back like a real fare?"

"Not this time. I want to be right here next to you."

She wanted to tell him to drive really slowly and take the long route so she could say goodbye to all her memories, but she didn't think that would go over very well. It was a working day for him, and she knew that each eager, arm-waving potential customer they passed up would cause him pain.

Queens had been her home as long as she could remember, and she knew the route they would take by heart. First over the Queensboro Bridge where she'd be able to gaze out over the city, then a left at Central Park and the congested ride down Fifth Avenue to 42nd Street and Grand Central Station.

She gazed out the window at some of the sights that you would only see in New York City. Gone were the business-suited men selling apples on the street corners and the long bread lines of the Depression. Of course, those sights would not have been right on Fifth Avenue. The beginning of the war finally signaled the end of the long economic recovery after the Wall Street Crash. Today she spotted commuters on roller skates cruising down the sidewalks putting their own and the pedestrians' lives in danger but saving gasoline. It looked like fun.

She loved the city: the grimy tenements, the soaring skyscrapers, the sludgy East and Hudson rivers. There was energy there that she knew she would never find any place else on the earth. She hoped she would be back, but for now she needed to venture out and figure out what was going on in the rest of the world.

New York City was the hardest city to live in, but the easiest to stay in. She had become confused by the difference between The City and the rest of the world. There was war everywhere. Cities were burning, but New York City chugged along like nothing else mattered: buildings going up, shows being produced, crowds ebbing and flowing through the streets. After the Depression, New York embraced the war. It signaled deliverance from sadness and gave everything new purpose. There were deals to make. The stock market had finally been resurrected. New York was a beacon on the hill. People came here to escape from where they had been, but Tilda felt like she needed to escape New York City to find out who she was.

The Depression years had been chaotic. At work she had met women who surprised her. Colored women who worked during the day next to her, putting out the food that was magically dispensed through the little windows of the Automat, but who at night met in the apartments and bars of Harlem to talk about ideas and change.

So many people had poured into her city during the lean times, and apartments and lodgings were hard to come by. She had attended more than a few rent parties; she'd paid her two bits and brought her own bottle of wine. Food had been plentiful and not always what she was used to. Eventually, she'd stopped asking what ingredients were in the dishes placed before her and set her mind to just enjoying what was exotic to her tastes. The music and dancing were not the sedate offerings of her parents' friends' parties. Negro writers and actors drank cheap liquor and argued fervently over social issues.

Riding in the front seat of her father's cab she was able to take in and cherish all of the sights, all of the people, all of the craziness.

Tilda was tall and athletic looking. Her honey-blond hair may have come from a bottle, but it wasn't brassy or cheap; it suited her, and the wind that blew through her open window brushed it back from her face. She was not leaving for good, just for a little while. Like her two brothers and brother-in-law were just off fighting for a time and would be coming home to pick up where they left off before long.

People were saying it would be over soon, any day, in a few weeks, or months, but they had been saying that for years now. It had started before the Japs had bombed Pearl Harbor. Europe had been struggling long before that. It was too late to have ended quickly.

Everyone just wanted it all to be over so that they could go on with their lives and pretend it had never happened. They wanted their lovers back, to make homes, to make livings, to have babies, and to never think about war again. If they could only hang on a little bit longer. If they could only survive the relentless war machine that sucked up everything: the men, the metal, the meat, the energy, the future of all who waited for it to be over.

Many of the men you saw on the streets were in uniform, either proudly wearing their medals or their newly issued clothing or struggling under the weight of those same medals and the horrors they had seen or committed. Sometimes they had limps or missing limbs to attest to the carnage they had seen.

She had saved her money, so she had enough to go someplace else, do something different. She would take her time; there was no place she needed to be. She just had to outlast the Axis. Today she would buy a ticket to someplace she had never been before. Maybe she would stay there for a while, or maybe she would buy another ticket and move on. Maybe she would get only as far as New Jersey and change her mind. Maybe she would go all the way to San Francisco and then change her mind.

Outside the massive entrance of the train station, she stood with her luggage and watched her father's cab swerve across the lanes and swoop in to pick up his next fare. Turning toward the building, she hefted her bags and strode determinedly through the huge doors.

When she entered the cavernous hall, she felt dwarfed by the size and bustle of it. She stopped on the landing inside the wide entrance. The broad rotunda of the building was full of people coursing in all directions. The kiosk in the center slowed the flow as the stream of people swirled around it. Of course, she'd been there many times, but usually to greet family from other cities coming to visit. This building was meant to overwhelm and impress, and it did. One of her visiting aunts had sworn that she had seen all she needed to of New York City; she could go home a happy woman after having only visited Grand Central Station.

Of course, before the war it had been even busier. Now travel was curtailed as much as possible to conserve fuel for the war effort. A poster on the wall of a scowling Uncle Sam demanded, "Is this trip really necessary?" People didn't just take off to Florida or go to Chicago for the weekend now. You had to be going someplace important, to do something that couldn't wait.

Tilda had already come up with several good reasons for her trip, none of which were true, but each of which could be pulled out of her hat, if she were challenged. She was quite proud of herself for being so ingenious and prepared. Her favorite was the story where she was a bride hurrying to marry her beloved before he shipped off overseas. She had spent one whole evening concocting the details, almost to the point of believing them. At one point she nearly managed to urge a single tear from her eye, but lost interest before it could spill down her cheek.

CHAPTER TWO

July 1943

Texas! Rhetta had never been out of the state, never seen any reason to go. Everything she needed was right there under the endless sky hovering above the vast landscape. All the people she loved had been there. But, one by one they had gone. First Pa, then Ma a few years later. Her sister Sarah lived in far-off Sugar Land. Her oldest son had gone off to fight the war and wouldn't be coming back. Now Dusty, her younger son, was driving away to who knows what and where.

Dusty shoved his final suitcase into the back of the station wagon along with the last spare tire in Texas and the box of gifts for his Aunt Sarah's family.

Rhetta stood at the base of the steps. She smiled, hoping that her husband would relent and come out to say goodbye, although she knew he would not. To him his son was deserting everything that mattered and was leaving him to bear the burden. Odd he hadn't felt that way when Chet left for the war. There'd been a big farewell barbecue with folks from all over the state. They'd had fireworks, and dancing, and she remembered a lot of laughing, although she couldn't recall what they'd had to laugh about.

Chet had been big, like Texas. Not so much in size as in life. He'd loved the ranch and learned the business of it since he was a child. When they found oil, he'd learned that business, too. He was ready and anxious to take over the world, beginning with the ranch.

She could see Chet when she looked at her younger son, Earl. Known his whole life as Dusty Rhodes, he had a quieter manner. He was a little less confident and was not quite so dashing and handsome. But there was strength there, and he would find a way to contribute without having to take his brother's place. Dusty had never been groomed to take over the ranch, and just because Chet was dead didn't mean you could stuff Dusty into his older brother's boots.

She would miss their talks in the sunny kitchen, about books and politics beyond the scope of the local elections that absorbed her husband's interest. She didn't know who she'd talk to now, with her son going to California. She and Bud had never talked much. It hadn't mattered when the boys were small, and they were a struggling rancher and his wife. Before the oil derricks, the local elections, and the prissy wives of Bud's town cronies. They'd worked hard together: riding, mending fences, planting the garden, staying up late to pore over the bills and the money that never seemed to quite go far enough. She'd been known to do ironing for folks, and to sell eggs and her favorite apple pie jam at a roadside stand. She could still rustle up enough grub to feed all the hands a hearty breakfast, milk the dairy cows, feed the chickens, and be ready to ride out before those town wives could get up and sip their morning tea. But she didn't have to do that now.

She had "help." Little Mexican women with whom she had worked out a mixture of Spanish and English that allowed her to communicate about what she needed done. Bud didn't like it when she mentioned the old days in polite company; that mix of snotty attitude and pretentious ideas that passed for socializing. If he wasn't exactly ashamed of her, he at least wished she could pretend to be more like the other wives.

It was nice to have money, she supposed. The boys had gone to college; they'd been able to pay cash money for the Ford station wagon that Dusty was leaving in. She was able to drive the farm pickup truck, and she didn't really need to drive anyplace much, with gas rationing and all. She only left the farm to respond to those late-night phone calls from women needing a midwife to help them bring another of their slew of youngsters into the world. Even that had slowed down since the war started, with most of the men away.

She liked tending her garden and her roses, gathering the eggs from her hens, each one of whom she knew by name. Having money gave her more time to read and more time to listen to the radio. She struggled to figure out what was really going on out in this crazy world. It meant she could share the bounty of her hands with the women who worked for her, paying them cash, but including eggs and produce from her garden in the rewards.

The luncheon yesterday had been a disaster. Her señoritas had cleaned the house until it sparkled, they had made a lovely lunch, and the house was full of roses from her yard. Coffee was hard to come by, so she'd opted for tea served from the silver tea service Bud had bought her last Christmas (she'd asked for a new Western saddle). Three of the town ladies attended and all had been well until one of them started in criticizing Eleanor Roosevelt. She wouldn't have minded if they lit into Franklin a bit, but Eleanor was off limits. She hadn't raised the roof, but she nipped that line of talk in the bud. Conversation had foundered after that and the ladies, who had driven over together to save gas, left before dessert was served.

Dusty finished closing up the car and turned back toward the house. He looked up at the shaded window of his dad's office and seemed to consider going back in to say good-bye. After a few moments he turned back to Rhetta and swept her up in a big bear hug. "Thanks for everything, Ma. I won't be gone forever and when I come back, I'll have done something you and Dad can be proud of."

"You know we're as proud of you as can be, already." The words sounded hollow even to her, but she smiled and tried to hold back any lurking tears.

"Yeah, well, you're gonna be even prouder. The war will be over soon, and someone needs to be ready to build up a new world." He hugged her once more and slid behind the wheel of the station wagon. "Thanks again for the loan of the car. Hope the gas stations don't question the midwife sticker too much."

"You just tell 'em you're running an errand for your mama. They'll be fine."

Neither of them witnessed the tweak of the curtain falling back into place at the upper window. Bud had not been able to hear their words. When he stepped back to his desk, he picked up the bottle of whiskey there and poured another two fingers. "Well, hell," was all he said before he sat down and pulled the ledger back in front of him.

Rhetta stood for several minutes after her son drove off, watching the car get smaller and fainter in the distance, until it disappeared completely. Then she turned and walked into the house.

CHAPTER THREE

July 1943

Dusty saw his mother's image disappear in the rearview mirror as the station wagon trundled along the dirt road to the pavement half a mile from the house. He hated leaving her, but he knew that he, unlike his older brother, would be returning home one day. Chet had made a difference, had sacrificed his life, and now Dusty needed to find his own way to contribute.

Staying here on the ranch, trying to make sense of running it, contributed beef and oil for the troops, but it would go on without him. No soldier would go hungry because he hadn't stayed in Texas butting heads with his stubborn father. The cattle would still be driven, the oil would continue to pump, and his father would still mourn his oldest son. But, Dusty would be free.

Dusty was backtracking a bit driving east from Pecos to Sugar Land to pick up his cousin. Los Angeles was west, but the adventure had begun, and his heart lightened as he traveled down the highway. He kept the "battle wagon," as he called the Ford, at the fuel-and-rubber-saving Victory Speed Limit of thirty-five miles per hour. He reckoned it would take him fifteen hours to drive from Pecos to Sugar Land and he was getting a later start than he had intended. The highway through Houston was the most direct so he planned his route that way. He had expected to sleep in the car and finish up his trip the next day, until he got just past Ft. Stockton and changed his plan.

A lone man stood on the side of the highway gazing after the quickly disappearing car heading east. Well, no loss, he was headed west, but not very quickly.

His plan for seeing some of the good old USA on his way to San Diego was taking longer than he had thought it would. And he realized, ruefully, summer might not have been the best time to do it. He picked up his bag and headed down the road. In his head he could hear his dad telling him what a dummy he was and that "any fool" would know better than to hitchhike in the middle of a summer day. At least his father wasn't there to berate him. He wasn't anywhere berating anyone since he'd been killed in a bar fight right before the war broke out.

Jack never got the story completely straight but there'd been rumors that his father, Big Jack, had stood his ground with the wrong fellow when he started extolling the virtues of Hitler and the Nazis. Jack didn't put much credence into the story as he didn't recall his father ever expressing much of a political opinion. He usually just took the opposite side to whatever the other guy was saying…it made it easier to get in a fight that way.

"Just plain ornery," was how Jack's mother had always described him.

"Why'd you ever marry him in the first place?" Jack had asked one night sitting at the kitchen table under the single ceiling bulb. They'd spent the two hours since supper trying to figure out how to keep the farm going with just the two of them working it.

His mother took a few moments to consider the question. She gazed into some middle distance searching for the past instant when it had seemed like a good idea to marry a bullying drunkard. Finally, she admitted, "I just don't know. It seemed like a good idea, I guess. Maybe I thought I could change him."

Jack had turned his attention back to the meager pile of money and heftier stack of unpaid bills on the table. He didn't think that was much of an excuse for the years of abuse they had all suffered.

Jack wanted to join the Navy from before the damned Japs had bombed the bejeezus out of Pearl Harbor, but with his father gone he was the man of the house. He didn't feel like much of a man, but his sister was still in high school and they had two younger brothers. He was as good as they were going to get.

The sound of a truck coming down the lonely highway pulled Jack from his reverie. He turned and put out his arm, thumb uplifted, and walking backwards. The old pickup turned left on a dirt track before he got as far as the waiting hitcher.

Well, his bad luck was holding. Still, he was happy to be here and not toiling away on that hardscrabble chunk of poor land in Arkansas. His sister had graduated from high school now and got a good job working in the drugstore in Jasper. His mother leased the farm out to some fellas that thought they could make some money off it and moved into town. Jasper, Arkansas wasn't that much of a town, but it had a couple of stores, a filling station, two churches, neither of which Jack had ever seen the inside of, and a tumble of clapboard houses. His mother had been energized by the move to town and took over the role of postmaster since the last one had gone off to fight and everyone else in town was either too young or too old. The house in town was tiny, not a lot of room for the five of them, but there was a little garden patch out back that had been planted for the year and looked to be a better bet than the farm had been. She'd even started planting some flowers and listening to music on the radio. One day he came in and found her dancing around the parlor. His daddy had only liked country music, but Mama was happily listening to Benny Goodman swing out on "Sweet and Low Down."

His mother had not only got herself a good job, but she'd perked up, as well. She'd started pin-curling her hair and was even wearing some lipstick the last time he saw her. He tried not to think it might be because there were a couple of older fellas, the mechanic in town and a traveling salesman that passed through every couple of weeks, who had been paying her a little attention.

He figured he would be glad for her if she could find some happiness at forty years old. He just hoped she made a better choice than she had the last time someone came courting.

With everyone at home taking care of themselves, he hadn't needed to be the man of the house any longer and told everyone who would listen that he was finally going to join up like he'd been wanting to do all along.

This trek across the country was a chance for him to convince himself that he was raring to go and fight. The only fights he'd ever been in were with his father, and he always lost those. He'd been young and afraid, and hadn't really taken a stand. He wasn't sure he'd be able to do it now. How did you get brave enough to go after someone bigger, madder, or meaner? He hoped it would help to be surrounded by a bunch of other folks fighting the same enemy. He guessed he'd find out soon enough.

Dusty had hit a long stretch of nothing after he drove through Fort Stockton. The sun was blazing, and he'd stopped in the small town to get a cold drink and a big hunk of ice. About fifty miles out he spotted a kid with a suitcase standing on the far side of the road, thumbing his way across the wasteland.

Hitchhikers were not uncommon during the war. Not many people could afford to travel by car, but Texas in July was not the best place to do it. Dusty knew that he had not passed a car on that stretch of road for some time and thought that guy could be standing out there in the sun for quite a spell.

Still, it wasn't his problem, so, though he slowed a bit, he continued on his way. For a while. He argued with himself for about three miles before he gave up and turned the beast of a car around at a wide spot in the road and went back to rescue the man.

Jack was still standing on the side of the road, although he had walked down about a quarter of a mile further. It seemed to him that a moving hitchhiker was more appealing than a standing one. At least you were trying to get where you wanted to be. It wasn't that cars were speeding by him; it was that there weren't any cars going his way. His last ride had picked him up outside Austin and let him off when they had turned onto a dirt road that seemed to lead off into nowhere.

He was surprised to see the only car that had passed in the last hour come cruising back toward him from the other direction. He didn't know a lot about cars, but this one looked like it would have room for him. There were no new cars on the road. The car factories and the resources they used had been turned to the manufacture of tanks, airplanes, ships, jeeps, and anything else that could be used for the war. This car had been built before all that happened and had cost a pretty penny when it was new. It was brown and the Texas storms and elements had taken a lot of the sheen off the paint. The wooden side panels had been ground down to bare wood and the dents and dings of a working ranch vehicle marred the fenders and bumpers.

Ever hopeful, Jack stuck out his thumb, although the quick return of the car indicated a local who wouldn't be driving far. Still, he was grateful when it slid to a stop just past of him on the shoulder of the road.

The eager, sunburnt face that was presented at the open car window was not quite as young as Dusty had first imagined. Maybe early twenties rather than late teens, but you didn't see many strong young men around these days. Even though he wore a cap, it didn't do much to shelter him from the sun.

"You know, there's a reason Texans wear big hats," said Dusty with a grin.

The kid laughed and gave an acknowledging nod touching the rim of his inadequate headgear.

"Where are you headed?"

"Headed for San Diego to join the Navy," Jack responded proudly. "Yeah, couldn't before because my pa died and I had younger brothers at home on the farm."

"You know, they will let you join the Navy without going all the way to California yourself."

"Well, I was thinking I'd never been outside of Arkansas so maybe I'd see some things before I shipped out. Just saw the capital of Texas."

Dusty had to admit that was part of his thinking, too. Maybe they had more in common than just being in this place at this time.

"I'm headed for California but going the other direction first. How do you feel about making a side trip and then tagging along with me?"

"Hell, yeah! That's the best offer I've had all day. You'd really drive me clear to San Diego?"

"Maybe just as far as Los Angeles, but you never can tell. It depends on whether we run out of gas. Move that ice bucket into the back seat and throw your suitcase in. We've still got a fair way to go before dark."

Jack yanked open the heavy door and moved the galvanized tub holding the chunk of ice. He took a moment to cup his hands and drink some of the cool water from the tub. Then removed his hat and splashed some on his face, head, and neck. "Dang, that is the best water I ever drank. You are a lifesaver."

"We'll have to see about that. I can be a pain in the neck, but Uncle Sam wants us all to travel together, so I reckon we can stand each other for a few days."

Jack threw his bag into the back seat next to the tub and climbed happily into the spacious front seat. "I've never been in a car this big before. It's like driving around in your parlor."

Dusty stuck out his hand. "I'm Dusty Rhodes."

"Jack, Jack Scoggins."

Dusty smiled and maneuvered the car in an easterly direction to head back toward Sugar Land.

Once they were on the road and the quiet of the highway and hum of the engine had settled over them, Jack glanced over at the driver. The man in the cowboy hat was not a lot older than Jack, maybe five years, but he seemed older. Maybe sadder. Jack hoped they could be friends. He wasn't really sure how you got to be friends with a new person. Everyone he knew he'd known for his whole life. He hadn't finished his schooling; there didn't seem to be much purpose for it, not for a dirt farmer. He'd bet that Dusty had some education. Maybe that was what made him seem older. Maybe he knew things Jack didn't know.

"Are you from around here?" Jack asked.

Dusty removed his hat and put it down on the seat between them. "I'm from near Pecos. My family has some cattle land out there." He didn't mention the number of cattle or the oil wells that had sprung up on the acreage since he'd been a kid. The truth was that Dusty was shy about the wealth and importance that had become a part of his family's life in the past few years, especially since the start of the war. He didn't feel like he'd earned it and this whole trip was about doing something that would use some of it for good.

It would be dark before long and they could sleep in the car. The government didn't want you to drive after dark. That probably made more sense near the coasts where there could be planes or submarines; not likely in the middle of the Lone Star State. But you never knew.

"Where are we headed?" Jack hoped it didn't sound like he was complaining.

"We're going to Sugar Land to pick up my cousin, Betty. She's hankering to go someplace other than Sugar Land to help win the war. When she found out I was headed for California she convinced her folks that it would be safe to travel with me."

"What's she planning on doing out there?"

"I think she's hoping to get a job, and probably a husband. I think she's pretty young to go traipsing off on her own like that, but I promised to keep an eye on her. She just got out of school."

Jack considered whether he'd be willing to let his sister go off with any of their cousins, and pretty quickly determined he would not.

CHAPTER FOUR

July 1943

It was only nine a.m. but Lucy's limp waitress uniform clung to her on the sultry Texas morning and the day was only going to get hotter, much hotter. The rotary fans at each end of the counter did little to disperse the miasma of sweat, bacon grease, and burnt coffee that hung over the room. She had tucked her red curls into a Victory Roll secured with myriad hairpins, but tendrils had come loose and trailed onto her sweaty neck. For some reason Tilda looked fresh; Lucy thought it might just be a New York City thing. Or maybe it was just from being tall and slim. Tall and slim were two things that Lucy was not. Her curves filled her uniform to capacity and the little stepstool behind the counter was used on a regular basis to heft her up to reach those tantalizing items just out of a short girl's reach. She could always have asked Tilda to reach them for her, but she'd be danged if she would.

The morning rush had ended, and Tilda stood with her elbows on the counter reading the morning paper a customer had left in one of the booths. "Says here that the allies have invaded Sicily. Maybe the war will be over soon."

Lucy glanced sharply at her friend. Was she kidding?

The bell above the door jingled as two men entered. The younger, sturdier man, with dark hair and eyes, and a sunburnt face, burst through it followed by a handsome taller man. The older man was dressed like all the other cowboys in Texas; long-sleeved Western-cut shirt, jeans, boots, and the ubiquitous ten-gallon hat.

Lucy was immediately drawn to the shorter, dark-haired man. There was an energy around him that almost crackled and he grinned and looked her up and down appraisingly as he took a seat at the counter. She was surprised that she felt a blush rising in her cheeks. She'd gotten used to cowpokes, truck drivers, and military fellas looking her over. There wasn't much else to look at here on the outskirts of Houston. Some even claimed having a good-looking waitress made the marginally palatable food she served them taste better.

"Howdy, ma'am," said the taller cowboy as he sat down. She could hear the West Texas drawl in his voice. He removed his hat and set it on the counter next to him. Lucy shifted her gaze away from the younger man with difficulty and pushed the damp red tendrils of hair from her forehead with the back of her hand, nearly dislodging her little waitress cap.

"Good morning. What can I get you?"

Jack leaned forward and slipped the menu from behind the napkin holder. "Well, I can think of a couple of things...." He stopped when Dusty gave him a sharp look. "Just joking..." He ducked his head and studied the grease-stained page in his hand.

"We'd like coffee to start with. How are your flapjacks?" Dusty pulled out another menu.

"They're good," Lucy leaned forward and lowered her voice. "Maybe a mite heavy, but they'll last you the morning, for sure."

"I'll have a stack of those." Jack tucked the worn menu back in the rack.

"Do y'all have oatmeal?" Dusty had barely glanced at the menu.

"Yes, we have oatmeal with margarine and brown sugar. That'll stick to your ribs, too."

"Okay, then. I'll have a bowl of oatmeal and some toast."

Lucy turned to the pass-through to the kitchen and shouted the order to the burly cook. "Stack of blowout patches and a bowl of hope." She was still learning her diner lingo, but she knew these items by heart. She popped a couple of slices of white bread into the toaster on the back counter.

Tilda walked up with the fresh pot of coffee she'd been brewing and placed two mugs on the counter. "Will you need milk and sugar?"

"None for me, ma'am. That sure don't sound like a Texas accent, does it, Jack?" Dusty smiled at the blond woman.

Jack had been watching Lucy and turned to look at Tilda. "Nope, it sure doesn't."

"Well, boys, there's a reason for that. I'm not originally from here."

"She's from New York City," Lucy piped up. "Just traveling through here on her way to California, like me."

Jack's face lit up. "Wow, we're on our way to California, too. I'm going out there to join the Navy and Dusty here's gonna …" He hesitated…he hadn't asked Dusty why he was headed for the West Coast. "He'd be joining up, too, except they won't take him because of his leg and all." It was hard to read the look that Dusty shot Jack but it stopped him mid-sentence.

"Sorry, Dusty." Head down, he focused on smearing a heavy coat of margarine on the steaming hotcakes Lucy had just placed in front of him.

Lucy didn't know what to say so she turned away and busied herself at the coffee station. You didn't know whether you should be congratulating or commiserating with someone who hadn't been swept up in the draft. Her own brothers and Tilda's brothers had all marched away. She paused…she'd never thought of asking them if they wanted to go. Next time she saw them she'd ask, if there was a next time.

Tilda had been listening to this exchange and took up the gauntlet. "How'd you injure your leg?" She was never one to let things slide and wanted to dissipate the awkwardness of the conversation. People had all kinds of problems. It wasn't anything to be ashamed of.

"Stupid kid stunt on the ranch. Trying to wrangle a calf for branding and me and the horse both went down. Unfortunately, I was on the bottom."

"That's too bad."

"Could have been worse. They thought I wouldn't walk, but a little thing like a banged-up leg wasn't gonna stop me for long. I can do anything anybody else can do, except march maybe." This last comment was made with a wry grin. "I am a dead shot with a rifle…though I mostly shoot at coyotes or bobcats."

"Everybody's doing the best they can with what they've got." Tilda looked directly into Dusty's eyes. Their gaze held steady. "Yes, ma'am," he responded and then dug into the steaming bowl of oatmeal in front of him. The food disappeared fast. He and Jack had slept in the car and would wash up a bit in the restroom of the diner before completing their run to Sugar Land.

Dusty had not paid much attention to Tilda until then, or Lucy either. A couple of diner waitresses in the middle of nowhere. What did they have in common, after all? Only what everyone had in common right then.

"Why are you working here when you're headed for California? Last I hear, it was about fifteen hundred miles that-a-way." Dusty jerked his thumb over his shoulder.

"This is just a place to light and make a few bucks for the trip. Don't plan on sleeping on the beach when I get there." Tilda smiled.

"Might not be so bad; starlight, bonfires, Japanese submarines…" Dusty smiled.

"Very funny. Do you want more coffee or are you ready for your check?"

He looked over at Jack, just mopping up the last of the syrup from his nearly spotless plate. "I'll take the check. And maybe I have a proposition for you."

Tilda's change of expression made Dusty chuckle. "Not that kind of proposition. We're driving through Houston to pick up my cousin, Betty, in Sugar Land. My mama promised her mama I'd take her with me and keep her safe. She's wanting to get away from Texas. I'll be driving out to pick her up today, then we are headed for Los Angeles. How would you feel about joining us on the trip?"

"I want to go, too," Lucy chimed in.

"Whoa, just wait a minute." Tilda waved her hand in Lucy's direction. "I'm not sure I'm really clear on this offer." She regarded Dusty; interested but still skeptical.

"I'm just saying that the government wants us to conserve fuel and travel together, if possible. I've got that big ole station wagon out there on the street, my mama's last spare tire, and I'm going your way." He flashed a shy grin.

Lucy was almost bouncing with excitement next to her. Tilda couldn't help thinking that normal people just didn't get into a car with total strangers and, literally, ride off into the sunset. Then again, these weren't normal times.

"We've got ration stamps to contribute and I've got money saved up," burst out Lucy, unable to contain herself.

"And you could help with the driving," added Jack. "You can drive, can't you?"

"Sure, I can, but Tilda can't. She's from New York." Lucy only looked a little smug with that pronouncement. "I can drive a tractor and a pickup, too."

Tilda wasn't sure what to think. Houston wasn't where she'd planned to end her trip, and Los Angeles sounded exciting and full of possibilities. Dusty didn't look dangerous, and, if you squinted your eyes, neither did Jack.

Standing next to her Lucy bounced on the balls of her feet, and it was only partly in response to "Boogie Woogie Bugle Boy" playing on the radio behind the counter. Her excitement was contagious.

"Heck, what's the worst that can happen?" Tilda shrugged.

Lucy shrieked and ripped off her waitress headgear, tossing it into the air. Jack jumped to his feet as she came running around the end of the counter and hugged him.

Tilda and Dusty looked at each other, silently wondering what they had gotten themselves into.

It was agreed that the girls would finish the shift, give their notice, and head down the street to the boarding house to pack up their gear. Dusty and Jack would drive to Sugar Land to get Cousin Betty and return to pick the girls up early the next morning.

"My aunt Sarah will have cooked up a feast for us, sorry we can't take you along." Dusty apologized.

"We're already paid up for dinner at the boarding house, and we have plenty to keep us busy until tomorrow." Tilda was already jotting down a quick list of things she'd have to do before she headed west.

Two truckers who'd just banged through the screen door eyed them curiously. Tilda picked up the coffeepot and a couple of menus and headed toward the end of the counter where they sat down.

The midafternoon sun had baked the asphalt to a hot goo when Tilda and Lucy hugged the cook good-bye and headed for the boarding house. It wasn't really a boarding house, just an old clapboard structure that belonged to Lucy's Aunt Mary. When Lucy had shown up on her doorstep a few months before, it suddenly became a boarding house, and now Mary had rented a room to Tilda and another to the telegraph boy with his sad face and battered bicycle.

Lucy burst into the kitchen; the screen door banging shut behind her. "We're going to California!" was all Mary heard as the young girl pounded up the stairs to her room, rattling off a long tale that was lost in the telling.

"What was that all about?" she gasped, turning back to the door as Tilda entered more sedately.

"We found a good ride to California and decided to take it." Tilda opened the icebox and poured herself a tall glass of buttermilk. She'd developed a taste for the tangy drink while she'd been in the south. It was not something she'd run into in New York. She'd miss cornbread, red-eye gravy, and butter beans, too. Of course, she doubted Mary had much experience with knishes, pastrami on rye, or celery tonic. It was a big country.

Tilda pulled her list and a pencil out of her pocket and sat down to explain the plan to Lucy's aunt. Upstairs they could hear Lucy banging doors and slamming drawers.

Mary was a little concerned about the girls going off with a couple of strangers, but the world was a different place than when she'd been a girl. She wouldn't be losing any money as she already had a waiting list of folks that needed a room and who had heard rumors of her fried chicken and biscuits.

Lucy was her dead sister's oldest girl and came to Houston from Oklahoma after her mama died and her daddy gave up trying to turn her into the housemaid and married a widow woman from town. Lucy was young, but she had common sense and a heart a little too big to keep her out of trouble. Still, Tilda was wiser, and a good surrogate big sister for the younger woman.

"I'd better go see what she's getting into up there…sounds like trouble." A crash from upstairs and the hollered reassurance, "It's all right, I'm okay," didn't allay Tilda's concern.

"I'll get dinner started. Maybe I can pull together a Service Cake. There's just the three of us tonight and it only takes a smidge of sugar." She lifted the lid of the canister on the counter and surveyed the slim remains of their sugar ration. "We can put some jam and cream over it, make it a real celebration."

Tilda smiled going up the stairs. Mary reminded her of her own mother. Always trying to make things "nice" for everyone. Flowers in a jar on the table, music on the radio, a little sweetness in a bitter world.

CHAPTER FIVE

July 1943

"Jesus, how the hell did I end up back in Texas," Julia muttered as she fanned herself with the bus schedule. She could hear the static squawk of the stationmaster's radio blasting "American Patrol" inside the terminal. She'd moved to the bench outside to catch what breeze there was, but even the air that stirred around her was hot and heavy. The Dallas street was quiet. There were cars parked along the curb, but smart folks knew enough to stay in during this time of day. She thought of Noël Coward's lyrics, "Mad dogs and Englishmen go out in the midday sun." Any living thing with any sense had found some hidey-hole to wait out the heat. The only traffic was the delivery trucks that trundled by, kicking up a choking cloud of the grit that covered everything.

The cheap cotton sundress she wore clung damply to her and she looked around to see if anyone was watching before she picked up the hem and fanned it to cool her bare legs. Her short, dark hair was plastered to her head like a swimming cap. When she'd last worn this dress, the fit had been perfect but now it hung on her.

She dropped the hem of her skirt and opened the bus schedule. She'd come back to Texas because she didn't know where else to go, but there wasn't a home here for her. She could take that 3:15 bus toward Houston, but the only thing welcome at her mama's house would be the government pay in her purse. She didn't need her mother to say, "I told you so." Julia already knew the Navy had been her biggest mistake, so far.

Her two brothers were in prison as conscientious objectors somewhere under that unrelenting southwestern sun. One of them had written to her to ask her why she'd joined the Navy. If she had answered his letter she would have told him, "I was hungry," but it was not just for food. She was hungry for pride, for a purpose, for a future, but none of that had turned out the way she had hoped. She wondered briefly if she should try to go to see her brothers in prison, but she doubted they'd be happy to see her. They couldn't understand why she would serve the nations of man, and she didn't understand why they would go to prison rather than serve in a peaceful capacity. She recalled as a little girl holding up a tiny flag her daddy had given her and explaining to her teacher how it would "keep her safe."

Her mama, brothers, and sisters had taken shelter with a jealous God to protect them from the world, to give them a place and a hope. If they could just stay faithful a little while longer, Armageddon would wipe out the unrighteous and give them a perfect world where they would live forever in peace and plenty. She wished she could believe. She'd tried… maybe she was too impatient, too restless, too sinful… but she didn't think so.

She could stay here in Dallas. She'd worked here for a while before the war and jobs would be easy to get with all the boys off fighting, but God, how she hated the state: the heat, the sand, the swagger, all of it.

She glanced up from the paper in her hand and gazed blankly down the empty street. Out of the waves of heat rising from the pavement the form of a lone automobile looked almost like a mirage; its progress distorted and shimmering. Eventually the grimy car pulled up in front of the bus station and came to a halt. It was a big car, a station wagon with wooden panels on the side, but what drew her attention was that it was piled high with suitcases tied helter-skelter on the roof. It looked to be packed to the brim with people. Two of the doors popped open and the driver and another person emerged. The driver was a tall man dressed like all the ranch hands she'd seen in her life. He was okay to look at but when he walked around the front of the car, she saw he walked with a limp. The person who emerged from the back seat was a young girl. Julia had seen a million like her too, hanging around the drugstores and soda shops near the Naval station in Bethesda. They were high school girls who the service men joked about being "khaki whacky." They were crazy about the guys in uniform. Their days and nights were spent flirting with them. The other passengers slowly climbed out of the car to get some air. The two women and a man milled around in the scant shade of the building.

The tall driver untied some of the ropes and removed a suitcase from the roof of the car while the girl hugged the other passengers and sobbed. Julia couldn't hear everything that was said but a few phrases floated to her. "We'll miss you, honey, but it's best for you to go home." "We'll write when we get there." "Stop blubbering, your mascara's getting everywhere."

When the battered suitcase had been removed and the ropes retied, the driver hefted the bag and took the girl's elbow, guiding her up the steps and into the terminal. She had stopped crying and smiled wanly at Julia as she walked past.

They didn't look like a family traveling together. One of the women was tall and slender. Her hair was blond and tied at the back of her neck with a scarf. Julia thought it looked like it got some help from peroxide, not that Julia could criticize. The only reason her hair was currently dark was because the Navy had frowned on changing it. She'd already been studying magazines trying to decide which hair color was in her future. The tall girl lit a cigarette and leaned back against the car as she expelled the smoke. She threw back her head and laughed at something someone had said and waved the cigarette in an exaggerated manner. She was wearing shorts and a man's shirt with the shirttails tied up under her bosom, exposing her midriff.

The other girl was shorter and curvier. Everything about her was round and soft. Her curly red hair was pulled back with a snood and damp loosened tendrils clung to her neck. She looked up and down the street and her gaze fell on Julia. Their eyes met briefly, and Julia quickly looked away. She was unprepared for the open frankness of the gaze and felt exposed by it. There had not been a lot of people whose gaze Julia could meet without glancing away in the last few months.

The other man had hefted himself onto the front fender of the car. He seemed shorter than the cowboy had been. His solid frame was heavily muscled and compact. His shirt was tight around his shoulders and arms. He unrolled the pack of cigarettes from his sleeve and lit one up, lowering his head of dark hair over cupped hands to catch the wayward flame.

There were two buses headed out in the next hour, one going west and one headed south toward "home." Tomorrow morning there'd be one going back the way she'd come from. "I can't go back, and I can't go home," she thought, "and I can't stay here." It seemed her decision had been made for her. She stood up just as the cowboy swung the screen door open and emerged with his hands full of frosty bottles of Coke. He stood back to hold the door open for her with his shoulder and then headed for the car. The young girl did not come out with him and Julia noticed her sitting on one of the benches with her suitcase at her feet. She tightly gripped a bus ticket in one hand and a bottle of Coke in the other.

CHAPTER SIX

July 1943

The cold drinks looked inviting. Julia walked to the big red cooler and slid the lid open. A gust of cold air rose to greet her. She took longer than necessary to select her drink so that the icy blast could play across her damp neck and face. She pulled a bottle out and reluctantly slid the lid closed. She pried the bottle cap off on the side of the cooler. Walking to the ticket counter she slid her nickel under the glass barrier. Still unwilling to purchase her ticket and commit to a destination, she sat down on the bench near the young girl.

Up close Julia could see the girl was not as young as she had thought. Her clothes were those of a high school girl, oxfords and socks, a full skirt, a blouse with a rounded Peter Pan collar and short, banded sleeves. She looked to be about eighteen.

Julia leaned back and took a long swig of her drink. "Sure is hot today," she said to the girl. The girls started slightly and smiled a little. "Sure is," she said.

"You from around here?" Julia asked.

The girl hesitated for a moment, "No, I'm going home to Sugar Land. That's near Houston."

The girl didn't seem anxious to keep up the conversation and the heat had sapped Julia's curiosity. Sugar Land, Texas, she thought as she sipped from the bottle, another exciting destination.

The screen door squeaked open and banged shut as the redhead entered. She carried an empty soda bottle and placed it carefully in the compartmented wooden crate next to the cooler. Then she turned and walked to the bench.

"I thought you might like someone to wait with you, Betty," she said to the girl. "Dusty and the others went to find some lunch and a filling station."

Betty moved over to make room for her. "Thanks, I'd like that. It should only be about twenty minutes."

Julia thought the bench was getting kind of crowded and stood up. She might as well get her bag back from the clerk. He had put it behind the counter while she decided what to do. Before she could walk away the redhead spoke. "Where y'all headed?" she asked.

When Julia turned, she was again struck by the girl's forthright gaze. "I wish I knew," she laughed nervously.

"Well, we're headed for Los Angeles and we have an empty seat," she said gesturing in Betty's direction. "Betty decided she missed her mama, so she's headed home." Betty elbowed the redhead and shushed her.

"Well, you do miss your mama. Besides, we need to keep the car full up to make this trip 'really necessary'." She glanced at the yellowed poster of Uncle Sam posted next to the ticket master's window. "We're headed west to work in the airplane factories, and Jack is going to enlist." She looked both proud and worried.

Julia hesitated, it wasn't a bad idea, but her last brilliant leap of faith had led her into the Navy, and that had been a disaster.

"We're all chipping in money and ration coupons, and Dusty has the last spare tire in Texas in the back of the wagon."

Julia wondered briefly when the ration coupons in her bag would expire. In Bethesda she didn't have to worry about such things. She shivered slightly. Even in this heat the memory of the regimented life of the barracks chilled her, but she missed the structure. At least she'd known where she would be the next day and the day after that. If she was honest, knowing she had shelter, clothes, and didn't have to worry about her next meal had been part of the military appeal. She could vaguely remember life before the Depression had hit: birthday parties, pretty clothes, tables groaning with food at family gatherings. Then it had all magically become tent living on an oil lease, scrabbling for food, dignity, and all of the other necessities of life. At this point she wasn't even sure her memories were accurate.

The redhead watched Julia curiously. She noted the shadow that had clouded her eyes as she considered the proposal. She reached out to shake hands. "My name's Lucy, and this is Betty. None of us are axe-murderers, or anything. Well, maybe Dusty is, but not when he's sober." She grinned.

Julia automatically grasped the outstretched hand and smiled. "I'm Julia Stafford. I was just wondering how long it will take to drive to Los Angeles from here."

"Dusty figures it's about fifteen hundred miles. If we take turns driving and sleep in the wagon by the side of the road we don't have to pay for motels. The speed limit's thirty-five now, so we figure three or four more days." Lucy explained. The stockier of the two men came through the door carrying a sandwich wrapped in waxed paper. "You owe me fifteen cents for the sandwich, doll." He smiled handing the food to Lucy. "But I might consider trading it for a big kiss."

"In your dreams, Casanova," Lucy answered, already peeling back the waxed paper. "This is Julia Stafford; I'm trying to convince her to take Betty's place, so you behave yourself." Betty's head came up at the mention of her name, but she said nothing.

Jack stuck out his hand after wiping it on his shirt. His gaze swept over her. "We could use a little class on this trip." he said, grinning broadly. "Do you know how to drive? Betty isn't much of a driver, but she kept everyone awake by talking non-stop."

Betty laughed for the first time. "You shush up, Jack. I could hardly get a word in edgewise and you know it."

Julia felt a nostalgic tug at her heart. She'd forgotten what it was like to be teased by her brothers and sisters. There sure hadn't been much teasing in her life lately and she purposely put the thought of her brothers' circumstances out of her mind.

"That sound like a pretty good offer," she said just as the Greyhound bus bound for Houston roared and belched to a smoky stop outside the terminal. Betty jumped to her feet, clutching her ticket. "That's my bus," she squeaked.

Jack hefted her suitcase and Lucy flung her arms around her. Betty smiled tentatively and burst into tears. "Oh, my gosh!" she sobbed. Lucy patted her back. "You'll be fine, honey. You just aren't ready to go galloping off for parts unknown. I'll send you my address when I get one and you can come out and join me next year unless this whole war has blown over by then. I'll write, I promise." With her arm still around Betty's waist, Lucy guided her out the door. Jack shrugged and carried the suitcase after them.

Before she could change her mind, Julia walked to the ticket window and retrieved her bag. At least Los Angeles wasn't Texas, and it was about as far as she could get away from Bethesda. The bus's gears ground and it started up outside. She could still hear Lucy and Betty shouting to each other through the bus window. She picked up her bag and started out the door. Her heart jolted and her step quickened when she saw the cowboy had climbed into the driver's seat and was revving the station wagon to life. She didn't want them to take off without her.

Lucy turned away from the departing bus just in time to see Julia coming down the steps lugging her battered case. "Jack, help the lady with her bag." She ran quickly to Dusty as she gestured wildly toward Julia and talked a mile a minute. Dusty turned off the ignition and opened the door. He unfolded his lanky frame from inside of the car and gave Julia an appraising once-over. She hesitated, slowed by his cool gaze. His piercing blue eyes weren't unfriendly, but she still felt unusually shy.

Jack took her bag from her, and she held out her hand to the tall cowboy before her. "I'm Julia Stafford, and I'd like to travel with you, if you'll have me," was all she said. He took her tiny hand in his great paw and just squeezed it gently. "Ma'am, we'd be happy to have the company," he said. He couldn't explain his carefulness with her. She looked hardy enough, but there was a shadow in her face that made her seem vulnerable. He'd always had a way with horses, a special sense, and it was that sense that told him she could bolt in an instant. He smiled just once and turned to help Jack swing her bag onto the roof of the car and tie it securely with the others. Over his shoulder he spoke to Lucy. "There's a couple of extra sandwiches stowed in the backseat. Why don't you dig one out for our new travel mate?"

"Sure thing," Lucy responded. "Come on, Julia, the girls will take the backseat while the boys are driving and then we'll switch later on." She swung the back door of the car open, climbed in and slid across the wide seat. Julia stepped into the sweltering car and closed the door. Lucy was on her knees rummaging through a basket stowed behind her seat. "Looks like we've got bologna or cheese. Which do you want? Oh, and there's a sack of pork rinds, and some apples."

"Anything's fine," murmured Julia. Lucy turned back around holding two apples, a greasy paper sack, and a waxed paper wrapped sandwich. She handed the sandwich to Julia and settled into her seat. "It'll be a little cooler when we get going so the wind can blow through the windows. Jack, where did Tilda get to? We need to get going before we suffocate in here."

"We dropped her at the telegraph office. We'll pick her up on our way out of town," said Jack.

Dusty restarted the car and pulled away from the curb, headed west. A few blocks down Julia spotted the tall blond woman outside the telegraph office leaning against the awning post and smoking a cigarette. The car pulled up beside her. Lucy pushed open the door and slid to the middle of the seat to give Tilda room. "So, did you wire your folks where you were headed?" she asked.

Tilda hesitated for a moment and tossed away her cigarette before answering. "Naw, the more I thought about it the more I realized that it would scare the daylights out of my mother and sister if they got a telegram. They'd for sure think it was one of the boys, you know?" Tilda leaned forward and looked around Lucy at Julia. "Wow, Betty you've really changed," she said.

"Oh sorry," Lucy laughed. "This is Julia. Julia, this is Tilda, she's from New York City. I don't know where Julia is from." Lucy looked at her expectantly.

"I'm just coming from Bethesda," she said. There was really no need to go into a lot of explaining. It was too hot and too complicated. She smiled at Tilda. "Nice to meet you."

CHAPTER SEVEN

July 1943

Given half a chance Lucy would talk her way through the state of Texas, but before long the torpid heat and rattling vibrations of the engine caused her to slip into a quiet reverie.

A galvanized bucket containing a chunk of ice sat on the floor at Jack's feet in the front, and another one sat nestled between Lucy's feet. As the afternoon continued and the monotonous miles of sand and scrub brush rolled past, they chipped away at the ice with an old screwdriver. They sucked quietly on the chips, or rubbed them over their arms, neck, and face, letting the melted drops run down their shirts. Occasionally they would roll through what passed as a town in West Texas: a bar, a few clapboard or adobe buildings, one with a cross, one with a rusty café sign, an old dog whose head would lift from his paws as they passed. The girls dozed in the backseat, arms and legs slung across each other, until the sweaty discomfort of another's touch caused them to shift and allow some of the desultory breeze to caress their damp skin and cool them a bit.

They stopped in one of the towns to buy bread, bologna, and a few cold soft drinks from a local grocer. There was a neglected washroom in the back of the store where the girls squatted carefully over the filthy commode. They splashed themselves with rusty, tepid water from the faucet and filled a couple of battered canteens. Finally, after eyeing the dubiously dingy towel, they dried their hands on their clothes and climbed back into the car.

When the setting sun shone directly into their eyes, making driving uncomfortable, as well as dangerous, they stopped on the side of the road and ate sandwiches with the car doors swung wide. The boys walked out into the scrub a little way to relieve their travel-jarred bladders, watching carefully for scorpions and snakes.

The sun set before them and Jack and Dusty climbed into the back seat to sleep. The three women got into the front seat with Tilda to supervise the driving with the confidence of the non-driver. When the war was over she'd learn to drive. She had learned that not all of the USA was accessible by foot, bus, or subway.

Lucy took the first driving shift and Julia gazed out the window as the sky darkened and the endless Texas wilderness was gradually cloaked in gray. There was no sound from the backseat other than an occasional snort or rustle of sleepy shifting. After a while Tilda started humming and Lucy joined in singing, "When the deep purple falls, over sleepy garden walls…"

In her dream Julia stood against the bar of the smoky Quonset hut that served as the USO in Maryland. She knew she looked trim in the dark uniform, her cropped hair shining under the harsh lights. A sea of uniforms and young, smiling faces bobbed to the irresistible rhythm of "American Patrol" playing on the jukebox. It was exciting to be here. She felt proud to be part of something important, and she wanted to dance. She was surrounded by eager sailors who vied for her attention and then took laughing turns swinging her around the dance floor. Suddenly she was shadowed by a hulking form. The music became muffled and she turned to run. She started awake in fear, and realized she had dozed off. "Hey, let's switch off now, it's my turn to drive," she said.

When they stopped for the night, pulling well off the road onto the shoulder, Dusty and Jack hauled sleeping rolls from the back of the station wagon and spread them out onto the ground. The girls made beds on the front and back bench seats and Julia curled up in the back of the wagon with the tailgate down. They'd driven as far as they could without turning on the headlights. There were few vehicles, mostly trucks, barreling down the long stretches of highway. The dullness of the road pulled them over even though they were anxious to get to their destination.

When the rising sun woke them, they sponge-bathed with the water from their melted ice blocks. They drove down the lonely highway, finally spying a soaring water tower and the first signs of a town in the distance. On Jack's advice they searched for the telltale signs of good food by watching for trucks pulled off the highway or clusters of pickups parked outside a roadside café. They didn't have to use their precious ration coupons for meals in restaurants.

Lucy was the first to spot a neon sign. "Stop, stop, there's a donut shop! I love donuts." The neon sign was half dim so it really said DO-__TS AND _OOD EAT_, but they got the idea.

Dusty pulled into an empty parking space in front of the shop. "What do all y'all want? I'll get it while you gals use the restrooms."

"Coffee, I need coffee," Julia groaned. She was hoping to get some caffeine before one of her headaches could get started.

She got out of the car with Lucy and Tilda and walked in the direction of the RESTROOMS sign pointing to the back of the building. Turning the corner, she saw two arrows, one pointing to a door in the back of the building with the word WHITE painted on it in coarse letters. The other sign, COLORED, pointed to a decrepit outhouse in the alley running in back.

Tilda stopped short. "What does that mean?"

Julia almost ran into the back of her when she stopped, "What does what mean?"

"White and colored…"

"It means that this toilet is for white folks and the one out yonder is for colored people."

"Hmph…" Tilda said nothing else but she stood for several seconds gazing toward the small outbuilding.

Julia shook her head and walked around her following Lucy through the small doorway.

It wasn't like NYC wasn't segregated; after all, there was Harlem, a whole huge piece of the city. Tilda had been to Harlem many times. Before the war it was where you went to hear good music, later, with the streets full of Black men in uniform, she had gone with savvy artists and writers to meet in smoky cafés and talk about color and war. She'd never given a moment's thought to using the dingy bathrooms, sharing cups of coffee, or sometimes mugs of wine. She'd bummed smokes from everyone there.

The paper cups of coffee and huge sugar dose of the greasy donuts soon woke them all up. After one especially long quiet spell on the highway Lucy's voice piped up from the backseat. "I wanted to join the Red Cross to be a Donut Dolly, but I was too young."

It took a couple of minutes for anyone to respond.

"Hmph, a Donut Dolly. Yep, I can imagine you driving a big ole truck around England stopping just long enough to fry up a batch of donuts for the GIs," mused Jack. "In fact, I'd stand in line for a donut from you any time."

Tilda joined in, "Do you even know how to drive a truck…or make donuts?"

"I can drive a tractor, a truck, or anything else, except maybe an airplane. I bet I could even drive a tank if I had to," Lucy huffed.

"We're just kidding, honey. You would have made a great Donut Dolly, but then you wouldn't be here with us." Tilda smiled.

"Yeah, well, I wanted to do it. A girl from my town joined and I thought it sounded great. But, when I tried to sign up, they said you had to be twenty-five years old, for crying out loud."

Her plaintive tone at the injustice of it all came through and Tilda and Julia rolled their eyes at each other.

"Let's hope when you get to be that old, the war is long over and you can just make donuts at the local bakery, if you're still hankering to," soothed Dusty.

"It isn't just about making donuts. They have uniforms, and rules, and they make things more cheerful and happy for the soldiers. I'd be really good at that."

Nobody could counter that argument and the conversation faded away in the heat and monotony of the drive.

CHAPTER EIGHT

July 1943

There hadn't been a lot of problems with getting gas along the way. Rationing was not new and more than a few reluctant filling station attendants had warmed up to them when they started talking about their trip. "Oh, man. I wish I was goin' with you guys!" from one bobbing Adam's apple at a truck stop in Arizona.

"Yep, my son is in the Navy," or "My wife's niece is off working at the Kaiser shipyard in Richmond, California. She said she's makin' sixty bucks a week and can't work enough overtime. Wish it was me."

Then they would shake off their trepidation about the gallons being sucked up by the battle wagon. Helping these travelers was like helping the government, even if the government didn't know it.

Usually there was gasoline to be had, either with coupons or by trading with Mr. Black (as they called the black market in whatever could be had). The sticker on the station wagon was an "X" because of Dusty's mother's work as a midwife, so there usually was not a problem getting fuel.

The next town was their first dilemma. The wagon was low on fuel and there was no heading off to the next berg unless they could fill up the tank, pronto.

About midday they rolled into a sad Arizona town, if you could call it that. The sign said WELCOME TO WINSLOW, ARIZONA, POPULATION 4,577.

Business had been a bit slow for Gus. That wasn't really his name, but it was the name sewn on the grimy coveralls he wore, so he just let strangers passing through think that it was who he was. In truth the coveralls had belonged to the previous owner, Gustav, a damned German who had sold out and headed for the hills when the war in Europe started up.

The heat was oppressive. He'd been sitting in the shade in front of the filling station feeling more and more inclined to dig the jug of moonshine out from the shed. It really pissed him off that he had to do his drinking at work because the missus didn't approve.

"It's not good for you to be drinking in front of the kids," was how she put it, but he knew it was just another way of keeping him from having any fun at all.

This filling station idea had sounded pretty good when his wife's father had dangled the "opportunity" in front of his unemployed eyes. "When my baby girl gets married, I'll make sure to set her husband up with his own little business."

Who wouldn't want to be their own boss, set their hours, and just rake in the money?

Turned out it was a lot more work than it looked like and the wife and then kids that came along with it were not a great bargain. Plus, he had to deal with the sneaky old skinflint of a father-in-law. Then the war came along and put an end to people driving much. Days out here got long and a man deserved to have himself a drink if he had a hankering.

He'd just stood up to find the jug when a big ole gas hog of a car trundled up next to the pump out front.

They almost coasted into the filling station on fumes, although Dusty was reluctant to share that information with his fellow travelers.

It wasn't really considered black marketing to try to trade something the station attendant wanted for a few more gallons of gas, but it wasn't something you'd want to write your congressman about either. Three gallons per family per week was not a lot of fuel when you were hauling your worldly belongings clear across the country. Besides, only folks who could show they owned a car could even get gas rations. Dusty had done a lot of calculating when he started out. At least he had the advantage of living on a ranch. His family place provided beef and oil to the government and got special allocations of gasoline for farm equipment. Still, once you filled up the tank and headed out, you were on your own. He'd gotten as far as Cousin Betty's family farm in Sugar Land and filled up there, but from then on, rationing was the word of the day. Mr. Black was a familiar character in all their lives. You mostly didn't like to think you would "cheat" to get what you needed, but then again, you had to have what you had to have. Once they got where they were going, they could abide by all the rules, but right now, getting there was all that mattered.

The attendant at the station looked especially seedy to Tilda, but then, what did she really know about filling stations?

The girls got out of the car to stretch their legs and Dusty approached the attendant. The man did not inspire confidence. His general appearance was grungy, and the way he slid his eyes toward the girls, especially Tilda in her shorts, was disconcerting.

When Dusty headed back to the car, he was a bit worried but not panicked. More annoyed than concerned.

"This guy is not buying the midwife designation. We may have to pay him some additional cash. Says he has some 'stray' ration coupons he can use for us, but it will cost a bit more."

Dusty and Jack hunkered down to discuss the situation. It wasn't like they had a lot of choices. At best they had some unused ration coupons and some cash to exchange for "favors," if needed.

Julia looked over at the man. His coveralls were stiff from a combination of dirt and sweat. Of course, most men didn't inspire confidence in her, although Dusty and Jack were breaking through the barriers a bit, Dusty more than Jack. It seemed that Jack didn't really know if he trusted himself.

It was clear the attendant wasn't concerned with impressing the opposite sex. He was unshaven and his rank smell reached her when the wind shifted.

Lucy was oblivious, as usual. But Tilda had been distracted since this morning. When she emerged from the backseat of the battle wagon she announced she needed the ladies' room.

The grubby little man motioned toward the back of the station and stared after her as she walked away. She wondered if she would encounter a restroom with possible toilet paper, or an outhouse unlike anything she had ever seen before.

Emerging from the surprisingly clean restroom, Tilda stretched her arms above her head and wondered briefly what the rest of the trip would reveal.

She started at a voice behind her. "Headed for California, are you?"

She turned and saw the station attendant standing between her and the front of the building.

"Yes," she answered, looking past him toward where her friends waited. "Have you ever been there?"

The man stepped toward her, narrowing the space between them.

"No, I've never been there," he said. He looked her up and down, his gaze lingering at the top of those long legs. His pointed tongue flickered out to lick his chapped lips.

She stepped back again, but it almost brought her against the closed restroom door. Each step back she took, he stepped forward.

"I bet you New York girls have a lot of experience. A lot of savvy."

Tilda glanced over his shoulder again. Where were her friends? Would they hear her if she let out a yell?

"Sure, we do, what about you country guys?" Getting him to talk about himself might be a good ploy, although she couldn't care less about him.

Out in front of the filling station Dusty and Jack, with help from Lucy and Julia, had determined that they might have the coupons and cash to satisfy the requirements of their current captor.

"Where's Tilda, and where is Gus?" blurted Dusty, glancing around the seedy lot.

"Wait a minute. I'll be back," said Jack as he disappeared around the corner of the building.

Tilda had been pushed completely against the door of the restroom by the forward motion of her pursuer. He hadn't touched her but he deeply breathed in the scent of her and closed his eyes. "You smell nice…."

At that moment she perceived him as being his most vulnerable. She was preparing to shove him backward and scream her head off when a deep voice behind him interrupted the moment.

"Tilda, is there a problem here?"

Gus jumped and turned toward Jack.

Tilda had not realized how physically daunting Jack was. Certainly, the man before her quailed under his imposing presence.

While the two men faced off, Tilda ducked around the attendant and ran for the front of the building.

Jack glanced back over his shoulder to make sure that Tilda had disappeared around the corner. The smaller man's glance followed Jack's.

"What is going on back here?" Jack voice was low and menacing.

"Nothin' going on. I was just helping the little lady find the restroom. Sometimes there's rattlesnakes and scorpions back here." He smiled obsequiously. He thought he still had a chance of getting out of this fix.

"Ah…" As Jack moved toward the man he quickly stepped back, much as Tilda had done a few minutes before. The man stepped back again as his gaze fell on Jack's fists, just beginning to rise from his sides.

"There's no problem here…. Let's just go get your tank filled up so you can be on your way…no extra charge or nothin'." He smiled and bared puffy gums with gaping holes and browned teeth that would soon join their missing kin.

Nobody spoke as the attendant filled the station wagon up, even checking the oil and water, and wiping the windshield with a grimy rag.

The girls had climbed back into the car. Dusty and Jack stood on either side of the vehicle as Gus finished his ministrations.

Finally, to everyone's relief, the packed car pulled back out onto the highway, raising a cloud of grit as the tires spun on the shoulder of the road.

Dang, not only had he missed out on a little fun, but he was also missing out on a substantial addition to the "savings" he kept in the rusty coffee can hidden in the back of the station. Just a few more desperate travelers and he was hoping to head out for parts unknown, leaving the wife and brood behind.

Tilda had shared her close encounter with the other girls, but there was no additional discussion down the road. It was still too fresh to be a comfortable topic of conversation.

CHAPTER NINE

July 1943

Tilda had expected the hot Southwest highways to cool down after nightfall but that hadn't been the case. In New York, even when the days were stifling, the evenings gave some respite. The wide expanse of sky twinkling with millions of stars was mesmerizing. She wasn't really tired. Yes, the day of travel beat you up, but she was used to walking all over the city and being on her feet most of the time. When they had first pulled over for the night, she headed up the highway a bit trying to stretch her legs. She had a flashlight trained just ahead of her feet in the dim moonlight. After about half a mile there had just been one too many skitters in the sagebrush and a distant coyote's howl had convinced her she had gone far enough. She didn't think her flashlight would be much defense against a gang of coyotes. Was it a gang? She wasn't sure but she wasn't going to worry about it now. The boys had erected a tarp and a tent on the side of the highway, and you could already hear their muffled snores. Being shortest, Lucy had stretched out on the front seat and Julia was allocated the space left in the back of the wagon when they removed the tent. That left the backseat for Tilda to crawl into.

They had used the melted water from the ice to sponge off their sweaty bodies and Dusty and Jack had made a show of averting their eyes as the girls wandered off the highway to relieve themselves. Tilda had always thought that God had been very unfair when he made it so easy for men to pee wherever they wanted. There were a lot of ways things were easier for men.

Tilda had written to her folks a couple of times since she'd left New York, but there wasn't much to say, really. I'm in Chicago, I'm in Houston, same old stuff. She kept the flashlight on and used the dim light to write a few lines to her mother. At least traveling with this band of strangers, rapidly turning into friends, gave her something interesting to write about. She described the different people and where they had come from and why they were going to Los Angeles. She didn't say much about why she was going there. They'd been over it a hundred times and her parents would never understand why she wanted to go off and "join the circus," as her dad called it. Why didn't she just get married to some nice Queensborough lad and pop out a couple of kids like her older sister or even go into the military like her younger brothers? She hadn't wanted to remind them that her pregnant sister and two nephews moving back into her parents' apartment had been one of the motivating factors for moving away. With her brother-in-law gone it didn't make sense to have two apartments. She could have just moved out and gotten a place with a few other waitresses, going home for Sunday dinners with the family. But if you were going to move out, wasn't it better to go someplace worth going? She hesitated briefly and decided it was better not to try to describe the run-in at the gas station earlier in the day. There would come a time when the story would be entertaining, but that time was not yet.

Some nights she went to sleep counting all of the ways that the war had changed her life, and everyone else's. The war had been going on for a long time in the rest of the world when it so rudely interrupted her quiet life. It was a Sunday, one of the few days Dad took off from driving his cab. He'd been lying in the bedroom listening to the Brooklyn Dodgers and the New York Giants play football. He was more of a baseball fan, but he was willing to listen to any Brooklyn team trounce those uppity Giants. Tilda had been doing her nails and absently listening to the New York Philharmonic with her mother. Mom was just finishing the lunch dishes and Brahms Piano Concerto No. 2 had ended when the broadcast was interrupted for a news bulletin. Before the announcer even had a chance to speak, she heard her father shout from the other room, "Holy shit! The Japs just bombed Pearl Harbor!"

Everyone's lives seemed to change overnight. Young men who didn't volunteer for the service were drafted so fast it made your head spin. Women who'd never worked outside their homes were working in stores, factories, and offices. Even Edwin Marchmont's life was thrown into disarray.

One morning Tilda encountered him near the bank of mailboxes on her way out to work.

"Good morning Edwin, are you okay?" He stood staring open-mouthed at the letter he held in his hand.

"Well, my dear, I have to say that I am a bit gobsmacked by this communication from my father."

"I hope it isn't bad news. Has someone in your family passed away?"

"No, no, nothing like that. Nothing for you to worry about, I suppose. It seems that my father has decided that the outbreak of war has provided the perfect opportunity for me to step up and fulfill my destiny, so to speak."

Tilda was running late, but she paused. In the years that the man had occupied his third- floor apartment as the generally acknowledged "remittance man" of the building, she had never seen him look so upset. Not even when the measly stipend provided by his family inevitably ran out mid-month.

"Your destiny?"

"Well, you know that my family in Georgia loves to tell the neighbors that I am a successful businessman here in New York, and, up until now, my father has subsidized my living expenses so that I don't come home and prove them all to be liars."

Edwin pulled a check from the envelope in his hand. "Sadly, this check, although more generous than usual, is the last that I will be receiving from my family."

"Then you'll be going back to Georgia; they are allowing you to go home?

"Alas, no. Not that I would return to that small-minded, inbred community willingly. My father has deemed this the perfect opportunity for me to join the ranks of my noble Southern forefathers and enlist in the military."

Edwin turned on his heel and started back up the stairs.

If there was an appropriate response to this news, Tilda didn't know what it was. She shrugged and pulled her coat more tightly around herself before heading out into the frigid street.

The war was like running into a huge boulder in the middle of the road. You could go over or around it, but you couldn't walk through it, and it would alter your path permanently. Like that soprano, Licia Albanese, who performed Madame Butterfly at the Met until it was banned in the U.S. until after the war. One day you were a world famous Cio-Cio-San and the next day you were scrambling to find a new signature opera role.

Finally, she put away her letter and switched the flashlight off. She'd thought it would be hard to fall asleep scrunched up in the backseat of the car, but she must have been more tired than she thought because the next thing she knew the sun was piercing through the widow and straight into her eyes.

CHAPTER TEN

July 1943

It didn't take long for everyone to wake up and pile back into the war wagon. Motivated by hunger they set off for the next town with an eye out for restrooms and breakfast.

They'd been eating in diners and cafés where you didn't need ration coupons or stamps, but where they could they went into the markets along the way and used their money and coupons to buy items they could eat on the road. The further west they got the less they wanted to stop. It was as though every rise in the road would be the gateway to their destination. Dusty had figured it would take several days to get to the Pacific Ocean. Unfortunately, it would also take seventy-five gallons of gas in the beast of a car that they were driving.

They stopped on the final night in Needles, a dismal burg on the border between Arizona and California. In honor of their entry into California they got rooms in a quiet motor court where they could sleep in real, if saggy, beds. It felt luxurious to shower off the grime of the highway and put on fresh clothes.

In the morning, the Mohave desert still spread out ahead of them, but they felt energized to find themselves so close to their destination. They didn't want to wait to have breakfast, so they bought a bag of Mexican pastries and cups of coffee to keep them going on the road. The conversation brightened.

"I'm gonna just stop a day or two to see Los Angeles and then I'm heading for San Diego to enlist." Jack strained forward as though he could almost see the shining Pacific Ocean ahead of them.

"I don't ever want to ride in a car again…. I will walk everywhere like I did in New York City," Tilda proclaimed.

For the most part, Lucy just entertained herself by watching for Burma Shave signs along the highway and reading them aloud for the enjoyment of all. Partial messages on signs spaced at intervals along the highway were a fixture and broke up some of the monotony. "If hugging on highways…Is your sport…Trade in your car…For a davenport… Burma Shave," or "Does your husband…Misbehave…Grunt and Grumble…Rant and rave?…Shoot the brute some… Burma Shave."

Dusty and Julia looked at each other and their eyes locked briefly. They could see the excitement and the trepidation reflected in each other's faces. What would this new place bring? The world was an unpredictable place for them.

At first, they drove across a desert dotted with cacti, that gradually turned to farmland, then orange groves, and finally the outlines of a skyline of sorts. On the outskirts it didn't really look different to the other towns they had seen. But, rather than peaking with a two-block downtown and then petering off into nothingness, it became a little denser with the miles, a little busier. Streetcars began to appear and there were more automobiles on the road. Warehouses and rail lines gave way to neighborhoods. They saw children playing in the yards and milkmen delivering their wares.

To most of them it started to look like a city, though Tilda still kept looking for something that more closely resembled New York, unlikely as that was. Where were the skyscrapers? Where was the bustle of the city, the mix of people, the taxi horns, and the crush of traffic? She didn't know what she had exactly expected, but this sunny, blue-sky covered scene was not it.

On the other hand, Dusty didn't think he'd ever seen a more beautiful place. He wanted to just keep driving; craning his neck to look around at the unusual buildings and awakening towns. If Tilda had been expecting New York, Dusty had expected the sprawl of Houston or Dallas. There were no oil derricks to be seen, no dust devils, no baked earth beaten down by droves of cattle being taken to train cars and on to slaughter. There were palm trees lining some of the streets for crying out loud. A building shaped and painted like a giant orange with a walk-up window lined with customers was just too amazing to pass up. He pulled over and treated the whole carful of people to cups of the best orange juice they'd ever had.

They stopped for gasoline on the outskirts of Santa Monica. "Hey, folks, I see you have an X sticker on the car. What kind of 'special service' do you provide?" His skeptical glance played over the varied people in the vehicle.

Dusty opened the car door and stepped out. "Well, sir, this is my mother's vehicle and she's a midwife, so she has access to additional fuel."

The man wiped his hand on the bandanna he'd pulled from the pocket of his coveralls. "I see you've got Texas license plates. Just where is your mama?"

"Look, we've been traveling for several days and haven't been able to pick up my gasoline ration coupons. We all came here to either enlist or get war jobs, but we haven't quite got to our destination yet. Is there anything you can do?"

It wasn't like sob stories about lost ration coupons, sick relatives, and desperate circumstances weren't an everyday occurrence. Richie had heard them all. He looked from face to face.

For a few long moments Dusty thought they might be hitchhiking their last few miles.

The attendant had a car, so he got ration coupons for gasoline. He didn't tell the ration board that his particular car had been sitting on blocks out back of the station for the past year because tires were impossible to get. It was convenient to have a few extra gas rations in his pocket. When he went out with friends he could help with fuel, and they were singularly valuable to barter for other scarce items.

"Well, lucky for you guys that the end of the week is here; I haven't used up my own rations. They're gonna expire and be no good to anyone in another day, so I can spot you a few gallons. Just don't be telling anyone."

"Thank you so much, man."

"Richie."

"Thank you, Richie."

"Yeah, so what are your sad tales?"

"I'm here to join the Navy," Jack volunteered.

"The rest of us are going to get war jobs," Lucy interjected.

Richie stopped the pump. "I've got my draft notice, but my dad owns this station and he's down with a bad back. If I go he'll have a hard time hiring anyone and making ends meet. My mother says she can do it, but I can't see her out here pumping gas wearing her apron."

"I wanted to enlist a couple of years ago, but I had family to take care of. They got older, so now I can go," Jack admitted.

"Yeah, when my dad's back gets better I'll be out to join you."

Lucy got out of the car. "You know, we are all doing what we can. You've got your folks to worry about, even though you really want to go and fight. I think that it's great you are doing the right thing for your family."

Richie smiled, "Well, thanks. I'll be fighting as soon as I can."

They bought a round of Cokes and continued to chat while they drank them.

After they'd returned their empty bottles they piled back into the battle wagon.

Dusty turned to Richie. "Say, how do you get to the ocean from here?"

A little surprised, Richie smiled and pointed to the west. "You just keep driving until the road ends. You can't miss it."

CHAPTER ELEVEN

July 1943

Richie was as good as his word and before long Highway 66 abruptly ended at the base of the Santa Monica Pier.

"There it is, I can see it. The Pacific Ocean." Lucy bounced in her seat. "Holy cow!"

Jack didn't say anything, but he sat so far forward in the front seat that his forehead pressed against the windshield.

Julia, Tilda, and Dusty all just grinned.

"Stop the car, stop the car, I need to get closer."

"Whoa, just a minute. I need to find a parking spot."

"Just wait a few minutes, Lucy." Julia put a restraining hand on Lucy's arm. "We'll park and we'll all get out."

"Okay, but hurry. I can't believe it. I'm at the Pacific Ocean."

It took a few minutes to park the car, and as soon as it came to a halt, Lucy threw open the door and ran toward the beach.

Jack restrained himself while the rest of them piled out on the walkway, but once the doors were closed and things locked up, he strode quickly in the direction Lucy had gone.

Dusty, Tilda, and Julia stopped a moment to gaze up at the huge SANTA MONICA YACHT HARBOR sign that arched over the highway.

"Now, that reminds me of something you might see in New York City, only there it would be lit up," Tilda said.

"Probably don't want the Japs to find it too easily." Julia laughed.

Two piers jutted out into the bay. The older one sported mostly fisherman. The second pier, the PLEASURE PIER, if you believed the signs, was more intriguing. From the highway you could see the roller coaster and Ferris wheel, silenced by the war.

"We'd better go find Lucy and Jack before they get into trouble." Dusty led Julia and Tilda toward the beach.

On a summer afternoon before the war, the carnival rides would have been running and the pier would have been packed with vacationers, but returning to those days would have to wait. For now, the rides remained shuttered.

They found both Lucy's and Jack's shoes abandoned in the sand. Lucy pranced around in the shallows and Jack had rolled up his pants and stood knee-deep in the lapping water.

"Oh, my gosh." Lucy returned to them, grinning broadly. "This is so amazing. I can't believe I'm really here."

Dusty removed his hat. "Yep, we made it all the way here. The next part of the adventure begins."

Lucy ran back to the water and Tilda and Julia slipped out of their shoes and waded out a few feet. Dusty stood gazing at the vast ocean. He started a bit when Julia approached him. "What are you thinking, staring out into the distance like that?"

"I was just thinking that on the other side of that beautiful water there are battles being fought and people dying."

Neither of them spoke for a few moments, then Dusty turned. "We should probably gather everybody up. We need to find the place I'm going to be staying before it gets dark."

Santa Monica had not been a random destination. The family of a college friend owned a beachfront home there, and they'd agreed to let Dusty stay on their property while he was in California.

The directions had been simple. "When Highway 66 ends at the ocean, turn north and drive until you see the wrought iron gate on the left side of the road. The gate will be unlocked. Just drive up to the house and we'll give you the key to the gardener's cottage."

Dusty's friend would not be there as he was fighting in Europe, but his parents would be home.

The afternoon was warm, but a cooling breeze blew across the highway from the ocean side.

Julia drove and Lucy fiddled with the radio dial. "Oh, I love this song." She started moving to "It Must be Jelly" … "Cuz jam don't shake like that," she sang.

"Are you sure this is the place, Dusty?" Julia gazed at the massive gates.

"Yep, this is the place."

Jack jumped from the car and swung the gate open. It was unlocked as promised and they all stared down the long driveway for a few moments.

"Get back in, Jack, we can't sit here all day. The worst that can happen is that it's the wrong place," Dusty coaxed him.

"You didn't say your friend's father was Daddy Warbucks," Lucy exclaimed.

"I didn't know it." Dusty hadn't mentioned his own family's cattle ranch and oil wells before and now didn't seem like the right time. "Jimmy was just one of the gang in college. He's in the Army Corps of Engineers now, someplace in Europe, or maybe someplace across that ocean there." He wondered if his friend's parents ever gazed across that expanse of water and wondered if their boy was out there getting shot at.

Julia wondered if she might have been mistaken in categorizing Dusty as just another cowpoke. "What college did you go to?"

"Chet, Jimmy, and I all went to the Agricultural and Mechanical College of Texas, in Brazos County, but Chet was a couple of years ahead of us."

"What did you study?" Julia was still processing this new information.

"I studied architecture, Chet was an agriculture major, and Jimmy is an engineer."

They had drawn up to the front of the house, which was even more imposing up close. A broad half circle of paved driveway curved in front of the entrance of the house. Wide steps and a broad porch were flanked by columns and tall windows.

Julia shut off the engine as they continued to just stare at the facade. "What do we do now?"

Dusty took a deep breath and opened the car door. Just as he emerged from the car, the big front door of the house opened and out stepped a trim young woman. "You must be Dusty; we've been watching for you for days. Welcome, welcome."

The woman hurried down the steps and stuck her hand out to Dusty. "I'm James's sister Barbara. I am so happy to meet you."

She turned to the car and leaning down addressed the occupants. "Please, all of you, get out and come into the house. Mother has prepared some refreshments."

As each of them exited the car Barbara shook their hands and then ushered them all up the steps and into the vast entry hall.

"There is a lavatory just to the left where you can freshen up, and we'll be having some cookies and lemonade in the drawing room just through those doors. Of course, if you'd rather have a beer, or something else…" Her voice floated behind her as she continued on through the drawing room doors.

Dusty and Jack looked at each other briefly before following the fading narrative into the other room. The three women trailed behind them.

The big room was more formal than the parlor at home, Dusty thought, and the rest of them were not sure what to think of the luxurious space. It reminded Tilda of the lobbies of some of the New York hotels.

Another woman entered the room carrying a tray. She was a miniaturized feminine version of her son, James, to Dusty's eye. He moved quickly to take the heavy tray from her. "Here, let me help you with that."

"Thank you so much, dear. Just put it on the table in the center of the room." She turned to her guests. "Please, everyone, come in and sit down. There are just a few simple snacks. Some iced tea, lemonade, and cookies. I'm not much of a cook and most of our staff have gone off to the war or much better paying war work." She looked a bit wistful. "Of course, we still have a bit of help, but we all have to make our sacrifices, I suppose."

They all sat gingerly around the room and Barbara and her mother offered them food and drink. "We would normally serve coffee, but our rations are a bit slim right now. Perhaps when Arthur returns from the office we can brew up a pot."

"Really, Mrs. Hardy, there is no need to feed us. I just stopped in to get the key to the quarters you have been so generous as to offer me." Dusty hurried to allay her fears of being a bad hostess.

"Oh, yes. The keys. They are right here." She stepped to the ornate fireplace and removed the keys from the mantel. "Barbara, could you show them where to leave the car and the path down to the gardener's quarters?" Handing the keys to Barbara she turned back to Dusty. "Our gardener joined the Navy last year and we've made do with day labor to try to keep up the grounds, so you are not displacing anyone by staying here." She glanced around the room at the four others. "Although the space is nice, it is quite small. Really just a lounge, kitchen, and bedroom, and of course a bath."

"Don't be concerned, ma'am, none of my friends will be here more than a few days. Jack is enlisting soon, and the ladies are looking to immediately find lodgings and employment."

Mrs. Hardy looked relieved at that. Julia thought it odd that Dusty was now speaking just like their hostess. Who was this guy?

Barbara showed Dusty where to leave the car at the head of a walkway that led down the side of the surrounding wall in the direction of the beach. "Here are the keys then. Will you be coming up for dinner?"

"That isn't necessary, we've already inconvenienced you enough."

"Well, then, just follow the path along the wall until you reach the cottage. We've provided a few grocery items in advance; eggs, some milk, a loaf of bread, and tea bags. Mother and I will send down a little picnic for you around dinnertime, and I'm sure Father will stop by to welcome you when he returns home."

With that, she turned and walked back toward the house.

They were all sitting on the porch of the cottage watching the sunset over the Pacific when the incongruous form of a nattily dressed businessman, Homburg hat and all, strode around the corner carrying a picnic basket.

"Welcome, welcome. I'm Arthur, James's father. You must be Dusty Rhodes." He extended his free hand to Dusty and smiled at the rest of them.

Dusty jumped to his feet. "Hello, sir. It's great to meet you. Let me take the basket for you."

"No need, son. I'll just take it inside."

Arthur Hardy placed the basket on the rustic table. "Barbara put a light dinner together for you all. I think there's sandwiches, potato salad, and some fruit. Even a couple of bottles of wine, in here."

"She didn't need to do that, sir."

"I know, but she's rather at loose ends since Michael, her fiancé, went into the Navy. It gave her something useful to do."

Mr. Hardy pulled the items from the basket and opened one of the drawers. "Yes, Barbara was correct. There is a corkscrew in here. I wouldn't be surprised if she and Michael didn't make occasional use of the cottage before he went away." He hesitated for a moment. "Dusty, I want to tell you how sorry I am about your brother's death in Europe. James wrote to me about it, but he didn't tell his mother and sister. They are very anxious…very frightened about what is going on and he didn't want to upset them."

"I understand." Dusty took the proffered corkscrew and picked up a bottle of wine.

"Won't you have a glass of wine with me and toast to your brother and all the others who are putting their lives on the line?" The man nodded toward the bottle on the table.

"Yes, of course." Dusty opened the wine while the older man stepped to the cabinet and took down two wineglasses.

Dusty poured the wine and they each picked up a glass. "To Chet, and all the others, whom we have lost."

"I like to think that Jimmy is busy building bridges like the ones he made with blocks when he was a child. I comfort myself that he is not 'in the fray,' so to speak, and that it makes him safe. But I don't believe it."

"No, sir. I don't think anyone out there is safe."

After a few moments Mr. Hardy prepared to leave. He paused. "I would appreciate it if you wouldn't mention Chet's death to Barbara and Lydia."

"I won't say anything."

When he was gone, Dusty returned to his friends. "He brought us some dinner and some pretty damned good wine, too. I'm not going to let it go to waste."

CHAPTER TWELVE

August 1943

Lucy absently swung her legs as she sat on the edge of a wooden flower box, rhythmically thumping her heels against the side as she waited for the trolley.

Sitting beside her Tilda studied the schedule spread out on her lap. "I think we'll need to make two transfers getting back to Santa Monica. This thing is more complicated than the subway," she sighed.

"What's a subway, again?"

"It's like a trolley line, but underground. Or most of it is underground."

"Underground?" Lucy couldn't keep the skepticism out of her voice.

"Yes, it's under the streets in New York."

"Do you climb down ladders to get to it?"

"Of course not. There are stairways that go down to the stations."

"Hmmm." Lucy seemed to have lost interest. "When's Julia getting back? She'll miss the trolley if she doesn't hurry up."

Tilda glanced around looking for their friend. "She won't miss it. I think she just stepped into the drugstore there." As she spoke she spotted Julia coming out the door of the Rexall store on the corner carrying a newspaper. At the same time Lucy jumped to her feet, "Here comes the Red Car, finally."

It was midafternoon so the car was not too crowded; they were able to get seats close to one another.

"It never occurred to me that the hardest part of this journey would be trying to find a decent place to live." Julia opened the newspaper to the classified ads.

"So far the places we've seen haven't been very nice but that last one was the worst, so far." Lucy just shook her head sadly.

Tilda and Julia had to agree with her. They'd been so hopeful setting out this morning. Even though this was their third day of traipsing from one end of Los Angeles to the other, the ads they had picked today seemed doable. The first one had already been rented, they couldn't even find the second one, and number three had been unlike anything they'd ever seen before.

A very large lot of evenly spaced little buildings spread out before them. The nearest one was identified as the OFFICE by a faded sign on the door.

"How can I help you ladies today?" The manager, as identified by the name placard on the desk, seemed friendly enough.

"We're here about your ad for accommodations." Tilda didn't know what else to call what they were looking at. It wasn't apartments, and it wasn't rooms.

"Glad to hear it. We've got a selection of spaces. Are you looking for single space or shared space?"

"What's the difference?" asked Julia.

"Well, you can pay the full rent for a space, or you can share the space with someone who works the opposite shift. The day space is yours to use from six a.m. to six p.m. and night space is available the other twelve hours."

"Wait, you only rent the space for half of the day?"

"Most of our folks work at the aircraft factories. They work twelve-hour shifts, seven days a week, so they only need to sleep half the day. It doesn't make any sense to have the rooms sitting empty when people are desperate for a place to rest. The rooms have a bed and dresser with a wash space and toilet. There's a shower building with laundry facilities on each row."

"What do people do about cooking?"

"Most everybody eats all their meals at work. They get good hot food at a decent price."

Tilda and Lucy just stared at the man. Finally, Julia spoke up. "Could you show us one of the…rooms?" She'd almost said shacks, but didn't want to offend the man. Maybe it wouldn't be too bad.

The room he showed them was clean and obviously occupied for at least one of the shifts. The washroom displayed someone's grooming items, and two of the dresser drawers were claimed.

"Truth is, most of the spaces are rented by men, although there are a couple that are shared by women working at the plant. Right now, we have two fully empty units and a couple of half-occupied units."

"So, can one person rent a room for the whole twenty-four hours?" Julia asked.

The man looked taken aback. "Well, sure if they want to pay twice the rent to leave the space empty half the time. Seems like a waste of money though."

"Well, thank you so much for showing us the room. We'll have to think about it." Tilda couldn't walk away any faster.

Once they were on the Red Car they could relax a bit. So far the day had been pretty discouraging. Julia was bent over the classified section of the *Los Angeles Times* and Tilda dozed in the corner. Lucy struck up a conversation with a young girl sitting next to her.

"That is so great, thank you so much." Lucy took a scribbled-on paper from the woman and turned to Julia. "You won't believe it, but this lady has an aunt in Burbank who sometimes has rooms to rent. She gave me her name, phone number, and address. We can try to call her when we get back."

They had rolled to a stop at a junction where they needed to change cars, so they moved out onto the sidewalk.

"I think we have to get the next car across the intersection." Tilda headed across the street, followed by the others.

At least they didn't have to wait very long before another Red Car clattered up.

Julia had finished marking up the newspaper ads and turned back to the front page. "It says here that the Germans might be retreating. That's a good thing, isn't it?"

"Who knows what a good thing is, anymore?" sighed Tilda. "I need someone to interpret the news for me. One day we're winning and the next day we're not." She kicked absently at the seat next to her. "Don't mind me. I'm tired, hungry, discouraged.… I didn't think this would be so difficult." Neither of the other women said anything.

After their final trolley transfer, they were getting closer to the water and the breeze from the ocean lifted their spirits a bit.

"I've been thinking about us trying to get a place together. I know we all want to, but I don't know if it will be possible." At the look on her friends' faces Julia raised her hand. "Wait, just hear me out. One of us could get the space we looked at yesterday. It was tiny, and the landlady was kind of snarky, but at least we wouldn't have to share the bed. The other two could take the cottage things we looked at. We could each get one and not share. The rent wasn't that bad for the whole thing. It doesn't have to be forever."

Nobody responded to her, but their sad faces said it all.

The last hurdle was a short bus ride from the trolley stop to the Hardy home.

They went directly to the house today, hoping Lydia would let them use the phone to try their last contact of the day. Barbara answered the door wearing an apron and looking a bit red in the face. "Of course you can use the telephone. It's in the nook just off the entry hall. I'll be in the kitchen if you need me. I've been trying to put together some scones for Mother, but I'm afraid they are turning out more like door stops." She wandered off, still muttering to herself and waving her hands around.

Only Tilda and Julia had ever dialed a telephone so there was a fair amount of discussion about how to do it properly. Finally, Tilda picked up the heavy black receiver and dialed the number on the paper.

Dorothy had just nodded off in her chair when the jangle of the telephone startled her awake. "Lord almighty!" It took her a moment to determine where that damnable noise was coming from, and three rings before she could rouse herself to answer it. "Hello!" It wasn't her friendliest voice.

"Hello, could you tell me if Mrs. Molly Moseby is at home."

"Yes, I can tell you and no she is not." Down slammed the receiver.

She had started the hobble back to her chair when the phone began to ring again.

"Hello!"

"Yes, hello, again. Could you take a message for Mrs. Moseby?"

"No, I can't be taking messages." Bang, down went the receiver.

This time Dorothy waited and damned if the phone didn't ring again.

"*What* is it you want?" she said this time. The hell with the niceties.

"Please, we just want to know if Mrs. Moseby rents out rooms and when she will be home."

"She'll be home before dinnertime or there'll be no eating here tonight."

"Do you know…?" But it was too late—the phone had slammed down again.

Not one to be easily deterred, Tilda turned to her friends. "She'll be home by dinnertime. We'll have to get Dusty to drive us to Burbank. I've got a good feeling about this one, except that whoever it is that answers the phone needs to learn some manners."

The girls left through the kitchen to thank Barbara for the use of the phone. The woman stood in front of a batch of singularly unappetizing brown disks. "Do any of you know how to make scones?" she wailed.

"I can make biscuits, are they anything like scones?" offered Lucy.

"Yes, I think biscuits are similar, only scones are sweeter and you eat them with jam and clotted cream. Please, you can pay me back for everything if you can teach me to make them."

Lucy blushed. "Sure, I can teach you to make biscuits and you can put whatever you want on 'em to sweeten them up. I can come over tomorrow, in the morning."

"What will I need to get to make them?"

"Just flour, baking powder, shortening, salt, and buttermilk."

"I have all of that, except the buttermilk."

"Don't worry about that. You can use regular milk if you have a bit of vinegar to sour the milk."

Barbara looked skeptical. "Vinegar…?"

"Yes, ma'am. It will work fine."

They left for the cottage with a bit more spring in their steps. Now all they had to do was get Dusty to drive all the way to Burbank.

CHAPTER THIRTEEN

August 1943

Dorothy stumped angrily out the screen door and down the back steps. Sometimes taking her annoyance out on the Victory Garden was the only thing that kept her from starting a row with her daughter-in-law. There'd be no winners in an argument but they'd both benefit from her chopping weeds for a bit.

The rambling house had a garage, but since they had no car, it mostly stored the detritus of the long years they had lived there: the old furniture Aloysius had always planned to repair, the wagons and baseball bats from the boys' growing up, the garden tools stowed near the side door where they were easy to get to.

Behind the garage sat a smaller shed and arbor, spilling over with bougainvillea. When they were growing up her grandsons had used that space for their own private fort. Over the years it had been a pirates' den, a clubhouse, and finally, a place where she'd found the youngest boy canoodling with the neighbor girl. Now it was deserted by all but the spiders and some mourning doves that returned to nest there year after year, but Dorothy noticed that the little gate to the arbor stood ajar.

She scraped the rickety gate shut and something started within the shadows, and then a pale face advanced from the darkness.

"Don't be afraid," a voice said, "it's just me. Harold Caine, from down the street."

As the face came closer it revealed the shape of a tall adolescent wearing the too-small jacket and cap of a telegraph boy. The face was familiar, as was the name it uttered.

"Harold Caine…you mean little Harry Caine, William's little brother?"

"Yes, ma'am, but it's Harold now."

"All right, Harold then. What are you doing there? You gave me quite a start."

"I'm sorry, ma'am. I was just resting here…remembering."

"Well, I guess that's all right then. I didn't know you were working as a telegraph boy now."

"I'm still going to school, but William is gone off with the Navy and I'm working to help Ma with things. I'm the man of the house now." The pride in his voice was obvious and he stood a little straighter.

Dorothy shook her head sadly. How many young schoolboys had stepped up to fill the void left by fathers and brothers gone off to war? She remembered that Mrs. Caine had been a widow for many years and her oldest son had done his best to help her support them all. During the long years of the Depression, she had seen him less and less often in the group of boys who congregated in the little fort behind the garage. Little brother Harry had been mostly tolerated, depending on how good-natured the older boys were feeling.

The red hair and spatter of freckles across his nose were still there, but the shining blue eyes seemed to have a world-weary look to them.

"I'll be going then, sorry about surprising you."

"You don't need to go. I am just going to garden a bit. What were you doing in there?"

"Nothing, really, just remembering how it used to be, when all the boys were here. Sometimes I just need to think it will maybe go back that way, someday."

"Well, maybe not exactly that way, everyone's growing up. Just look at you. You used to be the skinniest little kid I ever saw."

The boy smiled shyly. "Yep, I was pretty skinny, but I've been growing fast."

Dorothy considered him for a moment, then said, "I was just about to get me a glass of iced tea. Would you like one, as well?"

"Why, yes, ma'am, I would. I have to get back to the telegraph office pretty quick, though."

"It will just take a minute. I could use a break and someone to talk to." Dorothy didn't actually say "other than my stubborn daughter-in-law" but she thought it.

She came back with two frosty glasses of amber liquid. "Sorry, it isn't sweetened, but it does have some lemon in it." She nodded in the direction of the heavily laden lemon tree at the back of the little yard.

Harold took the glass and tipped it up, downing it in just a few swallows. "I'd best be going. The telegrams are probably stacking up for me."

As he turned away and started out toward the bicycle he had stowed next to the garage, Dorothy spoke again. "You know, you can always come here to remember whenever you need to. Sit for a spell and come to the back door for a cold drink and a bite to eat. Or just for some conversation."

"Thank you, ma'am, maybe I will." He slung his long leg over the bicycle and pedaled off down the gravelly drive.

Dorothy stood there long after he'd disappeared around the house. After a bit she turned to get her hoe but realized that her anger had vanished. The weeds would flourish for another day. She'd go into the house and bake up a batch of oatmeal cookies, sweetened with applesauce and raisins, and while they baked maybe she'd write letters to her grandsons. It never hurt to keep the cookie jar filled just in case someone stopped by.

CHAPTER FOURTEEN

August 1943

Molly Moseby slammed out the front door of the old clapboard house onto the porch carrying her bowl of string beans. She sat down in the old rocker. For twenty-five years she had been married to a violent drunk and had spent most of her time protecting her boys from their father's tirades. Now the boys were grown and she was a widow. When the war broke out her boys had joined the Navy, and one day her husband, Aloysius Moseby, drank one pint too many at the local bar and set off for the Navy recruiting office to join up. He'd missed a turn and driven into a drainage ditch and Molly sincerely hoped he was sitting in Purgatory waiting for his mother to pray him into heaven. She didn't wish him to hell, although she'd thought about it many times when he was alive. But she was a practical woman and was pretty convinced he'd be spending a few hundred years working off his sins. "Fair is fair," she'd thought at the Mass said for him at St. Benedict's, and she'd shed a few tears, for the charming young man he had been when they married. That boy, with the impish grin and the quick joke had disappeared long ago and left her with a mean-mouthed lout. But now she was a respectable widow with a ramshackle boarding house. The sign out front said ROOMS FOR RENT, RESPECTABLE LADIES ONLY; and she was the one who got to decide who was "respectable" and who wasn't, although she was still stuck with her cranky mother-in-law.

She hummed and rocked and gave each green bean a satisfying snap followed by a zip of the string and a toss into the bowl. The neighborhood had changed over the years. When her sons were small it had been full of families with young children. Rowdy boys rode bikes up and down the streets and pigtailed girls jumped rope and played hopscotch. The Depression had hit the street hard. One by one the houses had darkened. Either they were empty, or the families had turned into themselves and their poverty. She and her family had been "Lace Curtain Irish." Molly thought it was a nice name for a not-nice thing. Al had always been a drinker. "I'm Irish for God's sake, I'm supposed to drink." He'd laugh and pour another glass of whiskey or pint of beer.

He'd been shipped off to Europe for the last few months of "The Great War," and whatever the things he saw there, that he would never talk about, had changed him.

Sometimes, in her dreams, she ran across a field behind Al. They were both laughing, but he was just beyond her reach when he would turn and smile and beckon her onward. Before the dark times he'd been a cocky redhead with sparkling blue eyes. After that war, he'd been sadder, darker, and when baby Deidre, his angel, had died of the Spanish Influenza, a light had gone out in him; that something in him that believed that God smiled down on all of us, died once and for all.

He had carried on the best he could, mostly working hard, coming home as the sky darkened and gathering his family around him at the old dining room table. He took pride in his work at the docks and pride in his house and his boys. But, when the stock market crashed and the work became scarce he became closed and sullen. The laughing stopped. The drinking got worse. Sometimes he'd come home bloodied and angry. The regular pay stopped coming in, but somehow, he kept them fed and kept their home. But the shouting and the hitting increased. It wasn't about pretension; it was about shame and secrets. But all of that had passed now.

Molly's rocking stopped, and her fingers lay still in her lap as her mind wandered back through the neighborhood so long ago. It was a shame how powerless they had been to stop the crumbling of their lives:

the dying of the light in those young Irish eyes, the fear and shame in their home, the crushing wheel of poverty and isolation.

Although she was gazing at the street in front of the house, she didn't notice the car pull up at first. It was the laughter and the slamming of car doors that roused her from her daydream. The vehicle was quite a sight, covered in dust and full of people. Five people climbed out and all of them turned to stare at her and her house. There was a tall man and a shorter, stockier one. Three girls climbed out of the backseat. One of the girls was a tiny brunette, one a bouncy redhead and the last, a lanky blonde. "Peroxide," Molly snorted to herself, absently reaching up to touch her mouse-brown curls. She'd always wanted to peroxide her hair, but how did you just show up at Mass on Sunday with platinum hair?

Molly stood up and walked to the top of the steps. "Can I help you?" She smiled.

The tall blonde stepped forward. "Yes, we are looking for rooms to rent. We just got here and we're looking for jobs."

"Well, then you've come to the right place. I've got three beds to rent, but the men will have to find someplace else to stay." Molly dried her hands on her apron and waved the group onto the porch.

It didn't take a lot of discussion to decide that Tilda, Lucy, and Julia would rent her empty beds. Jack was going to enlist in a few days and could stay with Dusty until then.

Molly showed them the rooms, and the rest of the house. Oddly, her cranky mother-in-law was humming away baking cookies in the kitchen.

They paid her the first month's rent and promised to donate their ration coupons to the cause, once they had everything set up. They could move in tomorrow, and the drive back to Santa Monica was a much cheerier trip.

CHAPTER FIFTEEN

September 1943

Tilda had been working at the canteen on the movie lot for over a week, but she was still star-struck when the actors sauntered in dressed in their costumes. They ordered their pot pies and tuna salad sandwiches and she was getting to where she remembered their regular lunches. She didn't quite stammer so much as she repeated their requests back to them.

The weekend was coming up and a couple of the girls she'd met had invited her out on the town. She had learned that usually meant heading for the USO to dance with the boys who were stationed nearby waiting for orders to ship out, or the sadder ones on their way home with injuries that were still too new to feel normal. Those boys weren't much for dancing, but they appreciated a pretty girl who would claim her "dogs" were killing her and sit out a few dances, sipping a Coke with them, her eyes never straying to their empty sleeve or scarred face.

Tonight might be different though. On Tuesday her co-worker, Judy, had whispered that she had an actual "date" with one of the studio actors and they needed someone for his "friend." Tilda figured the guy would either be sixteen and too young to enlist, maybe someone from the Garland–Rooney filming on Stage 12, or he'd be old and handsy. Everyone else was off fighting the war or selling bonds. Tilda had seen many of those war bond shows in New York City. She hadn't had a lot of money, but she figured the payback on the bonds might someday finance her old age.

Her original plan in coming to LA had been to work in one of the war plants. The money was good and she'd feel patriotic working for the war effort. But, when she'd seen a job listed at the movie studio she couldn't pass up applying for it. In New York, she'd loved the theater and spent much of her time and most of her money going to plays, and to movies, if she couldn't afford the plays. She'd schlepped her way on the bus from Queensborough to Manhattan to work in cafés along Broadway.

Her favorite job was the Automat. She didn't really wait tables, but she loved working behind the bank of little windows, refilling them as they emptied, a few nickels at a time. She'd watched the people eyeing the food, doling out their coins and sliding the little doors open to access their choices. Sometimes the choices surprised her. There was one New York cop, a big burly guy, who almost always passed up the fancier desserts and treated himself to a jiggly dish of red gelatin topped with whipped cream. She imagined it was a beloved memory from childhood; the sweet coolness of it mixed with the creamy softness sliding down his throat without even having to chew. At least that was her memory of the dessert, though she had tried it once after watching him enjoy it and found it not to be nearly as lovely as she remembered.

The canteen served gelatin, too. There was nothing fancy here, which is why most of the big stars must have eaten someplace else unless they were in a hurry to get back to the set. Sometimes the movies were shooting out in some western setting in Santa Susanna, and somebody would come in before dawn and pick up lunch to take out to the set. Sandwiches, apples, cookies, jugs of iced tea. Nothing sounded as exciting to Tilda as a giant picnic clustered around a table in a saloon in a dusty corner of Ventura County. Of course, to her, any setting peopled with actors and movie cameras sounded wildly exciting and romantic.

Usually, when she got off work, Tilda hopped on the Red Car to Burbank. Dinner was included in her room and board at the old house and every meal she took there or at work meant she'd have that much more money to buy a new lipstick or a cute hat. Maybe she would take the bus down to The Emporium on Westwood Boulevard. to have her last decent pair of silk stockings mended. While she waited she'd cruise the makeup counter, spritzing herself with perfumes until she smelled like what her mother would call "a French cathouse." She wasn't really sure what that smelled like, but she imagined it would be some combination of roses and lavender, with the musky undertone of sweat and sex. She could definitely match the sweat part, but not so much the sex.

Today, though, she'd packed a little bag with the necessities to quickly change for a mysterious blind date. She had given some thought to the transformation. Since the date would be either sixteen or sixty years old, she decided looking like a young ingénue would work either way. Not that she had a lot of clothing choices, but a simple dress that went pretty well with her one pair of peep-toe pumps, and a perky bow tying back her freshly lightened hair would work. She changed and "freshened up" quickly in the tiny restroom. When she finally looked at herself in the mirror she was pretty happy with what she saw. One final flourish was to rummage to the bottom of the bag to find the minuscule bottle of Florida Water and splash it on her neck and shoulders. The dress was a little summery for the surprisingly cool autumn evening, but she'd thought to throw a filmy shawl into her bag in case she needed it.

She folded her uniform neatly and tucked it into the bag. The prickly question of what to do with her belongings while she was being wined and dined had taken some time to figure out. She and Judy would be taking a bus to the restaurant to meet their dates. She didn't want to be dragging a bag around with her all over Los Angeles. She'd decided to leave the bag with her work clothes in her locker. She'd leave her rooming house early the next day and change back into her uniform when she got to work. All this planning just to get a free dinner seemed like too much work, but Tilda hadn't been on a real date since she left New York City. There was a popular song that merrily intoned "They're either too young or too old," and she had found that to be true. Even if you found a seemingly suitable guy, of a reasonable age, you had to wonder why he wasn't in the military. Was there something physically wrong with him like with her friend Dusty, or was he a cowardly draft dodger?

When Tilda emerged from the restroom and stuffed her bag in her locker, she saw that Judy was a little more daring than she. The girl had slipped out of her clothes and changed in the locker room, where just anybody could have walked in. Undressing in front of other people made Tilda uncomfortable, but Judy didn't seem to mind it at all. Even after Tilda had posed for a few "arty" calendar shots in dingy New York apartments for sleazy wannabe photographers she still preferred to undress in private. She had soothed her minor misgivings by thinking of those encounters as "show business." The back of the stage or off-camera at a movie set was chaotic, seedy, and unimpressive. But drape a marabou stole across your shoulders and turn just right in front of a velvet drape and suddenly you were glamorous and alluring.

CHAPTER SIXTEEN

September 1943

Tilda and Judy reached the bus stop just in time. As usual, the bus was crowded before they even got on. With rationing of gas and tires, and the car manufacturing plants being converted to build weapons and tanks, everyone used the bus, or trolley, or walked. But, Los Angeles was not really a walking kind of town. The passengers looked tired. The workers from the munitions plants had worked twelve-hour shifts or were on their way to a long workday. Some of them might stop for a bite to eat before taking their shift in the bed they rented for twelve hours a day.

Tilda thought again how lucky she was to have a single room at Mrs. Moseby's house. She shared a bathroom, it's true, but it was just down the hall. Her sheets got washed in the old wringer washer and dried in the sunlight and wind on the clothesline outside.

Her thoughts were interrupted when Judy jumped to her feet. "Yikes, this is our stop. Get off…get off." Tilda was standing as she'd given her seat to a tired-looking woman with a small child. So, she stumbled quickly off the bus before looking around the neighborhood.

When she did glance up she was surprised to see that it was a quiet neighborhood that looked a little like home. Fairly large homes graced much of it, and there was a small central square where the lights shone from the windows of an inviting little restaurant. "Are you sure this is the right place?"

"This is it. I have the address right here and the name is on the window. *Tuscano's*, see?"

As they made their way to the front door Tilda felt a little self-conscious. Then she shrugged. This was the nicest dress she owned so she couldn't have dressed up more if she'd wanted to. She rather regretted not taking the time to draw seams down the back of her legs with an eyebrow pencil so that it wouldn't be so obvious she wasn't wearing stockings. Oh, well. The guy was probably so old he wouldn't be able to see her legs.

It was a little early for dinner, especially if you were from New York where people dined later unless they were on their way to the theater. But Tilda had reconciled herself to the fact that people did a lot of things differently on the West Coast. She didn't mind, since she'd want to get home early so she could get to work ahead of schedule and change clothes the next day.

When they entered the restaurant the scent of fresh garlic and tomatoes wafted to them. She saw a few couples seated in the dining room as she glanced around. At a table near the window sat two men. A gray-haired man with a mustache, and the most beautiful, dark-eyed man she had ever seen. She tried not to catch her breath and tamped down the disappointment in her elderly escort.

"The older, gentleman is Armand, and he's loaded," whispered Judy.

"I don't care about money, as long as he can pay for my dinner."

"He won't be paying for your dinner. That is my date. The other guy is yours."

Carlos turned out to be quiet and sweet, and she realized after a few minutes, very recognizable. Tilda reviewed the menu but was distracted by the activity at a nearby table. A woman there drew her attention. Her well-tailored dress, carefully embellished with hand-sewn beadwork, was obviously not from Sears and Roebuck. The woman rose tentatively from her seat and moved first to the left around their table, then moved back to the right. She took a moment to step back to her companion, who looked more than a bit annoyed by the whole procedure, ducking his head down behind his menu.

After the man had definitely indicated his refusal to participate, the woman and her carefully draped fox furs approached Carlos. This woman who, under other circumstances, would have borne down imperiously on the table, crept up shyly and thrust her purloined menu in front of Carlos, almost tipping his wineglass to the side. "Mr. Salida...Carlos, you are my favorite actor, I loved you in *Dark Destiny*."

Carlos glanced up at the woman and for a moment, you could see the shadow of her sixteen-year-old-self beaming at him from behind her heavy makeup.

"Thank you so much, madam." Carlos stood and, towering above her, said, "It is an honor to meet you." He took the hand not clasping the menu and pen and placed a careful kiss on the back of it.

Being from New York City, Tilda had never seen a deer in headlights, but the expression on the matronly face defined that expression.

"Um," she stammered, "would you...could you please give me your autograph?"

"Of course, madam. I would be most happy to." Saying that, Carlos took the pen and the menu and carefully wrote his name across the front.

From that point, the evening went downhill. One after another the women, and men, in the café came up asking for autographs. Tilda was pretty sure that when the tips were left for the dinners they would include the cost to replace many stolen menus.

Tilda ordered one of her favorite dishes from New York City menus, veal scaloppine. It was definitely not something she would see on her boarding house menu, which leaned toward stuffed cabbage, whatever grew in the Victory Garden, and the creativity of her landlady.

When the fragrant dish arrived, she closed her eyes and inhaled the memories of New York City.

What was she doing here, really? First the Depression and then World War II changed everything. She wondered how many people, women especially, had been driven to the point of subjecting themselves to debasement for the simple favor of a break on the rent, or a brief reprieve from hunger for their family.

For Tilda it had not been as bad as for some. She was mostly able to scrape together her contribution to the household through theatrical gigs, working as a waitress, and whatever else she could scrabble together.

She didn't admit to her family that a few of her "jobs" had involved some nudity, and occasional forays into the world of "off off-Broadway" productions. Thankfully, there was no way to document the various semi-naked photographs of Tilda probably still floating around the city.

She was tall, beautiful, and sexy. Early on she had accepted the fact that her "marketable skills" involved not just her physical attributes, but her willingness to collaborate with the general understanding of what worked in show business.

It had been her Harlem friends who had her rethinking her own behavior, both good and bad during those forays with co-workers into the dark neighborhood that occasionally lit up with a surprising flash of music or art. The discussions were never what she expected. In her world there was what people said, and then what they did. The Harlem girls talked about what was important and made her ashamed, not of her behavior but of her inability to admit who she really was. They were fierce and, after her last visit, when a group of menacing teenaged boys challenged her right to be there, she knew she wasn't as brave as they were, but she wanted to be.

The quiet buzz from the surrounding tables, his courteous manner, and his blushing response to the well-dressed elderly woman who first got up the courage to ask him for his autograph, had Tilda rethinking her first reaction to Carlos.

"You might as well get used to this wherever Carlos goes. He is considered quite the Latin lover...." Judy leaned toward Tilda and winked conspiratorially.

Tilda thought he really was gorgeous. Limpid dark eyes and thick dark hair with just the tiniest silver traces at the temples. He even had dimples when he smiled that bashful smile. Still, it was easy to be put off by the press of fans, especially the ones that gave her the surreptitious once-over, assessing why she was here with Carlos instead of them. More than one of the younger women slipped little notes to him that she was sure contained at least phone numbers if not outright propositions.

Throughout it all, between quick bites of pasta and sips of wine, Carlos stayed cool and appreciative. Armand and Judy were carrying on a conversation of sorts, but it was difficult to keep it going with the constant interruptions.

After their entrees were finished, while the waiter hovered nearby with a cart of scrumptious-looking desserts, Carlos leaned closer to her. "I have my own car and driver.... Could we skip dessert and go get some ice cream?"

Tilda jumped at the suggestion. Judy had already been making faces in her direction, giving her the high sign that she and Armand were ready to split off into couples. She could see the color in Judy's cheeks and the slightly tipsy smile she kept giving Armand.

"Sure, that would be great. I'm pretty full already."

Finally, the check was divided and paid, although Carlos had argued to cover the entire bill. The four of them departed the restaurant. Armand and Judy sauntered off down the street and Tilda and Carlos headed for his car.

Once in the back of the Cadillac with the chauffeur ensconced in the front, Carlos sighed. "Thank God that is over."

"I don't know. I kind of thought it was great for you."

Carlos smiled. "Yes, it is what the fame is all about. Still, it gets old."

Tilda patted his arm. "Whatever it takes to make sure people love you, I guess."

Carlos gave some quiet directions to the uniformed driver and before long they came to a quiet ice cream parlor.

"What is your favorite ice cream? I will have Robbie order for us."

"If you are paying, I want a banana split, with chocolate, vanilla, and strawberry ice cream. I want chocolate sauce, strawberry sauce, and pineapple sauce. I want whipped cream and maraschino cherries, and nuts...."

"Okay, sounds like you are someone who knows what you want."

Carlos laughed.

For the first time Tilda looked directly into his eyes.

"Yes, I know exactly what I want."

Going home, Tilda wondered about her connection with Carlos. He was amazing. Beautiful, sweet, kind, shy…

What did that really mean to her? She was, what… She was beautiful, ambitious and young. She wanted a career, love, all of the things that Carlos might offer, but what truly mattered to her in the long run?

CHAPTER SEVENTEEN

October 1943

Julia brushed her hair back from her forehead and took the traditional shorthand pose: right leg crossed over left knee, steno pad balanced, sharpened pencil poised. She waited expectantly for Mr. Chaney's rapid-fire dictation. "This is to Mr. Richard Bellhouse, the address is on my Wheeldex. Dear Mr. Bellhouse, pursuant to our earlier conversation Kaiser Industries is prepared to purchase your entire inventory of …" Julia's pencil skittered across the page and his voice droned on. The window was open but barely a breeze stirred the heavy air. Suddenly Mr. Chaney turned to her. "Please read that back," he barked. Without missing a beat Julia read his words back to him perfectly. She was tempted to imitate his pedantic tone and pace, but decided she was treading on thin ice there. "Hmph!" he snorted. He would have sworn she hadn't been paying attention. He turned back to the window and started up where he'd left off. Julia smiled to herself. She could notate his boring letters with only half her mind focused on his words. Finally, he finished, and she stood quickly.

"I'll need that on my desk by the end of the day…in triplicate," he snapped.

"Yes, Mr. Chaney," she said, then turned and walked out of the office.

Julia sometimes thought that knowing how to type and take dictation was a blessing *and* a curse. On one hand, you always had a skill to fall back on, but as a result, you didn't often go for the more interesting or exciting opportunities, like working in a shipyard, or in a movie studio canteen. Still, you were usually in pretty comfy circumstances. No worries about the weather or irate customers.

When she was younger she'd been more likely to take a chance on things, but she had become more cautious. Tonight, she was taking a chance on going out with a man she didn't know very well. An office supply salesman she'd met in the break room. Just dinner, but still. There weren't many men she felt safe with.

She'd brought her makeup to the office and a snazzier pair of shoes that showed off the pedicure Lucy had given her that weekend. The slim dress and a bright scarf would have to do for tonight. She'd read in the paper that in England the rationing was so tight that each person could only buy one complete outfit a year, including underwear. She didn't spend much on clothes, and there wasn't much to buy, but at least she didn't have to ration her panties.

Malcolm Ornish was not her idea of the ideal man but he did satisfy her wartime requirements. He wasn't a teenager and he wasn't over fifty years old. You could introduce him to people without being embarrassed to be seen with him. The criteria were not very demanding.

True, his hair was thinning a bit, and she believed he still lived with his mother, but it was a legitimate, but hidden, physical condition that prevented him from being drafted. In fact, he managed to work it into every conversation, just so people would know he had tried to enlist.

On the plus side, he owned a car and dressed well, including a spiffy, well-maintained fedora and a decent pair of nicely polished shoes.

They had arranged to meet at a nearby restaurant so that none of the busybodies from the office would see them together, and he had already claimed a table when she arrived.

When she came through the door he popped up from his chair like a jack-in-the-box and waved both arms to get her attention. At least he was enthusiastic.

She was happy with this restaurant. It wasn't flashy, but it wasn't a diner, either. The menus weren't greasy and there were tablecloths and candles and little vases of cut flowers in the center of the tables. Thankfully, the menu prices were reasonable, as well. One time she'd had a date abscond out the back door and she'd had to pay the check herself, so a reasonable price point was a relief. She'd also learned to order from the middle of the menu, so she wouldn't get stuck with a huge bill.

Conversation was mostly confined to his mother, office supplies, the state of the war, and the weather. She was thoroughly enjoying her Salisbury steak when she looked up to see Dusty Rhodes headed across the room in her direction. Damn, she'd hoped to not run into anyone she knew. It wasn't that Malcolm wasn't a perfectly adequate date, just that she didn't like people knowing her business, especially Dusty. There was something between them, but she wasn't really sure what it was.

She could see that Dusty wore his cowboy boots, although he also sported slacks and a dress shirt with no tie. She couldn't see that he was accompanied by anyone and found it somewhat satisfying that he didn't have a date.

"Good evening, Dusty."

"Good to see you, Julia."

"Malcolm, this is my friend, Dusty Rhodes. Dusty, meet Malcolm Ornish."

Malcolm stood to shake hands as the two men sized each other up above her head. Dusty was the handsomer of the two, but Malcolm was better dressed.

The men chatted for a moment, each managing to insert their reason for not being in uniform into their brief encounter.

Niceties completed; Dusty turned to Julia. "I've been meaning to stop by your place to see how everything is going, but I don't get to

Burbank very often."

"Well, as you can see, all is going well. I work in an office nearby, but I am sure that Tilda and Lucy would be happy to see you." She didn't exactly intend to make it sound like she was not happy to see him, but maybe it came out that way.

"Well, then. It was very nice to meet you, Mr. Ornish." Turning to Julia he said, "Please let Tilda and Lucy know that I will stop by to see them soon. Enjoy your evening."

Before she could say anything, Dusty turned on his heel and walked out of the restaurant rather than returning to his table.

CHAPTER EIGHTEEN

October 1943

After running into Julia and her date, Dusty had lost interest in dinner.

Sitting on the dark porch of the Hardys' gardener's cottage his mind wandered back to his family in Texas.

Back home the horizon spread out for miles, dotted with outbuildings, cattle, scrubby trees here and there, and the occasional oil rig. His home had been big; it had to be to hold his bigger-than-life family headed by his dad, Bud, a rancher lucky enough to have struck oil on his sprawling ranch. A big wheel now, who relished the sway he had over local businessmen and landowners. His mother, tough as nails on the outside but compassionate underneath. She'd tamed her cowpoke husband, borne two hardy sons, lost two daughters, and could still ride all day driving cattle into the pens. Though she didn't have to spend her days on horseback she still did it just to prove she could.

Rhetta missed her son Chet as much as her husband did, and Dusty missed him more than anyone else, really. The big brother, the listening ear, the football hero, the champion rider. He had been handsome, charming, loyal, and a good man. Chet had gone to college in Texas to study agriculture; he'd looked like his daddy only stronger and straighter. He knew how to run the ranch, how to handle the business, how to strike the deals. Dusty was different. He was strong, too, but in a quieter way. He had a sense for growing things, for plants, and for animals.

When he looked at the ranch he wasn't seeing the money value, but he was breathing it all in, sensing how to make it grow and prosper.

When Chet was alive it didn't matter how Dusty spent his energy. He'd heard a saying one time that he thought fit the bill here. His daddy had "…an heir and a spare." It freed Dusty to do what he wanted with his life because Chet relished being the heir. He'd been born to big boots and loved filling them. Now his boots stood empty.

When Chet went into the service, he'd become a pilot. He'd always wanted to fly and this was his chance. His daddy had been so proud, they all had. Dusty had bragged on his big brother all over town. Just as proud of his brother as he was ashamed of himself and his broken body. He'd tried to enlist, wanted to go, but the accident from his childhood had left him with a permanent limp. He got around good and could do anything he needed to do, but he sometimes exaggerated the limp in front of strangers; people who would look at a strong man in his twenties and wonder why he wasn't off fighting the war.

The last time Dusty had seen his brother, Chet had told him he was proud and happy to be leaving Dusty to take care of things "until he got back." He knew it was a burden. It would take all Dusty could give to keep things going. He would have to give up some of the things he cared about, but it would just be for a little while.

Dusty could see the excitement in Chet's face. His eyes glowed at the adventure ahead of him. He wasn't thinking about getting shot down by some Kraut asshole, he was thinking about soaring through the clouds. He was thinking about fighting for the good ole USA. He could almost feel the weight of the medals on his chest.

Chet's later letters to Dusty told a different story. The ones he wrote to his parents still sounded optimistic and positive. He talked about whipping Hitler's butt and heading home in a couple of months. Bud would carry those letters around in his pocket to share with "the boys" down at the courthouse when he ran for City Council.

The letters Dusty got didn't say a much different, but Dusty knew his brother in a different way. He knew his bravado was often just that, an act to hide his fears. Chet didn't mention to his parents the close calls and the deaths of friends. He only wrote to Dusty about the devastation of bombed-out cities where he knew not just soldiers lived, but mothers and children. Some of them came with passages blacked out. It was government policy to redact the negative comments or sensitive information, but Dusty knew Chet's code and much of what was left showed the ragged edges to someone who knew how to read it.

CHAPTER NINETEEN

October 1943

Julia sat in the room she shared with Lucy and relished the time alone. Working in the steno pool at the Kaiser offices wasn't as exhausting as some of the jobs her friends had, but it still didn't give you much time to yourself. The office was filledwith rows of desks. It made Julia think of being in grammar school, except that each desk held a typewriter, a stack of typing paper, a little stand to hold up the steno pad, and a basket for the neatly typed letters. You'd think an office would be quiet, and maybe the areas where the customers came in or the offices upstairs were. But, in the typists' area, the clatter of the keys, sliding of platens, and ringing of bells could be deafening. She only worked half a day on Saturday and the usually crowded bus was luxuriously empty in the early afternoon between shifts, when she rode home.

Time was crazy in this house. Some people worked twelve hours a day six or seven days a week, leaving before it was light and coming home after dark for a quick meal before falling into bed. Some left before dark and came home right after dawn, to do the same. Tilda worked in the commissary at one of the movie studios, so her shifts were more normal, but tonight she was going out on a date, so she would go straight from work to the restaurant. She'd be home before it was too late, but until then, Julia had plenty of time to pamper herself and enjoy the quiet. She'd taken a bath without a single person slipping into the bathroom, just for a minute, to grab something "really quick." She'd had time to give herself a pedicure and hand-wash some of her unmentionables, hanging them around the bathroom to dry before Tilda came home.

Dinner had been quiet; just Molly, Dorothy, and a couple of the boarders that Julia didn't know very well. As usual, Molly had managed to turn the rations into a nice meal. She'd been cooking for a family for a long time, and without a lot of money, so the restrictions of rationing hadn't thrown her off too badly. If you counted back the years you knew she'd been feeding some strapping sons and a husband during the Depression. She still kept an admirable garden in the backyard, only now she called it a Victory Garden. Fall, such as it was in Los Angeles, was setting in and the stew she presented tonight had been full of the last summer vegetables: tomatoes, squash, carrots, and what bits and bobs of meat that had been available without coupons this week. Her biscuits reminded Julia of those her mother had baked when she was a child in Texas. Rich with shortening and buttermilk. If she closed her eyes, she could imagine the "butter" she spread on them hadn't been massaged together from a lump of shortening and a capsule of yellow food dye. When she was a child living on an oil lease near Houston, they hadn't even bothered to dye the white glob. She missed the gravy her mother had seemed to magically make from a handful of flour and some pork renderings. Back then her mother had kept a coffee can of bacon grease on the back of the stove for flavoring the greens. Now they saved the meat fat to recycle to make gunpowder. She wondered if there would ever be a time in her life where there was plenty of everything for everyone, but she didn't spend much time on the thought. She'd never seen it yet and didn't know a place where it was true. She hoped that the soldiers out there fighting benefited from the rationing. She wanted them to have everything they needed in abundance.

CHAPTER TWENTY

October 1943

Carlos hunkered down in the backseat of the car, making sure his face was shadowed by the wide brim of his hat. He showed his driver's license to the border guard. Not the new license, but the old one with the old name on it. The one that identified him as Pablo Salas, another of the thousands of migrant workers that swarmed over the southern borders of the U.S. every summer and fall. But he was not coming into California but slinking stealthily back into Tijuana. It made him nervous that one of the tourists strolling the main street of the town perusing the tables of cheaply made goods might recognize him. It took only a few minutes for the car to leave the tourist-packed streets behind and slide into the dirt streets of ramshackle buildings that housed the citizens of the town. They stopped in front of a small, recently painted house and Carlos stepped out into the empty street. "Go get a *cerveza* and come back in two hours," he told his driver. "Don't worry, it will still be light," he said when the man hesitated.

A dog barked and growled ferociously from behind the fence next door. He pulled a large bag from the backseat. Not clothes, this was much better than clothes. It held treats and gifts that were dear in the U.S. and unheard of here. There were steaks, real butter, sugar, chocolate candy, coffee; the wealth of the black market bought with lots of money and the special cachet of celebrity. These offerings were better than gold because you could not buy these things in this neighborhood, even if you had gold.

He turned and walked up the path to the battered porch as his driver turned the car in the middle of the street and made his way toward the nearest cantina. He hoped the driver would be able to drive when, and if, he remembered to return.

A tiny lizard scampered across the boards of the porch as Carlos stepped up and the wooden plank creaked cantankerously. Before he could knock, he heard a plaintive voice from inside the house and the torn screen door swung open. "But where are you going? No more trouble…" Maria spotted Carlos then and gestured toward the young man who stepped out onto the porch. "Pablo, tell him, no more trouble," she pleaded. The young man's eyes flashed toward him, daring him to intercede.

"Don't worry Mama, Francisco knows what he is doing.… Here, take the bag, let me walk him out."

He shifted the heavy bag to the woman and took the younger man's arm in a genial, if firm, grip.

Everything about Francisco bespoke trouble: his insolent gaze, dimpled smirk, the wide lapels and wider shoulders of his over-long suit coat and the tightly pegged trousers. In a flash the wide-brimmed, jaunty hat was placed on his head, rakishly tilted over his right eye. "Sí, Mama, there's no trouble. Pablo knows I'm just going out to have some fun, to meet some girls." His gaze dared Carlos to contradict him.… He was raring for a fight, and there would be one before the night was through. But it would not be with his older brother.

As Carlos escorted his brother to the unpaved street, he took a five-dollar bill from his wallet and slipped it into Francisco's breast pocket, patting the outside of the coat. "For once pay for your drinks and keep the knife in your shoe." Francisco shook off Carlos's restraining hand and strutted down the street. "I will if they will," he laughed. Before he reached the corner, a battered Model A pulled up beside him and he climbed into the backseat. There was raucous laughter and the driver revved the engine and lunged forward in a spray of dust and gravel. The effect would have been greater had he not stalled the engine and had to restart and continue a little more sedately. Carlos turned away before he smiled; he knew Francisco would be looking back to see if he had noticed.

Francisco glanced back through the oval rear window of the old Ford in time to see his brother climb the rickety steps. He stretched his neck and adjusted his shoulders in the oversized jacket. José's red face and lopsided grin showed that he had already been swigging on the tequila bottle he offered. Francisco only hesitated for a moment before grabbing the bottle and downing a fiery swallow of the cheap liquor. His eyes watered but he was able to keep from choking on its harshness.

"Where to, *pachucos*?" said Diego, the driver, reaching out for the bottle.

"To San Diego but hide the bottle when we cross the border. We don't want the *guardas* to think we are going to cause trouble."

"We're not the ones causing trouble, it's those gringo sailors. Big shots, all of them." José laughed. "First go to Carlita's house. She wants to come with us."

"We will stop there, but she's not coming with us. We don't need *chicas* to slow us down. Besides there are plenty of girls in San Diego."

"Stop, anyway. I'll just tell her there's no room."

Carlita and her two friends waited on the stoop outside the two-story apartment building where they lived. She had dressed for the trip, much like the boys were dressed, with her mass of dark hair teased into a halo around her pretty face. Dark red lipstick framed the smile she flashed at them when the car drove up.

José hopped out and hurried over to the girls. Those in the car could not hear the conversation but they could read the story being played out before them: Carlita's disappointment and anger, Jose's supplication, the raised voices, the chorus of complaints from her friends.

Carlita did not take their rejection well. She frowned and then yelled at José, shaking her fist at him and then shoving him away when he tried to console her. Finally, she turned on her heel, storming away toward the downtown area trailed by her friends.

Jose looked sheepish as he climbed back into the car but took the jeers from his friends in good spirits. Carlita would get over it. She was crazy for him, or he thought she was. Maybe he'd bring her a present tomorrow. Some chocolate or a new lipstick. She could never stay mad at him.

Francisco didn't like to keep a girlfriend like some of his friends did. He wanted to feel free to flirt with the girls that hung around downtown San Diego, the Gaslamp Quarter district, and played the exciting Mexican boys against the lily-white gringo sailors. His friends had their girls at home, but they didn't mind not being true to them. Francisco wasn't like that. When he was ready to settle down, he'd want just one girl of his own. For now, though, he told everyone his mama was the only girl in his life. It bothered him that she worried so much, but he wasn't doing bad things. He just wanted to show who he was. That being from Mexico was not a bad thing, but a proud thing. His brother might change his name and pretend to be from Argentina, but Francisco was proud of who he was. Still, he didn't hold it against his big brother. It made life easier; he had five bucks in his pocket because of the lies, and his whole family lived a better life because of them. Sometimes he thought it would be nice if he could tell the little blue-eyed girls with their golden hair that his brother was a big movie star, but that would not be playing by the rules; the rules that made Pablo Salas one person in Tijuana and another in Hollywood. He grabbed up the tequila bottle again and took a huge swig, his eyes watering, and almost choking on the fiery liquid. Immediately he felt the warmth in his stomach. Tonight, he would not worry about it, tonight was just for fun, and swagger, and maybe a few sweet stolen kisses.

There were a few tense moments at the border, but the surly guard who searched the car was mollified to find the unopened "extra" bottle of booze in the back seat. "I'm going to visit my sister in La Jolla," said Diego. "Yeah, right, your sister," sneered the border guard looking over their highly polished shoes and too-long watch chains. The heat had begun to melt the Tres Flores brilliantine in Francisco's hair and the sweet smell mixed with the cheap booze made him feel sick. A slow drop of hair pomade slid down the back of his neck.

CHAPTER TWENTY-ONE

October 1943

Dorothy scuffed into the warm kitchen and noted the empty teacup and toast plate in the sink. The kettle had been left warming on the burner, and she pulled down her favorite mug from its usual hook below the cabinet. The sun had not yet risen, and Molly was nowhere to be seen. Still, Dorothy knew where she was and why she was there at first light. She plucked a tea bag from the canister and poured steaming water over it. She still hadn't gotten used to drinking her tea without sugar and grimaced at the can of evaporated milk still sitting on the table. Oh well, someday there would be sweet tea with real milk. Toast was always a good start to the day. She was lucky that Molly was one of those people who gathered seasonal fruit and turned it into jam. There was still a bit of strawberry goo in the bottom of the jar that she thoroughly scraped out. She was careful to put the jar aside to be used again.

Dorothy kept a close eye on the toaster so that it didn't burn the bread. The little device needed some repair, but the local fix-it guy had gone off to the Marines and toasters were not something they made in the war plants. She sighed. There was no point in fretting over what you didn't have; nobody had those things anymore.

She set her plate and mug down on the oilcloth-covered table and slid the chair around so she could watch for Molly through the window.

After a few minutes she saw her daughter-in-law come around the corner of the neighboring house, watering can in hand. She had garden shears in her apron pocket and a small bunch of roses in her other hand. Molly stopped to gaze back at the empty house and assure herself that all was well before turning and making her way home.

"You know, if anybody sees you out there they're going to report you as a Jap sympathizer."

Molly started at the unexpected voice in the kitchen. She shook her head and stepped to the sink, taking a small vase down from the windowsill for the flowers.

"I am not a Jap sympathizer; I am a good neighbor."

"That woman and her family are gone, for good. What's the point of taking care of her yard?"

Molly busied herself with the flowers and then placed the bright spot of color in the center of the little kitchen table. "Keiko loved her garden. If…when, she comes home I want it to be there for her."

"Waste of time, worrying about some foreigner." Her mother-in-law averted her eyes from the look Molly shot her.

"Keiko is more American than you are, she came here as a young bride and her boys played with my boys since they were babies,…" Her voice choked out the last words and she turned back to the stove, picking up the kettle to refill it.

"Well, it's a damned shame to waste your time on something you can't fix." Dorothy shook her head and stood up. She'd have said more except that she'd noticed the stiffening of Molly's shoulders and knew better than to pursue the subject.

If there was anything that Molly was, it was loyal. Dorothy had averted her eyes and made sure she was busy in the kitchen the day Molly helped Keiko and Michi load their meager suitcases into the trunk of their car. They drove off, Michi driving and Molly and Keiko in the backseat. Keiko had worn one of those kimono things that she dragged out for special occasions. It didn't make any sense to Dorothy to waste space for useful things for something that wouldn't be of any use wherever they were headed. She had put her hair all up in a bun with those fancy sticks in it, and put on makeup, red lipstick and eyebrows, even earrings. Michi had worn his best suit, and his stiff back had held his graying head high. Their boys no longer lived at home. One worked at a bank in San Francisco, and one was still in college. They were not being sent away yet, but the day would come. Dorothy never said it, but she hoped that when that day came they'd be able to go to the same place as their mother and father. Families should be kept together, not torn apart.

Keiko had saved some money that she gave to Molly to take care of their house. Not to pay her, but to keep the power and water on, and pay the taxes. Molly had driven the car back to the waiting garage when they were gone. She and her friend had made a plan; Molly would see it to the end, no matter what. It had been a long time now, and the lovely garden next door stayed green and the 1940 Ford, Michi's pride and joy, stayed tucked under blankets in the dark garage. Dorothy thought Molly was a damned fool about most things. But you wanted her on your side when things got rough and you definitely didn't want her against you. That was why Dorothy bit her tongue more often than anyone knew, like about the money Keiko left. It was probably long gone and the upkeep funds coming from Molly's own slim savings. Or maybe from the money her boys had sent to her every month.

"Well, I think you're just wasting your time.... Good money after bad is what I say. Nobody is ever going to thank you for it."

"Dorothy..." Molly took a long pause and a breath and turned to face her. "For once you and I agree. Nobody is ever going to thank or repay me because I don't do it for them, I do it for me; because it makes me feel good and it makes me happy. I do it for me, so there is nothing to repay."

Once Dorothy had left the kitchen Molly picked up the cup towel and wiped away the tears that had sprung up in her eyes. Dorothy was right about one thing; there wasn't much Molly could fix. Her boys were off someplace being shot at, her husband was gone, her youth was gone, and her neighbor was gone. Still, there were things she could and would do to make life livable.

She washed the last of the jam from the jar and set it to drain. Then she poured another cup of tea and sat down with the stack of ration stamps and the newspaper to plan her shopping for the week. She didn't just take in boarders to supplement her income, although it went a long way toward making things easier. She liked to think she was making their lives better, too. If she hadn't had someone to plan and make a meal for, she and Dorothy would have lived off tea and toast. Who could be bothered cooking just for yourself? She usually cooked the kind of meals her boys had eaten growing up, and since that was during the Depression, they didn't call for a lot of fancy ingredients. It was quantity over quality when it came to feeding her family. Still, she didn't object to cooking some different things when requested. Actually, she'd added a lot of new recipes to her book since she started housing girls from all over the country. Grits, she'd learned to make passable grits, which were cheap and very filling. She'd learned you could slice up the leftovers and fry them in bacon fat. She'd learned to take those last tomatoes from her garden, the hard, green ones that would never ripen, slice them up, dip them in corn meal and fry them. There was a lot of frying going on in her kitchen, and she had noticed the effect on the size of her hips. Not that it mattered.

She could hear the squawking of her chickens in the coop clamoring to get out into the morning light. She wished that she had a rooster so she'd get some chicks but had given up on that in conciliation with the neighbors over the crowing. She at least had eggs to supplement the vegetables from her garden, and they were valuable to barter for other things that were scarce.

CHAPTER TWENTY-TWO

October 1943

Delia White wriggled her bare toes in the burbling water of the creek. She'd been coming here to fish for crawdads since she was a little girl, and the thought that this might be the last time she would do it was both sad and exciting. She'd been here quite a while on this humid Alabama afternoon and was grateful for the dappled shade offered by the spreading mimosa tree above her head.

She spied one of the shelled creatures under the edge of a rock, so she slowly lowered the piece of raw bacon tied to a string right in front of it.

"Them critters have got to be the dumbest in the world," she thought as the crawdad grabbed onto the bacon. She slowly drew the string out of the water with the creature hanging on for dear life, moved the string above her bucket, and jerked it abruptly, causing the crawdad to let go of the bacon and drop into the bucket with his wriggling kin.

The small bucket was half full and she thought she'd soon have enough for Mama to make her famous crawdad étouffée, an elegant, creamy concoction. Or maybe, if they were lucky, she would make filé gumbo, with its darkened roux of filé powder made from ground sassafras root. Delia liked the spicy gumbo better than the étouffée, but anything Mama made for her party would be delicious.

As Delia made her way home by the familiar path she hummed "Chattanooga Choo Choo" to herself and danced the last few steps to the porch.

"Hey, Mama, I've got us a mess of crawdads, what do you want me to do now?" The screen door banged behind her.

Her mother stood over the stove, stirring a big pot of beans. "Well, you could boil up a pot of salty water to cook 'em in it. Then you can peel them for me."

Delia pumped some water into a pot and set it on the only empty burner on the stove. Between the beans and a mess of greens simmering in the back, there wasn't a lot of room. "What time is everyone coming? I need to get cleaned up and change my dress."

"I told everyone six o'clock, so you should have plenty of time. I'll put the cornbread in the oven just as folks start gettin' here."

It only took a few minutes to cook the shellfish, but the process of peeling them was a lot more work.

"What are Melba and Ruby bringing tonight?"

"I'm guessing Melba will bring dirty rice and a pecan pie. God only knows what Ruby will show up with. Your dad has gone down to the smokehouse for the ham and brisket."

The family members you could count on showing up early and helping get things set up started arriving about 4:30. Some of them brought musical instruments: a banjo, a washboard, and a couple of fiddles. Every get-together was an opportunity to "make a joyous sound unto the Lord," as her Auntie Melba always said. Jacob would bring his camera and a fresh roll of film, although it wouldn't likely get developed until after Christmas when the roll was full. Delia wondered if she would ever get to see those pictures.

About 5:30 Delia slipped into the back bedroom and sponged off with a tepid washcloth. The water was neither hot nor cold, but it was still refreshing. She had laid her new travel dress and shoes out on the bed. Sears and Roebuck had come through again. When they were kids they'd all marked up that catalogue with the things they dreamed of for Christmas, but now Delia lingered over sheer underthings and stylish clothes when she had the time to look.

By the time she went back into the kitchen, many more people had arrived. The smell of the familiar food and sound of raucous laughter overwhelmed her senses.

Her daddy had returned from the smokehouse. "There's my baby girl," and put his arm around her shoulders. "This little lady is the very first, but not the last, of the family to graduate from high school, and we couldn't be prouder." From his broad smile you'd have thought he was the one with the diploma.

Mama banged a couple of pot lids together. "Okay, everybody, grab a plate of food and stake out a place to sit. We are going to have a feast."

The food was delicious and plentiful, but Delia didn't eat much. She found herself gazing at each of the attendees and remembering all the good and bad times they'd been through together. She wasn't old enough to remember the times before the Depression, but she did recall that most of her life each and every one of these folks had counted on each other just to keep body and soul together. At least now there was plenty of food, even if other things were much worse.

When the plates were cleared the music began. Darkness had fallen and even the most energetic of the children had settled down onto laps and on the floor to listen.

The party didn't run late. A lot of the folks had quite a long trip to get home tonight and some of them would even camp out in the yard and leave the next morning.

As people started packing up to leave, Auntie Ruby stood up. "Okay, everyone, now is the time for us to give Miss Delia our best wishes for her future."

Those who'd already stood up sat down again. Once Ruby started talking, it could be a while.

"Graduating high school isn't the only thing that Delia has been the first to do. Tomorrow morning, at ten o'clock, she will be taking the Greyhound Bus all the way to Los Angeles, California!"

When the hootin' and hollerin' had died down, Auntie Ruby started up again. "Delia's mama and daddy and a bunch of you other folks chipped in money to buy her a bus ticket and give her a grubstake when she gets there. She's gonna build airplanes or ships or somethin' so that we can win this war." Ruby paused a moment while everyone thought on all the young men that were not there that night because they were off fighting the Huns and the Japs. "Anyways, give her your best hugs and prayers before you leave tonight." Ruby had finally run out of gas and everyone got back to packing up to leave.

Before each person left they gave Delia a big hug. Many of them pressed a quarter or a dollar into her hand as they wished her well. The little kids didn't really know what was going on but they heartily participated in the hugs and kisses.

About midnight, when she should have been long asleep, Delia sat on the porch and watched the last of the season's fireflies flit through the darkness. She heard the screen door close and then felt Mama sit down beside her.

"You should be asleep."

"I know, Mama. I just can't sleep for thinking that so many people are counting on me to do something special."

"You don't have to go at all if you don't want to. You could just cancel the ticket and stay here." Delia heard a note of hope in her mother's voice.

Delia snorted. "And do what? There aren't any jobs here. Besides, I'm excited to go. This is probably the biggest adventure I'll ever have."

"All of the folks here tonight feel like they are going with you, helping the war, somehow. If they had money to give, they feel proud, and if they didn't have any money, they are giving all their prayers. Just go and write back about what you're doing."

Delia leaned onto her mother's shoulder. "You know I will write, Mama."

"Well, it wouldn't hurt to write about meeting movie stars and swimming in the Pacific Ocean. If you don't have any adventures, I'll have to make them up out of whole cloth to keep things interesting for the relatives."

CHAPTER TWENTY-THREE

October 1943

The steno pool office at the Kaiser offices was stifling in the summer and grim in the winter. The large high-ceilinged room had not been built for rows of desks armed with typewriters. The women focused solely on transforming the stacks of blank pages to the right of their typewriting machines into stacks of contracts and documents on the left of their machines. Multiple copies were produced using carbon paper stencils, and errors were laborious to correct. Steno pads and sharpened pencils adorned every desk in readiness for a call for someone to take dictation.

Julia was fast and accurate in both her shorthand and in her typing. Over the months that she had worked in the office she had gradually moved forward from the back row to one of the desks closest to the front. Today had been especially hectic as the secretary for the vice president had been sidelined with a bad cold.

The office had been buzzing all morning, and it seemed that everyone was on high alert. One minute Mr. Chaney would be standing over one of the girls demanding that she type faster and the next he would be almost ripping the paper from her typewriter and setting off down the hall toward the executive offices. Julia had heard a buzz on her break that Mr. Kaiser was in the office. Henry Kaiser, *the* Henry Kaiser, was in the Los Angeles offices today for meetings and all the whir was about contracts with a big investor.

Julia was surprised how excited she felt at that news. Henry Kaiser!

Next to FDR, Kaiser was big. Someone who made a difference.

After lunch Mr. Chaney stood in the doorway of the steno area and surveyed the girls. His eyes lit on Julia. He headed in her direction. At her desk he towered over her. He waved the sheaf of papers in his hands around as he spoke. "I need these right away, in triplicate. Type them up and bring them to me in my office as soon as they are done, It's urgent." Julia just nodded and reached out for the bundle.

One thing she had learned in secretarial school was that you didn't really need to read the words, just follow the letters, one at a time, as quickly as possible. Her stencils were her pride and she didn't want to make mistakes. Only twice in the multi-page document did Julia have to stop, roll the page up on the platen and use a razor blade to remove her error.

When she was done, she whipped the last pages from the typewriter and strode to Mr. Chaney's office, which was conspicuously empty.

Julia halted at the door, turning to scan the room behind her for his nervous presence. Nothing. He'd said he needed it as soon as possible, but he was nowhere to be seen. Damn!

She knew the papers were important, "urgent" he had said, but she didn't know what to do with them. It didn't make any sense to just set them aside and go on with the rest of her work. Someone was waiting anxiously for them. Still, under normal circumstances she had never ventured out of the steno pool into the outer bank of offices and reception areas of the building.

Almost always there was at least one old biddy of a senior stenographer lurking around the edge of the room with a sharp eye for any of the girls taking a break to refresh her lipstick or slip off to the lavatory without permission; or, heaven forbid, sneak a smoke in the stairwell. But, right now, not a single one of the old harridans could be seen.

After a few moments' hesitation Julia took a deep breath and headed for the "front office." She'd never ventured there before, there'd been no need to. She was just a typist, but this document was important. She glanced at the title at the top, AGREEMENT BETWEEN KAISER INDUSTRIES AND EARL RHODES. Someone "up front" would know where it should go.

Surprisingly, it was not that far away; once she had passed the restroom she turned left down the hallway she'd never gone down. She knew that to the right and through the doorway the switchboard with its massive bank of phone lines was manned by a varying crew of "operators." At the end of the hall a wide reception area opened. In the center of the far wall was an impressive desk flanked on either side by imposing doors that presumably led off to the inner sanctum sanctorum of the Kaiser Los Angeles offices. Surprised to see nobody at the desk she stopped, unsure how to proceed. She couldn't just leave the papers on the desk and would have died before she'd have had the courage to knock on one of the doors.

When she turned to return to her desk, she was even more shocked to see Dusty sitting at his ease on one of the couches in the room, reading a magazine, a cowboy hat sitting beside him on the plush cushion. She hurried over to him glancing back over her shoulder. She knew that it was him though he looked different than she was used to seeing him. His hair was neatly trimmed and combed, and instead of his usual cowboy shirt and dungarees he was wearing a nice, well-cut suit. His worn boots had been replaced with nicely polished shoes. The kind that walked away from shoeshine stands in train stations.

"Dusty, what the hell are you doing here?" Her voice was lowered but still full of shock and anger.

Dusty looked up, startled. "Julia…"

"What are you doing here. Get out. Get out now!"

He had stood up and picked up his hat, as she began to push him toward the large door that led to the street. "It's okay, I have an appointment. I'm supposed to be here."

She stopped trying to herd him out the door, but her expression was skeptical and confused. "This isn't funny. I work here…this is my job… what kind of appointment?"

Dusty started to speak but a deep voice behind her stopped them both.

When Julia's gaze went from Dusty's face to the man standing behind her, she was shocked. Henry Kaiser, himself, in the flesh. She'd never met him, but she had seen his face staring out at her from the front pages of the newspaper. She knew it was him, and she was completely tongue-tied: embarrassed, amazed, humiliated for Dusty, nonplussed.

Mr. Kaiser looked at her kindly and reached out for the documents. "Are those the contracts we've been waiting for? Thank you for being so quick, Miss —?"

"Stafford, Julia Stafford,' she stuttered.

He took the sheaf of paper from her hands and turned to Dusty. "All right, Mr. Rhodes. Seems like we have the documents in hand, thanks to this young woman. It looks like all of the copies are here. We can get them signed and get things started."

Dusty looked at Julia one more time, shrugged, and turned to follow Henry Kaiser into the big office with the imposing double doors.

Julia stood for a few moments staring at the two men and then turned on her heel and returned to the steno pool, more confused than ever.

Dusty stopped at the door to the office and watched Julia's departure for several seconds before shaking his head and following the man inside. He was in trouble with Julia, again.

CHAPTER TWENTY-FOUR

November 1943

Jack smoothed the stubble that was returning to his almost shaved head with the palm of his hand and slipped the white cap over it. He swung in behind Tacoma as the bigger, brawnier leader of his crew jostled to get down the gangplank first. For now, they were fairly quiet, but the seedy bars strung out along the boulevard outside the station would soon eliminate any reserve. Navy blue uniforms and shiny shoes masked the fear and tension that they all felt in these last few days before they would ship out. They had a few dollars and no leashes outside the Shore Patrol that would sweep through the darkened streets as the hour grew late to scoop them up, depositing them back at the ship. There was no escape, only the few hours of raucous laughter, drinking, and maybe a few kisses with the girls that populated the night and then went home alone. Those girls who had lied to their parents, and lied more about their age, sipped punch spiked from hidden flasks and boogied into the night with the sailors. It felt free, and dangerous, and it was, but not in the way they believed.

Tonight, the girls would sneak home into darkened houses where parents pretended to sleep so that they wouldn't have to ask the unanswerable questions. In the morning, the girls would splash cold water on their faces and gather up their schoolbooks and go back to being children in a world turned upside down.

Jack, Tacoma, and the others would drill, work, and prepare for whatever was coming. Something that was beyond their imagination. Another world, across an ocean. An ocean where submarines lurked below the surface, waiting to blow you to smithereens. Where planes full of bombs could swoop in and send you to Davy Jones's Locker before you knew what was happening. Maybe to tropical islands where people with guns would be trying to kill them.

Fucking stupid saying, "Davy Jones's Locker." What did that mean? Jack just knew that he was afraid when he went to sleep at night and afraid when he woke up in the morning. He was disoriented when his eyes opened and stared at the unyielding metal walls cocooning his bed and exhausted when he fell onto his bunk at the end of the day.

He spent his days trying to fit in, to be one of these other young men full of bravado, quick to make jokes about death, sounding braver than they were. Jack was learning how to laugh at the coarse jokes, to pretend to believe the blustery stories of daring escapes, even if most of them concerned eluding the Shore Patrol rather than fighting any enemy; tales of romantic escapades rather than winning medals.

Lucy had come to San Diego a few times to visit him, and he'd had a couple of short shore leaves when he went to Burbank to visit her. Molly had let him sleep on the sofa in the parlor, where you had to tiptoe past Dorothy's room to get upstairs. He hadn't really tried to go upstairs, Lucy shared a room with Julia, but he hadn't mentioned the arrangements with his buddies. It gave him a little status in the group that he had a girlfriend nearby. If the other guys had a girl she was far away, and most of them made do with pinups of Betty Grable or Rita Hayworth. Lucy had given him a snapshot of herself at the beach. She wasn't wearing a swimsuit in a swanky pose like the pinups, but she still looked beautiful.

He'd been thinking hard about Lucy and what she meant to him. He'd never had a girlfriend, and he wasn't sure Lucy was his girl anyway. There had been a few hurried kisses on that same sofa he'd slept on at Molly'sand he'd done his best to grope a bit without making her mad. He had little experience and thought she might have had a bit more than he. She was more outgoing than he was; of course that applied to most people. Did that mean she was easy? He was a little unclear on first base, second base, and whatever was next when it came to scoring with a girl. He guessed she was a virgin but didn't know that for sure and wasn't about to ask. How did you ask a girl something like that?

He'd shown her picture to his friends but didn't much like the way they'd laughed and made comments about her. He let them joke about their relationship, but it made him uncomfortable that they assumed she was the kind of girl who would let a guy do things.

Lately he'd been thinking about being shipped out. He knew Lucy would write to him if he sent her letters, but how did she really feel about him? She seemed to like him a lot. But she was a funny kind of a girl. She liked a lot of people. His gut clenched thinking that she might find another guy while he was away fighting or getting killed, or worse, rotting in a prison camp. Maybe an older guy or someone working at Lockheed with her. Hadn't she mentioned a couple of her co-workers; 4-F guys working cushy jobs with a lot of cash to spend? Tilda was dating some movie star. She might introduce Lucy to one of those playboys with lots of money and big houses. Pretty boys!

Lucy was on his mind tonight. He was missing her and suddenly worried about losing her to some jerk who didn't have to go off to war. The last dark bar had been too crowded and too loud. The drink and the smoke had made him dizzy and he focused on staying close behind Tacoma. The bar had closed and pushed the last of them into the darkened street. He hoped that one of them knew the way back to the ship.

CHAPTER TWENTY-FIVE

November 1943

At first Jack just heard shouting and jeers and he was shoved aside and stumbled into a parked car. Straining to clear his vision, he saw a pool of light under a streetlamp open ahead of him. He spied a knot of people, a couple of girls and a man, really only shadows. A grumble arose from around him; "Fucking zoot suits, fucking cowards." "Look at him, pawing our women like that." "Fuck that." "Hey Zoot Suit," the cry went up and was echoed by other catcalls. The laughing man in the wide-shouldered suit turned and a look of fear flashed across his face. The two young girls, their tied-back hair swinging, stepped behind him, laughing nervously. He raised his hands palms outward, and Jack could hear him speaking. What the hell was he saying? The men around Jack surged forward into the light and one of them shoved the boy. An arm swung out and a fist caught the side of his head. One of the girls screamed as he fell, but then he was up again, and a knife blade flashed in the streetlight. He tried to back away from the men, but they had surrounded him. Someone grabbed him from behind. Jack heard the sound of punches landing, cushioned by flesh and resounding off bone. The boy fell to the ground, curling into a ball to protect himself. Jack stumbled against him and kicked out with his heavy shoe. The shoe connected with flesh and bone and it felt good. It felt powerful. He kicked again, and again.

Suddenly an old car turned the corner in the distance and the headlights flashed onto the mob. There were shouts and the gunning of an engine as the lights careened toward them. The blue garbed crowd of sailors surged away from the oncoming car and the mob broke into the individual pieces that had composed it. They scattered running into the darkness. Jack ran too, without looking back.

The car did not chase them; it stopped where the man had fallen and lay huddled on the ground, unmoving. Jack followed his ragtag comrades back to the ship. He managed to get signed in and find his way to his bunk. In his drunken dreams the girls danced under the streetlight and the laughing dark-skinned man's face turned sharp and menacing before it dissolved into a blur and disappeared.

CHAPTER TWENTY-SIX

November 1943

Jack slept late and jumped to his feet when his head finally cleared. He was supposed to get a bus to LA to meet Lucy at Pink's. When he stood up from the bunk his gut lurched and he felt bile in his throat. He reeked of last night's cheap booze and the greasy smell of fried fish clung to his T-shirt. Even in his drunkenness he had thought to neatly fold his bell bottoms and hang them over the side of the bunk. As he pulled them down his eye caught a flash of something dark on the hem of the right pant leg. Examining it, he wondered what he had stepped in.

Memory seeped into his clouded brain and he looked down at his brogans. They too were scuffed and spattered with the dried darkness. For now, he stuffed the soiled trousers under the bunk and pulled out the one other pair he owned. Later he would sort out the chaotic glimpses of memory and would scrub the stains from the hem. He grabbed his shoes and stumbled to the sink. As he washed the muck from them under the running water he saw the dark reddish color of the water that swirled down the drain and recognized the stain for the blood that it was.

Pink's was a fixture in downtown Los Angeles, a hot dog stand that had operated since 1939 and now cheerfully dispensed franks to the droves of new customers who actually had money to spend. The 25-cent frankfurter had been feeding thousands on the cheap for years. By the time Jack's bus deposited him two blocks down he was over an hour late for his rendezvous. As he rushed closer to the familiar joint he spotted Lucy sitting on a low wall to the side idly kicking the heels of her oxfords against her concrete seat. He slackened his pace a bit, trying to gauge her mood. Was she ticked off, worried, bored? With Lucy it was a good idea to get your bearings before you rushed into the lion's den. Weighing the possibilities, he deemed his best action was to rush up apologetically and begin giving her his tale of woe. Of course, he wouldn't begin with having to wash blood from his shoes and would manage to throw an imaginary missed bus into the explanation for arriving late for their date.

When she spotted him Lucy jumped to her feet, but at least she was smiling. "Jack, you finally made it. I thought I was going to have to get one of these other guys to buy me a hot dog." She gestured in the direction of a cluster of factory workers farther down the sidewalk.

"You wouldn't let someone else buy my girl a frank, would you?" Jack's grin did not show how disconcerted he was by the suggestion.

She playfully placed her hands against his chest and gave him a little shove. "That depends on whether or not I really am 'your girl.'"

"Of course, you are." Jack's smile had disappeared. This was a major escalation of his commitment. As she turned back toward Pink's he threw his arm possessively across her shoulders.

"Well then, you'd better start showing up on time. I'm starving," was all she said.

Hot dogs devoured, they wandered down La Brea Boulevard and talked. Los Angeles was still new enough to them both that part of the adventure was watching the world go by. Lucy did her best to keep up a stream of cheerful chatter. She felt responsible for making this time with Jack fun and happy. Beneath it all was the lurking knowledge that he would soon be shipping out. Whenever her cheer would flag she would glimpse him staring blankly into space. What was he thinking? She didn't know that he was thinking about the same thing.

CHAPTER TWENTY-SEVEN

November 1943

"Where are we going, Carlos?" Tilda was still a little confused over this outing. All Carlos had told her was they would be gone most of the day, and to bring her identification.

"Do not worry, *chica*. I will explain everything in the car."

However, they drove for some time without any explanation. When they reached San Diego the driver stopped in front of Captain Clancy's, their favorite seafood restaurant. "Robbie will drop us off here and come back for us in a little while."

Still, Carlos explained nothing more as they made their way onto the sunny veranda and were led to an umbrella covered table. Finally, when the menus and icy glasses of water had been delivered, he turned to her. "Did I ever mention to you that I have a brother?"

"A brother? No, you never mentioned any of your family, even when I was rude enough to ask you outright."

"Well, I do have a brother, and a mother, as well."

Tilda laughed. "I imagined that you had a mother."

The waiter stopped at the table. "May I get you something else to drink?"

Carlos had been perusing the menu. "Yes, a bottle of Chenin Blanc, please."

"Today you will meet both my mother and my brother and also see their home.'

"In Argentina?" Tilda couldn't help but look surprised.

"No, not in Argentina. In Mexico."

"They've moved to Mexico? How wonderful to have them nearby."

Carlos gave Tilda that look. The one he gave her when she seemed to be particularly obtuse.

"Don't look at me like that. I don't understand what you are telling me." Tilda blushed as the waiter returned with their wine. She waited while he filled their glasses.

She took a sip of the golden liquid. It was lovely, light and perfectly chilled. "Okay, so speak slowly and clearly to me, and tell me why your family is in Mexico."

"They are in Mexico, in Tijuana, because they have always been there. That is where my home is, not in Argentina."

Tilda took another, larger, sip of the wine.

"My brother, Francisco, has been in the hospital here. He was attacked several days ago on the street, by a gang of sailors, and today they are sending him home."

"That's terrible, Carlos! Did they catch the men who attacked him?"

"No, and I am afraid they didn't try very hard. Francisco wears what the police call a zoot suit. They think it is his own fault that he was injured."

"That isn't fair."

"No, it is not fair, but it is how San Diego is, now."

"Are we going to get him from the hospital?"

"No, Robbie is picking him up and paying for his care. When he has Francisco he will come here and pick us up."

The waiter had returned. Tilda wished he'd quit coming back and hovering over them. Then she realized that he recognized Carlos and was anxious to please his celebrity client. It also occurred to her why Carlos was not able to go to the hospital to get his brother. Surely someone would recognize him and call the newspapers. She was happy that the waiter had refilled her wineglass. Carlos had not touched his wine.

Tilda didn't need to look at the menu. Her favorite meal at any seafood restaurant was Shrimp Louis. A heap of shredded lettuce generously piled with succulent shrimp, chunks of tomato, and quartered boiled eggs. The whole thing was doused in the tangy pink "Louis" dressing that she couldn't resist. When she felt especially indulgent she would request a small dish of extra dressing on the side and dip her chunks of sourdough bread in it.

When the waiter had departed, she turned to Carlos. He was not looking at her but gazed out the window as though he were a million miles away.

"Do you want to tell me why you have told everyone you are from Argentina?"

"I don't think you really have to ask, but yes, I will tell you.

"When I first came here, I was working at the home of Bedford Myers, the head of the studio. I worked in his garden and around the house. One day he asked me if I had any interest in taking a screen test. After the test he said that he would like to put me into one of his movies, but that first I would have to go to South America for a few months."

"Why did he send you to South Argentina?"

"He sent me so that I could obtain a new passport, one with the name Carlos Salida."

"Your name is not Carlos?"

"No. The name my mother gave me is Pablo Salas. It would be Paul in English."

"Pablo…"

"It is very important to the studio, to me, that nobody discovers my secret. It would ruin my career."

"I am not going to tell anyone, Carlos. Any secret you have is safe with me."

"I know. That is why I wanted you to come with me today. I want you to meet my family and to see my home."

Both the wine and the enormous salad were gone by the time Robbie returned with Francisco ensconced in the front seat of the car.

Introductions were brief and Tilda tried not to stare at the young man who looked so like Carlos but whose face was bruised and swollen from the recent beating.

The guard at the border took their identification and stepped into the guard hut. When he returned he gave Carlos and the others their documents back but motioned to Tilda. "Would you please step out of the car, ma'am."

"Is there a problem, Officer?" interjected Carlos.

"Sir, I am speaking to the lady." Turning to Tilda he repeated, "Would you please step out of the car?"

When Tilda turned to Carlos, he nodded, though he kept his face turned away from the window.

"Please step into the office, for me. I just have a question about your identification."

Once they were inside the office the guard closed the door behind them.

For a moment Tilda felt afraid, though there was no menace on the face of the man. He looked more…worried. "Ma'am, I need to ask you if you are willingly traveling with these men."

"Why, yes, of course I am. We are just escorting one of them home to his mother. He's been in an accident."

"So, there is no coercion? Who are these men to you?"

"One of them is my dear friend, the one driving is his chauffeur, and the young man in the front seat is his brother, who has been in an accident. He has just been released from the hospital. We are taking him home to his mother."

The man looked relieved and handed her back her identification. "Sorry ma'am, I just wanted to make sure that you were safe."

"Certainly, I…I guess I understand."

The guard opened the door and smilingly escorted Tilda back to the car and opened the door for her. He tipped his cap. "Thank you for your assistance."

When they had pulled through the gate Carlos turned to Tilda. "What did the guard want? Was there a problem?"

Tilda hesitated for a moment. It was embarrassing to tell them what the guard had asked, so she said, "Oh, nothing. He was confused by my New York ID card. Guess he thought I was a gangster, or something." She smiled.

Carlos looked relieved. "Good, that is good."

Driving through the main streets of Tijuana was a revelation to Tilda. She knew it was another country, but it truly felt foreign to her. The businesses and buildings were so different from what she was used to seeing. Not just the signage and the architecture, but the colors they were painted and the goods displayed in the windows. Of course, this part of town would be where all the tourists from the U.S. would come to shop and be entertained, but even the demeanor of the people on the street was different.

After a few blocks the businesses fell away and the neighborhoods began. The homes were small, but mostly tidy. Many were surrounded by small fences and sided by lush vegetable gardens, inhabited by a few scraggly chickens. On one corner a knot of young boys, barefoot and grinning, squatted around a small dog who leapt up to lick their faces and make them laugh. Tilda could imagine Carlos and Francisco as children playing in the same way, wearing the same kind of tattered shorts and mis-buttoned shirts.

In just a few minutes the car pulled up in front of a small house. Next door a mangy dog growled and lunged toward them behind a rickety fence.

Before they could even get out of the car a woman ran out the door and down the steps. She was smiling and crying at the same time. Tilda didn't speak Spanish and the woman spoke at an incredible rate, although the name "Francisco" punctuated the tirade at intervals.

Carlos and his mother helped Francisco out of the car and up the porch steps. Tilda followed self-consciously as several smiling neighbors had come out onto their porches and shouted encouragement to the injured man.

Robbie had pulled several bags out of the back of the car and Tilda reached out her hand to take one of them. The driver smiled, handed her the lightest bag, and they followed the group into the house.

Francisco had been lovingly helped onto the sofa and covered with a colorful blanket. His mother continued to exclaim over him and kissed his bruised but smiling face, repeatedly. Clearly, the best tonic for him would be the love of his family during his recovery. Tilda had noticed that he had a distinct limp, held his right arm close to his body as he walked into the house, and paused carefully on each of the steps of the porch. She'd not had a chance to talk to Carlos about the boy's condition but was appalled by the severity of the beating he had taken.

"Mama, Mama…I want you to meet someone." Carlos struggled to get the woman's attention. Finally, she turned. "Sí, Pablo, sí…what is it?"

Carlos spoke to her in Spanish and gestured in Tilda's direction. She heard her name and the word *amiga* and saw awareness dawn in the woman's face as she realized that Tilda was not just a friend of her son's.

"Tilda, this is my mother, Maria Salas."

Tilda smiled and offered her hand. "Señora Salas, it is so very nice to meet you. I am sorry but I do not speak Spanish."

"Is no problem. *Hablo un poco de inglés.* I speak some little English."

Both of the women laughed.

Carlos interrupted them. "There is no problem, I will translate. I speak very good English and Spanish."

Robbie returned from taking the bags into the kitchen. He leaned over and gave Maria Salas a kiss on the cheek. "Es bueno verla de nuevo, señora. Te ves tan hermosa, como siempre."

Tilda could have sworn the woman blushed as she giggled.

"Ah, Robbie, let's go see what you have brought us to eat. We will have a celebration now that Francisco is home."

CHAPTER TWENTY-EIGHT

November 1943

A ball of yarn had rolled unnoticed off Dorothy's lap and across the polished wood floor of the parlor as she dozed in her rocking chair. The front and back doors were open to allow what breeze there was to flow through, and the familiar sounds of the neighborhood dodged in and out of her dreams. Someone was mowing a lawn down the block and the scent of cut grass filled the room.

She woke up disoriented and unsure what had woken her but then heard the firm rap on the back screen door. "Hmph, who'd be disturbing a body in the middle of the afternoon?" Too late for the milkman and too early for the bread man.

"Just a minute, I'm coming…" she called as she made her way to the kitchen.

Harry, rather Harold, Caine stood on the stoop peering into the dim kitchen through the screen, his telegraph-boy hat in his hands.

"Harold, son, come in, come in." Dorothy unlatched the door and swung it open for the boy to enter.

He hesitated before entering the room. "I hope I'm not bothering you, Mrs. Moseby. I was just in the neighborhood and thought I could maybe get a glass of water from you."

"Of course, come in… I've got iced tea and there might be some cookies in the jar." She waved her hand in the direction of the wooden table where the ceramic jar stood. "Come in, come in. The flies will beat you to it if you don't hurry."

The mention of the flies moved Harold more quickly through the door. "I can't stay but a minute, I need to get back to the office."

"Just sit down for a bit. There's nobody here but me right now, and I was just wishing someone would stop by." It wasn't really a lie, she thought. She had been wishing for something to break the boredom of the day, even if it was in a dream.

Harold moved to the table and, pulling out a chair, sat down with some relief.

"It must be hot riding your bike around in that telegraph jacket. Why don't you take it off for a minute?"

"Thank you ma'am, but I'm fine, just need to rest.

"Water or tea?" Dorothy had retrieved two jelly-jar glasses from the cabinet and opened the refrigerator door. The cool air felt good.

"Tea would be great if it's no trouble."

"Not a bit of trouble." And she filled both glasses from the frosty pitcher.

She set their drinks down on the table and lifted the heavy lid of the cookie jar. "The cookies look a bit stale, but they'll wash down proper with a little tea."

Harold leaned forward and plunged his hand into the almost empty jar. "Thank you, I'm sure they're fine." He lifted one of the chunky cookies out and brought it to his mouth. "Mmm, it's good. Lots of raisins…" He smiled appreciatively as he lifted the glass of tea to his lips.

"You don't hardly need to use much sugar when you have raisins."

Since neither of them had any more raisin comments the conversation lapsed as they munched in companionable silence.

Dorothy sensed that Harold had something on his mind, but she realized that asking him straight out would just chase the thought away, so she waited, taking a second cookie from the jar and nudging the jar in his direction.

After a bit, and a second cookie had disappeared, Harold sighed. "I'm glad to have a job, but sometimes I wish it wasn't this job."

"It must be kind of a sad job, with everything that is going on."

"Well, yes it can be sad, but sometimes it isn't. Sometimes I'm bringing good news to folks. Babies being born, people getting married. Once in a while I even have to sing 'Happy Birthday' to someone. They look so pleased that someone was thinking of them on their birthday."

"That would be fun to get a singing telegram. Maybe I'll send myself one on my next birthday." Dorothy smiled to think of this young man standing on her porch singing. "Do you sing pretty good?"

Harold ducked his head and a blush rose on his freckled cheeks. "I guess I'm okay, no complaints, so far."

"So was today one of those good days?"

"It wasn't bad, but a sad thing happened anyway."

Dorothy waited.

Harold glanced around the kitchen. "You know Mary Roberts that lives over on Mason Street?"

"I know who she is, she goes with her mother to Mass at St. Benedict's."

"Well, she's in my class at school and today I was riding by her house and saw her out on the porch. I thought I'd stop and say hello, but when she saw me on the street she had the worst look on her face. She was afraid of me. She turned and almost ran into the house letting the door slam behind her."

Dorothy could picture the scene and felt bad for both children,

"Harold, I don't think she is afraid of you, she's just afraid like we all are now. There is so much to lose."

"I know, I'm afraid every day. Afraid we'll lose the war, that my brother and his friends will die, that I won't be able to make enough money to help my mother. If the war is still going next year I will be going away to fight and I'm afraid of that, too. I don't know if I'm brave enough for that."

"I think you are brave already. Not everyone could go up to strangers' doors with good news and bad, doing a job that has to be done."

"I guess, but it felt bad that Mary was afraid of me."

"It's the uniform and what it might mean. She wouldn't be afraid if she saw you at school or the picture show or the soda fountain, would she?"

"No…"

"You don't look very frightening to me. In fact, just the opposite, but your uniform is another thing."

Harold ruminated on that for a few moments.

Dorothy stood up. "Let me wrap the rest of these cookies for you. I'm needing to bake some fresh but want to wait until the cool of the evening."

Harold waited by the door, cap in hand, until Dorothy handed him the waxed paper wrapped parcel. "My mom will like these. Did I tell you she got a better job at the grocers? She likes it but she doesn't have much time for baking anymore."

"That's great news Harry, I mean Harold."

"Tell you what, Mrs. Moseby. When I am wearing my uniform I am Harold, but when I'm just me, you can call me Harry."

CHAPTER TWENTY-NINE

November 1943

The woman had come to the door humbly, to the kitchen door, not the front entrance. Her dark face looked hopeful, but cautious.

"Miz Moseby. I'm Delia. I saw your name on a board at the bus station, but you may not be the right person for me to talk to."

Molly hesitated for a moment. The boarders were all gone to their jobs and Dorothy was having a "bit of a lie-down" in her room.

"Come in, please." She stepped back, wiping her wet hands on her apron.

Delia stepped through the screen door but did not proceed further into the kitchen.

"I know I may not be in the right place, but I'm new here. I just came on the bus from Alabama. There was a message on the board at the bus station." She held out the handwritten piece of paper she had copied from the notice at the Greyhound station.

Molly took the piece of paper in her hand. "Yes, I posted this there."

Delia didn't seem to know what to say next. After a couple of moments, she said, "I know this wasn't meant for me, but I thought you might know someplace else I could go."

"You're probably right. This might not be the place for you to stay, but you are still welcome here. Maybe I can help." She turned back to her kitchen, gesturing toward the kitchen table.

Delia followed Molly into the kitchen. And stood in the space Molly had pointed to.

"Please, sit down. What can I do for you?"

"I just came all across the country from Alabama to get a job at one of the defense plants. I didn't know everything would be so big and strange."

"Yes, it must be strange here, but there are lots of other people coming from all over. It's too late to do much today, but you can stay here tonight, and we'll figure something out tomorrow."

At Delia's happy response, she clarified. "I don't really have a room available. I mean, I have a bed you can use tonight and then I will take you to…" she hesitated, "another neighborhood, where we might find a place that you can stay."

With a little coaxing Delia set down her bag and sat at the kitchen table. Molly made tea for them both and then continued her work at the kitchen sink. Her boarders would be coming home before long; she needed to get supper on the table.

When Molly had finished her meal preparations, she carried the suitcase and led Delia to what passed as a basement, of sorts. The house had been built on a knoll where the house backed on a decline to the alley. The resulting space beneath the back steps had long since been converted to a secure little space with a small cot and dresser in it. Growing up, the boys had considered it their own little hideaway and the bed used to be called into duty at holidays for the overflow of relatives.

Molly stood in the kitchen and stirred the stew that had simmered on the back of the stove all afternoon. She'd already made up her mind but was not sure how to present it to her mother-in-law and the boarders. There was no way that she was going to leave her home to trundle down the trolley lines to the next "neighborhood." She'd made that trip before, hoping to identify a place she could refer folks like Delia to. It had not worked out.

Delia looked around the basement room. It was basic, spare. There was only a cot and a small dresser. There were no windows and the single bulb that hung from the ceiling gave the only light. Still, it was better than some of the places she'd stayed.

She sat on the edge of the cot and let a bit of the euphoria she'd been feeling surge up. She had done it. She had left home and traveled for days and now she was in California, ready to start a new life. Her excitement and fear had been struggling with each other for the past week, but just for one moment, she let the excitement win.

Miz Moseby had invited her to dinner with the rest of the boarders, but she had to give that some thought. She couldn't recall ever having been to a meal with a houseful of white folks, where she wasn't serving the food.

Still, she hadn't eaten since breakfast; a quick roll and coffee at the bus station. The aroma of the long-simmering stew had whetted her appetite and Miz Moseby had whipped up a batch of biscuits and popped them into the oven while they talked. She hadn't used the lard Delia's mother had used at home, but the smell of the warm bread still wafted down the steps as she'd walked to her room.

Delia lay back on the bed and must have dozed off until she heard the scrape of chairs above her head and the mealtime chatter. Fear gripped her, but she knew this was a new world, a different reality. Finally, she ascended the stairs and entered the kitchen; the curious faces turned to her and she stopped.

"Ah, I'm glad you're here. I want to introduce you. Everyone, this is Delia. She is going to be staying here helping me with the housework."

Nobody was as surprised as Delia, except maybe Dorothy. Molly caught Delia's surprised look and gave her a wink.

"Delia, if you'd help serve these bowls, we can get started eating."

Delia stepped to the stove and took the stew bowls, two at a time, and placed them before the hungry women at the table.

When everyone had been served, she was motioned to an empty seat at the end of the table, and Delia sat down before her steaming supper.

When everyone had wandered away from the table, chatting and sharing their day, Delia stayed behind and helped Molly clear the table and clean up the kitchen.

Molly walked to the cellar door with Delia. "I'm sorry I surprised you with my plan, but I think it makes sense for you to stay here with us while you find a job. You can help me, and nobody, not the boarders or the neighbors, will question you coming and going. Are you okay with that?"

Delia didn't really know what to say. She recognized that Molly might be taking a risk in keeping her there, but she also knew she could help, and that it was a chance for her while she got her footing in this new place. She placed her suitcase on the bed and began arranging her few belongings in the drawers and on top of the dresser.

Upstairs with the boarders settling in their rooms the scene in the kitchen was somewhat different.

"What the hell are you thinking, Molly?" Dorothy glared at her daughter-in-law from her usual perch at the kitchen table. Over the war years it had become a custom for them to share a cup of tea and a little conversation after everyone else had wandered off to their evening activities, which usually consisted of poring over movie magazines and painting each other's toenails. Just before she'd come back into the kitchen Dorothy had heard the bunch of them cackling over some particularly nasty column from Hedda Hopper. She'd wondered who was in the old hag's sights this week but hadn't stopped to ask, as she had a mission of her own.

"Well," Molly nervously pushed a tendril of hair that had escaped her topknot behind her ear, "I am thinking that I could use some help around here and, since I can't afford to pay someone, Delia can help me some in exchange for rent and get herself an outside job to make some money." She realized it didn't sound all that farfetched when you said it out loud. She could use the help, and the extra ration coupons, and nobody was using the downstairs room.

Still, Dorothy wasn't going to be convinced that easily. "Why is it you never mentioned to me that you were looking for help?"

"Because I wasn't looking for it, it just came to me. I needed help and Delia needed a place. Serendipity."

"Hmph…I'll tell you right now, Bobby is not going to like it."

That stopped Molly in her tracks. It was a low blow for Dorothy to invoke her estranged son in this argument. Her support of her neighbor Keiko after the war started had caused a row with Bobby. No matter what she'd said, he couldn't understand her loyalty to a Jap. His parting words to her had been, "I hope one of her Jap cousins isn't the one that puts a bullet through me, because I'll be shooting at every Jap I see and that includes Keiko, if I have the chance."

"Well, unless you tell Bobby, I don't know how he is going to find out about it."

It was Dorothy's turn to be flummoxed. She wasn't sure that Molly knew that she wrote letters to Bobby without telling her and snuck them to the mailman when nobody was around. Not that Bobby ever answered; he was his father's son. "I won't be telling him, but he wouldn't like it if he knew."

"Then there is no problem, is there?"

At that moment Delia knocked timidly at the kitchen door.

"Mrs. Moseby, I, um…there isn't an outhouse out back and I need to, um, use one pretty quick."

"Oh, sorry Delia. No, we don't have an outhouse." She couldn't help but laugh at the girl's look of consternation. "We have indoor plumbing. The commode and bath are at the top of the stairs. Go right on up. You'll have to wait your turn if someone is in there, but it is for everyone."

For a moment Delia considered whether she could turn back and find a place to urinate in the back yard or maybe take one of the empty canning jars to her room like a chamber pot. Neither option sounded like a good solution in the long run.

Finally, she let herself in the door and sidled through the kitchen and up the stairs.

When she was gone Dorothy started up again. "See that, she doesn't even know how to use an indoor toilet."

"Well, and neither did you when you first came over from Ireland.

You told me yourself what a miracle you thought it was."

Dorothy knew when it was time to give up the fight. Molly was just as hard-headed as Al had been, just not as mean. She'd be damned to hell if she would retire with her tail between her legs, so she allowed Molly to pour her another cup of tea and smoked another cigarette before withdrawing to her room.

Placing the empty cups in the sink Molly gazed out into the darkened yard and thought of her boys. She had her own secret letters that she wrote to Bobby. They were the same letters she wrote to Ian. Not arguments or excuses, but chatty news about home, relatives and neighbors, meals, and jokes. Yes, she and Bobby were angry with each other, but she couldn't stand to think that he would not be receiving letters from home. She didn't even care if Dorothy wrote, although she expected the letters would be less cheery. Either way, she never saw any letters from him for either of them. Sometimes you just sent your love out into the world without any expectation of response. Still, it would be nice...

CHAPTER THIRTY

November 1943

Jack squatted in the tiny patch of shade on the base side of the security gate, smoking a cigarette and trying not to get overheated in his dark blue dress uniform. The chambray shirt and lighter-weight pants of his daily uniform were cooler, but for his own wedding he had to be more formal.

The chapel on the naval station was getting quite a workout with all the last-minute weddings and they'd been lucky to book a time on this Sunday afternoon, although he figured the ceremony wouldn't take very long at all. What was there to say, two "I do's" and a quick kiss and it was all legal. The marriage license was set to be signed, the chaplain and Jack's commanding officer had both met with him and Lucy, and everything was ready to go.

A small travel bag sat beside him. He'd managed to wangle a couple of days of leave, even though they were shipping out at the end of the week. Dusty was paying for a night at a motor court near the beach for what would pass in wartime as a honeymoon.

Jack's head was throbbing, and he moved back against the wall to avoid the glare of the bright sun. He'd had too much to drink last night. His buddies had thrown him a little bachelor party, but he didn't really remember much of it. Mostly that he had been embarrassed and didn't understand half the jokes that were being thrown around to raucous laughter, elbow jabs, and back slaps. What did the curtains matching the rug mean?

"What are you doing here, sailor?" The voice was sharp and disapproving.

Jack leapt to his feet and saluted. "Nothing, sir." He quickly dropped his cigarette and stepped on it as he rose.

"Then why are you here instead of at your post?" The officer looked him up and down. "You're wearing your dress uniform."

"Aye, aye, Sir." I'm getting married today and I'm just waiting for Lucy and the wedding guests, sir."

The older man's demeanor softened. "Oh, I see. Well then, stand up and look sharp. Can't let your bride think she's marrying a slacker."

"Aye, aye, sir."

"Congratulations and carry on. Oh, and pick up that cigarette butt." With that the officer returned Jack's salute, turned on his heel, and walked out through the gate, saluting the Shore Patrolman manning the entrance.

"Shit, that was my last cigarette," Jack grumbled.

He hadn't been a smoker back home in Arkansas, but the tobacco companies made sure to supply "our fighting men" with all the cigarettes they might need. It was almost un-American to not make use of them. He thought his mother might have a different opinion, but she was far away, and who knew if he'd ever see her again.

When he and Lucy had decided to marry, he'd sent a letter home, but he doubted they'd even received it yet. It all happened pretty fast. In fact, it almost felt like you had to hurry up before you could change your mind. The chaplain and his commander had both voiced the same thought, but there wasn't really any time to think it through. In a few days he'd be gone to sea.

There had been an additional discussion without Lucy present; they asked a lot of questions about her background and how long she'd been in California. It seemed there were quite a few "young ladies" who made a habit of marrying men who were shipping out just to get their dependent stipend. He'd been told some of them were married to more than one man and were living pretty high on the hog with multiple checks coming in. And, if the guy got killed, they got his insurance.

The "war wagon" pulled up with Dusty driving and the gate guard stepped briskly to the car window. "Please state your purpose in being here."

"We are here for a wedding, at two p.m., so we're running kind of late."

The guard looked at his clipboard. "What is the name of the service member?"

"Jack Scoggins," came Lucy's voice from the passenger seat.

"And the name of the bride?"

"Lucy Rivers."

The guard bent down and surveyed the other members of the party. "We're going to need to sign in these other people and check identification."

"I'm going to be late for my own wedding," wailed Lucy.

"No, ma'am. We'll be quick, but it's required security. If everyone could step out of the car and show me your ID, we can get through this pretty fast."

Jack stepped forward. "I'm the groom. Is there anything I can do to help?"

The guard cast him a glance. "Not at this time. We will be as quick as we can."

In due course Lucy Rivers, Molly and Dorothy Moseby, Tilda Morrison, Earl Rhodes, and Julia Stafford had shown their IDs and signed their names in the logbook. The license plate of the car was recorded, and the standard spiel about security and safety was delivered. As they climbed back into the car the final warning came. "Absolutely no photos can be taken outside the chapel."

Everyone nodded solemnly.

Before long the clean, but battered, automobile drove beneath the raised gate and Jack stepped up to greet them.

Lucy moved to the middle of the front seat. He opened the passenger door and slid in, placing his travel bag at his feet. "I'll get us to the chapel. Drive to the end of this road and make a right. It's not far."

The chapel had to be fairly big to accommodate the masses of God-fearing sailors that were being processed through this base. It was surrounded by trees and a well-kept lawn.

Once the car stopped in front of the building, they all sat for a few moments staring warily at the stained-glass windows and grand double door. Molly was the least intimidated by a church and the first to open the door and climb out. She'd brought bouquets of flowers from her and Keiko's gardens for each of the women, a larger one for Lucy, and made boutonnieres for Dusty and Jack. Jack wasn't sure he was allowed to pin a flower to his uniform. So, he just held it in his hand as they walked to the doors.

Inside was cool and quiet. "Welcome to you all," the chaplain greeted them. He and Jack exchanged salutes, and he led the party to the front of the church. "Do you have the license?"

Jack drew the document from his pocket. "Here, it's right here."

"That's fine. We will complete the ceremony and then both of you will need to sign it, and I will sign. Who are your witnesses?"

Dusty stepped forward, "I am." And Julia echoed him, "I am."

He quickly lined the party up at the altar. Jack and Dusty to his left, Lucy and Julia to his right. Molly, Dorothy and Tilda were in the front pew.

The room felt cavernous and they all started when the strains of the organ swelled with the wedding march. When the last chord of the music had echoed through the vast hall, the chaplain began the ceremony.

It was pretty much what Jack had expected and was over in less than fifteen minutes.

Molly herded them all back into the car and directed Dusty to a small café near the base. She'd eaten there with her sons before they shipped out, so she knew they could get a nice meal without too much fuss.

Dusty ordered a bottle of wine, and when all of the glasses had been poured, as the best man, he raised his own glass in a toast. "To the marriage of Jack and Lucy. May their love protect and sustain them through the days ahead, until they are united again in a time of peace."

"To Jack and Lucy," echoed the voices around the table.

CHAPTER THIRTY-ONE

November 1943

Lucy shivered slightly and pulled the blanket closer. The dim morning light slanted in through the blinds and she glanced over at Jack's sleeping figure. He'd wake up soon. What would he say? What would she say? She hoped neither of them would have to say anything and that they could just pretend things were as they'd always been.

Outside this little room the world was just spinning away on its axis. After Dusty had dropped them at the motel they'd walked on the beach, eaten ice cream cones, and talked about their families. But, as it got later the laughter became more strained and by the time they returned to this tiny room, the silence deafened.

Lucy had grown up on a farm, as had Jack, but somehow she'd imagined that sex between people would be more romantic. Bulls didn't woo their cows, and roosters were notoriously unmannered, but somehow she'd thought there would be more kissing and sweet talk, and less hurry up-and-get-it-done.

She was not a prissy person, but her experience of petting had not prepared her for the "wham, bam, thank you ma'am" of their encounter.

It hadn't helped that he'd started drinking long in advance of the sun going down. He'd even seemed angry that she didn't know what they were supposed to be doing. How could you be a good girl, and still know your way around?

She slipped quietly from the bed and into the bathroom, washing her face and brushing her teeth before shimmying her sundress over her head. She grabbed her purse and carefully pulled open the door, just enough to allow her to silently exit.

The bell above the donut shop door jangled as she entered, and she was engulfed with the heady fragrance of hot grease and sugar with an overlay of cinnamon and an undertone of chocolate.

"Good morning. How can I help you?" The young woman behind the counter stifled a yawn and smiled.

"I would like two chocolate and two cinnamon donuts and two cups of coffee, please."

As the girl filled the order other early risers entered the tiny shop.

Lucy made her way back to the room, walking slowly and letting the first beams of the sunlight play over her skin. She only had to make things seem normal for the few hours until Dusty picked them up, so she had begun to relax a bit.

She stepped into the lobby of the motor court and picked up a newspaper, depositing her nickel on the empty counter.

When she re-entered the room, Jack was just beginning to stir.

"Wake up sleepyhead. I've got donuts, coffee, and the newspaper. We can have a little breakfast and then go wish farewell to the beach before Dusty comes."

Jack rolled over and gave her an assessing look. When he turned back to his pillow, she realized they were already reading each other's minds like old married people.

Jack rose from the bed, not bothering to cover his nakedness and walked into the bathroom. The door stayed open and she could hear him peeing into the toilet and then spitting. Why did men spit all the time? Women didn't spit. Did men have different salivary glands or something? It felt oddly intimate to be observing these morning rituals. In a way, more intimate than sex, itself.

She set the coffee cups across from one another on the tiny table and opened the paper. "It says here that the war in the Pacific is going well."

"Yeah, it always says that. Nobody wants us to know what is really going on." Jack sat down and picked up his Dixie Cup of steaming coffee.

"Is that really true? Do you think the government is lying to us?"

Jack considered the question. "Maybe not lying, exactly, but not telling us everything."

'Maybe they are just trying to protect us, so we don't worry so much."

Jack started to answer but seemed to reconsider. This was Lucy he was talking to, not some asshole guy in the chow hall. "Yeah, maybe. I'm sure they don't want us to worry too much."

He picked up one of the chocolate donuts and took a bite. "Hey, remember when you talked about being a Donut Dolly? Well, your dream has been fulfilled. You are serving donuts and coffee to a fighting man." He waggled his eyebrows at her and she laughed. It felt good to feel like friends again.

The beach that day was mostly deserted even though the weather was quite warm, only a couple of old men surf fishing and a mother and her children looking for shells could be seen on the expanse of sand. Jack and Lucy wore their bathing suits under their clothes today. Neither of them had ever swum in the ocean and Lucy argued it might be their only chance for a while.

They had bought a couple of sandwiches and bottles of Coca-Cola on their way down today so they could have a picnic.

Wading knee-high in the lapping water Lucy called out, "Hey, Jack, look at me." When he turned she kicked water up over him and then turned to run away. It was harder to move in the water than she thought it would be and when he reached her, he swung her up into his arms and began wading farther into the ocean where he dropped her and then fell over himself.

Lucy sprang up and pushed his head under the water before he could get up. "You got my hair soaking wet, Jack. Now I'm going to look a fright the whole rest of the day." She tried to sound angry but there was still a smile plastered on her face.

"You started it." Jack lunged at her again and as she turned away his hands came around to cup her breasts.

"Stop, Jack. Someone will see."

"Then we'll make it so nobody can see us." Jack pulled her farther into the water and then took her into his arms, looking down into her laughing face.

"You don't look a fright. You look beautiful. Like a redheaded mermaid." Then he pulled her to him and planted a lingering kiss on her lips.

Lucy's arms went up around his neck and she returned his kiss and then gave him another.

His hands roamed over her body and he was breathing hard when he came up for air. "You feel so wonderful. I love your body."

"I need to lose a few pounds."

"You don't need to lose anything." And he bent to kiss her again.

Several minutes passed before she pulled his head down and whispered in his ear. "Let's go back to the room."

By the time they got to shore, gathered their belongings, and stumbled back to the room they were covered in sand. Once they were inside Jack took her into his arms again.

"Wait, I'm covered in sand. Let me rinse off in the shower." Lucy turned and went into the bathroom, stripping off her suit and leaving it in a heap on the tile floor.

Jack shed his own suit and stepped into the shower behind her. "I don't have to wait…we're married."

"Oh yeah, silly me…" and Lucy turned to him and pulled his head down for another kiss.

Lucy woke in a tangle of arms, legs, and bed sheets. Someone was knocking on the door.

"Hey, Jack, Lucy, are you in there? We need to get Jack back to the base."

Jack sat up, startled. "Holy cow, it's four o'clock. We slept the whole day away."

"Well, maybe not the whole day," Lucy teased.

Jack untangled himself and went to the door just as the knocking began again. "It's okay, Dusty. We were just taking a nap. We'll be out in five minutes," he shouted through the door.

"Okay, I'll wait in the car. But hurry it up. We need to get you back by dinner time."

Lucy peeked out the window through the curtains. "He's gone back to the car. We need to pack up in a hurry."

It took about seven minutes for them to dress and gather up their few belongings.

Jack carried their bags to the car as Lucy made a quick sweep of the room to make sure nothing was left behind. She stopped and looked at herself in the bathroom mirror. Jack had been right. She didn't look a fright. She looked beautiful, and happy.

They barely got back to the naval station in time. Lucy gave Jack a long hug and then, surprisingly, Dusty gave him a hug, as well. "We won't forget you Jack. We'll think of you every day and I will watch out for Lucy until you come home."

The trip back to Burbank was quiet, both Dusty and Lucy lost in their thoughts. At the rooming house Dusty carried Lucy's bag to the door and stopped there. "I'm not going to come in, but you can call on me if you need anything."

Lucy threw her arms around him, "Thanks, so much, Dusty."

Two hugs in one day was a new experience for Dusty, but he decided he liked it and might have to do it more often.

CHAPTER THIRTY-TWO

November 1943

The fire in the stone fireplace had burned low and the rocking chair squeaked gently as Rhetta slowly rocked it. This chair had been her mother's and her grandmother's before that. Rhetta had rocked and soothed her own babies in it. She wondered if she would ever have the chance to rock her grandbabies, as well.

It was late, or very early, when she heard Bud's heavy tread on the porch outside. The door swung open heavily and his footsteps echoed in the quiet hallway. He didn't see her when he entered the room and walked to the bar, so he jumped slightly when she spoke. "If you're getting yourself a drink you can refill mine." Rhetta held out the heavy whiskey glass to him.

"You startled me. What are you doing up so late?" Bud carried the decanter of liquor to her and poured a shot. When she still held out the glass he poured again.

"I was waiting up for you, of course."

"Well, I'm sorry I'm so late. These city council meetings just get longer and longer. Seems nobody can agree on anything." He returned the decanter to the bar, picked up his glass, and took a swallow of the amber liquid.

Rhetta rocked the chair a couple more times before she spoke. "Just what is it you and Widow Bradley can't agree on?"

"Now Rhetta, don't go making silly accusations…"

Rhetta held up her hand. "That's enough, Bud. I can smell her violet water on you from clear over here."

"Rhetta…it's not what you think it is."

Rhetta snorted and took a swig of her whiskey. "Of course it is exactly what I think it is. I just wonder what Verna Bradley thinks it is."

"It's nothing."

"Sit down, Bud. You're making me nervous pacing up and down like that."

When the man had settled himself on the settee his wife reached out and turned on the lamp next to her chair. "I know you're tired and want to get some sleep, so this won't take long. I'm no fool, and I am not the only one in town that knows all about you and Verna. I just want you to understand something. This ranch was my daddy's before we married and he left it to me, free and clear. Just to make sure, I met with Judge Harlan last week. You remember Judge Harlan, my daddy's best friend."

Rhetta took some satisfaction noting that Bud had paled a bit as he stood to get another drink. She waited until he had topped off his glass and returned to his seat. "He assured me that, in a divorce, you couldn't take the land, along with the cattle and the oil wells away from me. Of course, we'd have to share.…"

"Wait a damned minute, Rhetta, nobody's talking about divorce here." Bud moved to stand up.

"No, we haven't talked about divorce, and I don't want a divorce. I've lived on this land my whole life and I intend to live above it and then lie under it when I die."

Bud sat back in his seat. "Then what's this all about?"

"This is about me making sure you tell Verna that she is never going to be the rich rancher's wife as long as I'm alive."

"Verna is not interested.…"

"Oh, of course not. She is only interested in your charm." Rhetta almost snorted again but held herself back. "You are a good-lookin' man, Bud Rhodes, always have been. Getting rich has only made you better looking. But you are not available and won't be for a long time."

Bud downed the rest of his drink and stood up. "I'm going to bed." He strode toward the hallway.

"Oh, just one more little thing."

Bud turned back to face her. "What is it?"

Rhetta picked up a sheaf of papers from the side table. "I found this in your wastebasket. Looks like it must have accidentally been thrown away."

"What is it?" he snarled, although he recognized what she held.

"Well, it's a very interesting proposal for an investment with Henry Kaiser. You know, the Henry Kaiser that is second only to FDR these days. It looks like he's wanting to partner with us, with our son Dusty, to build homes and hospitals for our fighting boys when they come back from the war."

"It's just a silly pipe dream. Who even knows when the war will end and who will win it?"

"I do, I believe it won't be long before it's over and those men who survive it will be coming home to get jobs, marry, raise kids, and make the country over."

"That is a lot of money, Rhetta. What if it doesn't work out?"

"Well, we'll just invest my half of our money, then if it doesn't work out we'll still have your half."

"Just because Dusty cooked up some scheme doesn't mean I'm going to fall for it." Bud's voice had started to rise.

"Simmer down, cowboy. This is a solid plan; you just don't want to support Dusty. Well, I do. He deserves every chance to make his own way in the world. We can support it together, or we can split everything up and I will do it myself."

Bud was silent for several seconds. "I'll take the proposal down to the bank tomorrow…but I'm not going to be strong-armed into doing something foolish."

Rhetta smiled sweetly. "Of course not, Bud."

The man turned on his heel, crossed the hall and stomped up the stairs as Rhetta moved to the doorway. "Oh, and by the way. I have moved all of your belongings to Chet's old room, so you'll be sleeping there from now on."

CHAPTER THIRTY-THREE

December 1943

Tilda was sure that tonight would be the night, the night that Carlos would propose. They hadn't been seeing each other that long, and she'd never spent the night in his home, but she thought she maybe knew the signs. The questions about her family, her dreams, his history; the real history, not the one Hedda Hopper wrote about. There was a gentleness and kindness he'd always shown her. He wasn't like the other men she'd dated. He was respectful, intelligent, listened to what she had to say, and she felt cherished and admired by him. It had amazed her and frightened her that a movie star like Carlos had taken her seriously, had continued to see her. She was not a one-night stand for him, she sensed that. Not that there had been "one-night," but that was because of his gallantry. She'd been willing, eager in fact, but he'd kept himself at arm's length.

She'd been honest about her humble beginnings, and she had learned his own origin secrets. He was not the suave South American he portrayed to the public. She'd stayed with him while he drove his brother home to Tijuana after he was beaten by American sailors. She comforted him and felt his tenderness toward her for her sympathy. She felt there were no secrets between them. She loved him for his mind, for his beauty, for his devotion to his family, and because he was unlike any man she had met in her life. All of those oafish, aggressive suitors who had seemed to care and then tried to force themselves on her, their tongues down her throat, pressing against her, pretending it was love when it was really dominance and strength. Carlos was different. He needed and wanted her for other reasons, and she was willing to follow him. She had given some thought to whether she was willing to be a mistress, a concubine, or whatever. She already knew that the answer was yes. No other man had treated her with the concern, the caring, and the respect that he had.

Carlos showed her into the lovely living room she had visited before. A fire was burning in the fireplace; a bottle of champagne chilled in a bucket of ice on the low table in front of the couch. He let her know that his staff had been dismissed for the evening.

He was his usual self, but a little more tense, a little unsure. He led her to the sofa before the fire and poured two glasses of champagne.

"Tilda, I am so happy that you are here with me tonight."

"Me, too."

"I need to talk to you seriously, like we have never spoken before. I am afraid to speak to you in this way."

"There is no reason to ever be afraid to speak to me."

"I know that, but this is different. This is something I have not spoken to any other person about."

Tilda couldn't imagine what Carlos was talking about, but she was sure that it couldn't be anything she wouldn't understand.

"*Mi amor*, you have only known me a short time, but you know more about me, and my family, than any person here in Hollywood, save Robbie."

"Oh, Carlos, don't worry, I would never tell anyone anything you didn't want me to."

"Yes, I know that you would not, but there are other things that you do not know. Things that are just as important, just as secret."

"I love you. I would never betray your secrets." Tilda didn't hesitate in her promise, but she wasn't sure what he was talking about.

"Dear one, I will tell you what I need from you, but I will understand if it is not something that you can promise. Just, please, continue to keep the other secrets that you already hold."

Tilda downed the rest of the wine in her glass and held it out to Carlos. He took the glass from her and set it on the table before them. "In a moment. First let me ask you, do you know what is a beard?"

"A beard?" Tilda couldn't help but laugh. "Don't tell me you are thinking of growing a beard."

"No, no, I don't know how to say this. Please listen. The kind of beard I mean is a person that keeps a secret to protect another person."

"Like a liar?"

"No…yes, lying of a sort, but for a good reason, for a loving reason. But also, for a kind of payment."

"If you are trying to make this clearer you are doing a very bad job of it. What are you talking about?" For the first time Tilda picked up the frisson of fear and desperation coming off Carlos and she began to feel afraid herself.

"I care for you very much…."

"Yes, I know you do. I care for you, too."

"But there is something about me that you do not know." He raised his hand to silence her as she moved to speak. "Something very…bad, or maybe not bad, but secret."

"Carlos, you're scaring me. It sounds like you are a murderer or something."

"No, not a murderer, but something that would end my movie career, if people know… I am queer.… I take men as my lovers."

Tilda froze. Homosexuality was nothing new to her; she'd started her career on Broadway and knew that there were many people there who just didn't talk about it. She couldn't really grasp that he was saying he wanted to be with men. If that was the case, what was he doing here with her?

She stood suddenly. "I have to leave; I need to go home."

Carlos grabbed her hand. "Please don't leave yet. Let me tell you what I am asking you. I want you to marry me, to move here and make movies with me."

"But you just said…"

"Yes, I know what I am, but that does not mean I don't care for you. Together we can make a life, careers, money, everything."

"You want me to marry you and pretend to be your wife. To lie every day to everyone."

"I know, I know it is impossible, but it must not come out that I am like this. It would be the end of everything for me."

"I know. But what if I can't do this? I love you, but I don't... I swear to you Carlos, that nothing that I have learned from you and your family will ever be shared with anyone."

Tilda reached out to Carlos but sensed him holding back from her even as they embraced.

"Okay, Carlos, I need to know what you are talking about and what you need from me."

He downed his glass of champagne and sat down on the sofa before the fire. He began to speak to her, and she clung to his every word.

Tilda started awake in the hour before dawn, unsure where she was. The moonlight was flooding down over the veranda in the hills. She was lying on one of the chaise longues and she could see Carlos asleep on the other one. Her head hurt and she realized she'd drunk too much of the expensive champagne.

She considered his handsome face and watched him sleep for several minutes before she got up. She wasn't sure where her shoes were, but she wouldn't need them right away. She went through the French doors into the dark and quiet house. She walked through it silently, one room to the next. Every room was beautiful, and expensive. She stopped for a few moments in the kitchen that was kept immaculate by the cook and housekeeper who came in each day. The rooms were large, nothing like the apartment in Queens where she had grown up. Several of those apartments could fit into this house with its ornate bathroom fixtures and flowing drapes. Outside in the garage there were several cars and she could see that the lights were on in the apartment above them where Carlos's driver awaited the call to drive her back to Burbank.

She could have all of this. She could live in this house and be driven in those cars. She could go to all the parties with her handsome husband. She would have a chance to be in the movies made at the studio, not serve the lunches to the extras in the canteen. It could all be hers.

But it would be a beautiful ruse. She would be wealthy and glamorous and famous, and Carlos would be safe. Safe from the rumors and the whispers. Safe from the threats to his career. The newspapers would eat it up. "Latin movie star falls for beautiful waitress and sweeps her off her feet." It would be her on his arm, wearing designer clothes, being envied by all of Hollywood.

She stopped and looked down at the huge engagement ring that he had given her. Even in the dim moonlight it sparkled.

She walked back outside where Carlos still slept. Funny thing, he thought he was offering her everything, but she knew she would have done what he asked even without the money and the glamour. She loved him and she wanted to protect him from the people who would destroy him if they had the chance. He would be deserted if they knew he was a poor *pachuco* from Tijuana. If they knew that he was homosexual.

She stood over him for a while. She almost reached out and touched his beautiful head. But if she woke him, she would have to give him an answer.

She needed time to think, but she didn't want him to worry. His eyes had looked at her so pleadingly. He seemed strong and confident, but she could see that he was terrified of losing everything, for himself and for his family.

He had said that she could take lovers if she wanted. She couldn't imagine wanting that, but beyond that it meant that he would be taking lovers. He would sometimes not be coming home at night. He could maybe love someone else. Did homosexuals love each other? She'd never given it any thought. He had said that he loved her, like a friend, like a sister, maybe like his mother. Could people change? If she loved him enough and was there for him and made this choice for him would he grow to love her, grow to want her?

Who could you ask these things? Who would know the answer? A frown creased her forehead as she tried to imagine whom you might turn to with these questions. Had someone hurt him, had he just not found a woman who would love him and make him feel safe? Maybe she could wait to give him her answer. She shook her head. "I'll just wait a while." He'd promised to give her time to think. After all, there was no hurry.

CHAPTER THIRTY-FOUR

December 1943

Lucy loved everything about going to the USO on Saturday nights, like the music, sometimes from a real band instead of scratchy records. She loved to jitterbug, and a lot of the military fellows really knew how to cut a rug.

If you were a GI you could go to the Hollywood Canteen on North Cahuenga Blvd., a lot of celebrities volunteered there. She'd heard of the boys being served coffee and doughnuts by the Andrews Sisters, or Lucille Ball. Everything was free, you just had to be in uniform.

When she was at the USO Lucy felt like a movie star herself. She imagined being in one of those wartime pictures she'd gone into Wichita to see. She didn't see herself as one of the glamorous stars, just the cute sidekick, but that was good enough for her. Cute and perky, she danced pretty much every dance all evening. If, for some reason, she didn't get asked she strutted right up to one of the quieter guys that lined the edges of the dance floor, grabbed his hands, and dragged him onto the floor. They usually weren't very good dancers, but they were happy to get asked and really appreciated the attention.

Lucy knew how to stay in the middle of the floor and not get lured into a dark corner or out into the dark evening for some fresh air. The first few times she'd fallen for that line and had to wrestle off some handsy guy with his sad tale of leaving for the front the next day. She'd heard that line before and what had it gotten her: a wedding ring she had to slip into her pocket before she went out and a husband in the Navy. She loved Jack, or maybe she just thought she did, but she'd never intended to get married so young. He was a nice guy, maybe too nice, a good dancer, but kind of shy.

When she'd returned to Burbank after her brief honeymoon, she felt self-conscious that everyone knew what she and Jack had been doing and she had to face them alone. Her friends didn't really treat her differently, but she had yet to write to her father and his wife in Kansas that she had gotten married. She'd tried to write the letter several times, but it just seemed sort of tawdry. What was she going to tell her dad and his new wife about Jack? What did she even know about him? His last name, that she now shared; that he had a mom, a sister, and two younger brothers in Arkansas; that he was in the Navy; that he was a good dancer. They would be surprised and maybe shocked that she had known him for such a short while. How could she explain that she didn't want him to go to war and maybe die without having a girl back home. It sounded kind of romantic when she agreed to do it, but now it just sounded like she was some khaki-whacky young floozy when she tried to write it down on paper.

This was the first night since he left that she'd hadn't had to work a twelve-hour shift at the plant. She'd been tired all week and really wanted to just go home and go to bed, but she couldn't pass up a chance to go dancing. She'd told Molly she was going to a movie with some girlfriends from the plant. It hadn't seemed right somehow to tell them she was going dancing when Jack was off to war. She wasn't going to do anything bad; she just wanted to have some fun. For crying out loud, she was only nineteen years old. Couldn't she just have a good time without people looking down their noses at her?

The USO seemed louder and brighter and much hotter tonight than it had the other times she'd been there. She'd left the house before supper, so she'd scarfed down a couple of free donuts instead. Her head had started to throb and she suddenly felt nauseated. It was lucky she got outside the door and around the corner before she threw up her sugary meal. The air outside was cooler and, after she stopped shaking, she felt much better. So much for thinking donuts made a good dinner.

When she went back inside, she got a cup of coffee and found a chair along the wall. A band had come in and set up and had started to play one of her favorite songs. She closed her eyes and sipped her warm drink. This was better. It was like the last time she was here with Jack. She remembered his warm brown eyes, and the way he looked at her like she was the most precious thing in the world. She realized she missed him and being here alone just wasn't the same. She would listen to the music for a bit and then go home and write him a long letter. She didn't really know where he was, but the address where she sent her letters sent them on to him, wherever in the world he was. She would use the funny little papers they provided for letters and write in her tiniest handwriting. She thought to sprinkle some cologne on the missive but remembered that he would never actually receive that note. He would receive a printed out photograph of it. She imagined that somewhere there was a huge warehouse that held all those millions of original letters, but thought they were probably destroyed after being filmed.

She knew he had a picture of her in his wallet and she imagined him looking at it every night before he bunked down. She was laughing into the camera and wearing a sundress. Her red curls bounced around her face. She wondered if he showed it to his friends and said, "Hey, you fellas want to see a picture of my beautiful wife?"

CHAPTER THIRTY-FIVE

January 1944

Molly paused her vigorous kneading of the cellophane pouch of margarine. The capsule had broken, and the color was beginning to spread through the fatty mass. The hurried footsteps above her head and the slam of the bathroom door signaled Lucy's morning dash to the commode. She waited and shortly heard the flush of the toilet and the running of water.

Sitting at the kitchen table Dorothy blew noisily on the tea she had poured into her saucer. Her red lipstick had already begun its journey out the deep furrows that surrounded her puckered lips. Her hands trembled slightly as she lowered the saucer to the table. "How long's it gonna be until that girl admits she's in the family way?" she grumbled.

Molly started and looked sharply at her mother-in-law. "You don't know what you're talking about, you old gossip," she retorted as she resumed kneading.

"My eyes might not be good, but I can still see what's going on under my nose...." wheezed the older woman. She leaned back in her chair and motioned toward the ceiling with her arthritic finger. "That girl's got a bun in the oven, and you know it, too."

"Shush, she'll hear you." Molly whispered! as there was the clatter of feet on the stairs and Lucy entered the room.

Lucy's freckles showed sharply against her unusually pale face, but she smiled wanly at them both. "Good morning, ladies," she chirped.

"Do you want some breakfast?" Molly offered, waving her hand toward the pan of porridge that bubbled on the old stove.

For a moment Lucy's face showed her alarm at the thought of eating. "No...no, I'm fine. I'll pick up something on the way to work," she said and turned quickly toward the back door.

"Lucy..." Molly hesitated, then said, "...never mind. I'll talk to you later," as Lucy banged out the door.

"They're not going to let her work at the plant when they find out, you know," quavered Dorothy.

"I know, and it's not fair," Molly muttered. "She's a hard worker and she needs the money, especially with a baby."

"It doesn't matter. Rules are rules," the old woman said emphatically. "What are you going to do about it?"

"What do you mean? I'm not going to do anything about it."

"Well, she won't be able to pay for the room if she's not working."

"I don't care about that; she can stay as long as she needs to."

"Hmph! If Aloysius was alive there'd be no free rent."

"That's right, and if Aloysius was alive, you'd be living with your sister Hannah in the old folks' home."

There was a pause as Dorothy raised the tea saucer to her lips and slurped noisily.

"You're right about that. He could be a mean son-of-a-bitch," she said. Then she stood and walked unceremoniously out of the kitchen.

Twelve-hour shifts at the Lockheed plant took a toll on everyone, and the added trolley ride and bus connection to get back to Burbank didn't help. Lucy slipped through the back door while everyone was at dinner and went up the stairs to have a little rest before she could think of eating. As she dozed off she thought how the days were still short and it was dark at six p.m. When Tilda came to bed she took special care not to wake the sleeping redhead and pulled a light blanket over her friend before sliding between her own covers.

Lucy woke in the dead of night to a silent house, still tired but ravenously hungry and chilled to the bone, still dressed in her work clothes. Getting up she pulled the blanket around her shoulders and made her way out of the dark room and down the stairs to the kitchen. About each third step of the old stairs creaked ominously, but she tried not to wake anyone else up. In the dark it was hard to find the chain hanging from the ceiling light, but she waved her arm around until she made contact. Light flooded the homey space and she noted the row of lunch boxes already lined up on the counter for the coming day. It would be easiest to just eat her already packed meal, but then she'd have to do something else about lunch.

She opened the icebox and sighed with relief when she spotted the waxed-paper–covered plate on the top shelf. She should have known that Molly would be thinking of her.

She grabbed a fork from the jar on the counter and carried the plate to the table. Even cold meatloaf and potatoes sounded heavenly right now. The brown slices were likely more loaf than meat, but she didn't care. It always amazed her how Molly could make almost nothing into a meal you were grateful to eat.

Molly pulled her robe around her as she stood in the dark and watched Lucy dig into her cold dinner. She needed to take a few minutes to think about what she wanted to say.

Finally, she cleared her throat before entering, trying not to startle Lucy. The girl was so focused on using her slice of bread to mop up the last drips of gravy from her plate that she still jumped when Molly entered.

"Sorry, I didn't mean to startle you."

"That's okay, I just didn't expect anyone else to be up so late…or so early, I guess. I hope I didn't wake you up."

Molly went to the sink to fill the coffee percolator. "It was almost time for me to get up, anyway."

"Looks like I had dinner for breakfast. I hope it stays down. It was pretty good meatloaf."

"Thanks, it could be that eating in the middle of the night could be the answer to your tummy upset." Molly hoped that would give Lucy the opening she needed to start talking about the obvious. But Lucy just stared down at her empty plate.

With the coffee started Molly pulled a chair out from the table and sat down across from the silent girl.

"You know, Lucy, bringing a new baby into the world is not a sin. It is something to celebrate."

The tears so close to the surface began to roll down Lucy's freckled cheeks. "I know, and I'm happy, but I don't know what I'm going to do. I don't have anywhere to go, anyone to help me. I can't go home to my daddy and his new family, and I don't even know Jack's mother."

"Honey, that is not true. You can stay here, and you have a whole family of grannies and aunties to help you."

For the first time Lucy looked up from her plate, warily. "They're not going to let me work when they find out. I guess I will get some money from Jack. He doesn't even know yet. I sent a letter but I haven't heard anything."

Molly shrugged. She knew that it could take weeks for Jack to even get the letter and more weeks to get an answer back. How long had it been since she'd heard from her boys? Bobby wasn't much of a writer, but you could tell by the dates on the letters that Ian wrote regularly. The letters would come in a packet every couple of months. She'd put them all in date order before she began reading them. "He'll be in touch when he can. He's going to be excited; I know."

"I didn't think I could get pregnant so fast. We only had a day together."

"Well, that's the way it works a lot of the time. Bobby was born eight months after Al and I married. People are still speculating about it, especially since he weighed nine pounds when he did come. You'd have thought he'd at least try to make it to nine months."

Lucy giggled at that. "Doesn't matter a bit, married is married." Then she yawned.

"I'll tell you what. Why don't you go up and try to get a little more sleep before work? Tonight, we'll have a special dinner and you can officially tell everyone about the baby. Don't be taken aback if Dorothy is not too surprised."

Lucy stood up. "I thought she was giving me the evil eye the past few days," but she said it with an affectionate smile on her lips.

As Lucy went upstairs Molly turned off the fire under the percolator. She was already planning how to manage a celebratory cake for dessert tonight. She thought she had all the ingredients, and what she didn't have she could barter for with eggs from her chickens. It was time there was something to celebrate in this house.

CHAPTER THIRTY-SIX

March 1944

Jack wasn't sure what being in the Navy and going to war would be like. But, for a low-level swabbie like himself, it was a crazy mix of boring and terrifying. The tropical temperatures were exhausting and the mind-numbing work of cleaning and maintaining the ship felt pointless. During the day the solitude was only broken by the occasional frightening distant drone of an aircraft or the more unexpected breach of a whale that looked suspiciously like a submarine. At night he would fall into his bunk exhausted but end up not sleeping as every thud and clunk of the lumbering ship woke him in a cold sweat.

He had never been a reader or a card player and had lost his measly money stash in a few hands of five-card stud. When he tried to join conversations beyond the horrible heat and his hatred of the Japs, he soon fell into silence, recognizing that growing up on an Arkansas farm didn't provide much fodder for discussion.

He would spend this day mopping in the unrelenting sun and was in a foul mood before he even grabbed his mop and bucket. He suspected that his idol more than friend, Tacoma, had been purposely leaving him out of his group and had crowned a new prince. Whenever he approached a knot of his former pals, the group would dissipate like smoke, leaving him standing alone in the mess or the rec area. He couldn't think what he had done wrong, but some fresh-faced city boy with a permanent smirk and a cutting wit had replaced him in the roster.

So far, none of the sly remarks had directly landed on him, though he spent an inordinate amount of time dreaming up answers to ill-disguised insults, should they ever come his way. It almost seemed as though he was beneath consideration, even as a butt to the men's jokes.

Early in the afternoon, he had backed himself into a shaded niche to grab a quick smoke and dream about being anywhere but here, when a familiar taunting voice intruded on his reverie.

"Where's farm-boy? Hiding from work, as usual?"

"Beats me, haven't seen him since chow. Must be hiding below decks, mooning over that slutty picture of his wife."

"Maybe we should keep a closer eye on him. If we ever get attacked my bet is on him finding the best hidey-hole."

Before the conversation could go further Jack sprung from his spot and grabbed the sailor from behind, putting him in a choke hold. The other men tried to pull him off his victim, but for someone who had wrestled a 200-pound calf to the ground, the effect was negligible. Before he knew it he had thrown the man down and straddled him.

Jack had never understood the rage that came upon his father in all those long-ago bar fights, but today he could feel the need to pummel this man's face into a pulp. Again, and again his meaty fists pounded into the no longer smirking face.

Jack had not felt this powerful and brave since the day he enlisted and the process of beating him into submission had begun. When the drill sergeant had stopped hammering at him, his compatriots had started. It seemed like to feel like a big man, you had to make someone else feel small, or stupid, or cowardly. Finally, he'd had enough.

It took three sailors to pull him off the other man and they had a tough job of it. In his rage Jack would have happily taken them all on, until suddenly he went limp in their arms, his fury spent.

Commander Mack was not surprised to hear that someone had been beaten up. It was only a matter of time before the boredom and trepidation flipped one of the crew into a frenzy. He knew exactly how to handle it. Throw the guy in the brig for a few days and tell him he needed to use that anger on the Japs when he got a chance. The excitement of the fight would rouse everyone and then let them settle into a less fraught attitude. It released some steam from the pressure cooker of a warship on the hunt.

It was too bad that the young guy that took the beating was in pretty bad shape, but he would survive, and he'd probably be less of a smart-ass in the future. For Commander Mack it was a win-win.

Captaining a ship could be like tiptoeing through a room covered in mousetraps and ping-pong balls. One little trip up, or stray missile, could send the whole place into pandemonium. Jack Scoggins was a weapon. Someone who could throw all training and caution to the wind with the urge to destroy something or someone could be very useful in a battle. Those were the guys who got the medals; no common sense or self-preservation there.

For today, though, the latest radio communication let him know that enemy submarines had been detected in the area he was quickly headed into. He'd need to have a couple of attack drills run, and hope that nobody manning the radio would leak the news to their buddies. It was a big ocean, and there was a small likelihood of being attacked, but nobody needed any more stress.

CHAPTER THIRTY-SEVEN

March 1944

Jack lay on the hard mattress and looked up at the metal coils of the bunk above him. He didn't know how long they'd been at sea. A few weeks, he thought. He didn't know exactly how long he'd been in the brig, either. Not long, maybe a few days. It was hard to tell down in the bowels of the ship where the sun never shone, and the only sounds were the mechanical chugging of the huge seagoing beast making its way relentlessly across the Pacific. Nobody talked to him; the only person he saw was that asshole who brought him his meals. The light stayed on night and day. He only knew breakfast from supper based on what they sent down to him in his tin can of a cell.

They hadn't bothered to tell swabbies like him where they were headed. He knew that the sun rose behind the boat and set along the bow. He knew the repetitiveness of his daily tasks and the anxiety he felt as they moved closer and closer to the battlefront made him angry. It made them all angry. It was easier to admit to being pissed off than to show your fear. Who were you going to tell that you wished you'd never heard of this war, never gotten onto this floating target?

He'd tried to read; had them bring him a bible. He figured they couldn't really refuse to give him a bible so he could reflect on his sins. The Gideon folks had been spreading God's word throughout the land in cheap lodgings from coast to coast. Not that Jack had stayed in many hotels. He was just a good ole farm boy, but he did know his bible. His mama had seen to that.

He wished he hadn't thought about his mama. The steady rocking of the boat made it easy to drift off and find yourself back on the hardscrabble farm of his childhood. He was the oldest of the four kids. One younger sister and two little brothers. It seemed as though Mama and Daddy had suddenly remembered each other after years of exhaustion and poverty and decided to start a new brood of kids. Jack didn't really mind. He liked them, they were funny and silly and crazy about him. They didn't cause him extra work and somehow, he felt the stuff he did around the place was worth something if it made their lives better. When his daddy had died he was old enough to be a big help to Mama. He hadn't given much thought to the war in Europe, didn't go in much for reading the papers and usually fell asleep listening to radio programs in the evening.

When the Japs bombed Pearl Harbor and his friends all started enlisting he'd wanted to go, but he knew he couldn't leave his family alone. He'd filed for an exemption as the only breadwinner for his family and stayed around long enough for his sister to graduate from high school last June. She and Mama had both gotten jobs in town that they wouldn't have been able to get before all the men and boys went off to fight the war. Sure, some of those boys weren't gonna be coming home. The telegraph office courier was a common sight riding his bicycle down one of the streets bearing bad news to families in the town. People would turn their backs when they saw him ride by, they'd close their front doors, like they could ward off the sorrow he might be bringing to their homes, to their families. Jack had felt sorry for him, sorry enough to befriend him on Saturday afternoons in town when he'd see the kid sitting alone on a stool at the Woolworth's counter. One Saturday morning he'd found an old bottle of hooch tucked in the back of a shelf in the basement and had shared it with the kid that night, back behind the post office. They'd gotten sloppy drunk and done some snotty crying before they both threw up and wandered off in opposite directions. Jack remembered the kid talking about the long waits on the front porches when he'd rung the bell; the urgent whispers behind the doors, and finally, the door opening slowly and the look of fear on the person who braved the threshold. He never waited for them to open the telegrams or to give him a tip. Once the envelope passed from his possession to theirs, he turned and walked quickly, stiff-legged, to his bike and pedaled away without a backward glance.

Jack had worried that he might have confessed to some of his own fears that night, and from then forward he was another person in town who avoided the lone kid.

Jack was not much of a lady's man. He was shy and awkward around girls and women, but he had a much broader array of ladies to choose from once Uncle Sam had scooped up all the eligible men in his small town. He still didn't have much to say for himself and usually spent the first few minutes explaining why he hadn't enlisted, but being one of the only boys available to dance with had stood him in good stead at parties. Not that there was much to party about during the war. It just didn't seem right to be celebrating and having fun when your brother, or father, or boyfriend was maybe being shot at by Germans or Japs. Still, there were occasional get-togethers in the church basement, or sometimes a wedding hurriedly celebrated after a draft notice was received.

When Jack finally felt that he could leave his family, he could have just gone down to the local recruiting station, but he decided he wanted to see some of the country he was supposed to be fighting for. He packed up his few possessions, took half of his savings, leaving the other half with his mother, and began hitchhiking across the country toward California.

It was a lucky chance that he met up with Dusty just a few days into the trip. Soon Tilda and Lucy were added, and finally, Julia joined them.

Lucy hadn't really been his type, if he had a type. She was kind of loud, and forward for a girl. She had a lot of opinions and wasn't afraid to share them. He didn't think his mama would like her, but she just wouldn't let him back off. Lucy liked him. That alone made her the most unusual of girls. She kissed him first, pressing her body against his in a way he'd only imagined, and not that accurately. She wasn't really pretty, but she was bubbly and funny. She laughed loudly and often. She was quick to point out his flaws, and just as quick to repent and do or say something to gain forgiveness. She was almost like a buddy except that she smelled good and felt soft and pliant in his arms. He thought she was probably what his mama would have called "fast," or "no better than she ought to be," whatever that meant. He'd heard her say it about the girl behind the counter at Woolworth's and about his cousin Estella who had an early baby six months after the wedding.

When Jack got his orders and knew he'd be shipping out in a few days, he'd panicked. He was going to go fight somewhere and the only girl he'd ever kissed was Lucy. He was going to some strange place to die without ever having made love to someone, without loving someone, without someone loving him.

When Jack pressed her to marry him before he shipped out, she hesitated. Looking back he thought she probably would have suggested they just sleep together instead of getting married, but it just wasn't something she could say to him, so she said yes, I will marry you. The wedding had been quick. Only a couple of their friends could get off work, and he was able to get one day of shore leave that they spent in a cheap shoreside motor court. That's where he'd learned about Gideon and his Bibles.

On their wedding night, Lucy had been suddenly shy and he'd been awkward and realized he didn't even really know what he was supposed to do. There was anger and crying, and it wasn't just Lucy that cried. When all was done Jack wasn't sure that the few seconds of release were worth the effort. But he now had a ring on his finger and a girl back home to write to, and a picture of a laughing redhead in a sundress in his wallet.

Jack jolted awake, almost being thrown from his bunk. The lights had gone out and, for a few seconds, he didn't remember where he was. The giant engines churned on but after a second blast they shuddered to a stop. It was not quiet, but the sounds that Jack heard were not the familiar throb and hum of the monstrous boat.

"Hey! Hey, what's going on?" He grabbed hold of the cell bars and shook them. "Hey!"

There was no answer. His voice echoed off the metal walls and ceiling.

Explosions shook the huge craft followed by the sound of water rushing into the lower compartment that housed the brig. Everything was pitch black but before long Jack could feel the water rising around his shoes. He found his way back to the bunk and clambered onto the top tier.

"Hey!" he continued to shout.

The water was rising faster and when he felt the boat list to one side and was flung against the bulkhead he realized the water was already up to where he cowered beneath the ceiling.

He struggled to find purchase on the slippery frame and pressed his face against the ceiling as the water rushed in, gasping for any last breath of air. His final thought as he slid beneath the icy water was that he was dying for his country. Nobody would ever know that he had died locked in a cell in the belly of the beast.

CHAPTER THIRTY-EIGHT

April 1944

The doorbell at the front of the house had never worked properly since Al had installed it. Instead of a resonant *ding-dong* you got more of a flat-sounding thunk, but it was enough to recognize it as coming from someone at the door.

The day had been warm enough to make some rolls, set back and rising on the stove where the pilot light kept them warm.

Molly was in the garden pulling up the last of the carrots and onions from last year.

Dorothy wiped her hands on her apron as she walked toward the parlor. As she stepped around the dining table and craned her neck toward the door she froze. She could see Harold standing on the porch although he could not see her from where he stood. The doorbell chimed its sad note a second time and she called out, "Just a moment."

She took several shaking breaths before she smoothed down her apron and ran a hand over her untidy hair and forced herself to walk to the door.

"Good morning, Harold… It's not my birthday, you know." She smiled weakly.

"No, ma'am. I have a telegram here for Mrs. Lucy Scoggins." He held the envelope out to her as she opened the screen.

Dorothy did not take the envelope at first. It would be easier to call Lucy down, to let her take the envelope into her hands directly from the messenger, but when she raised her eyes to Harold's she saw the pain there. She couldn't do anything for Jack, or much for Lucy, but she could save Harold this one moment.

"I think she is sleeping. Is it okay for me to take it and give it to her when she wakes up?"

"Yes, Mrs. Moseby. You'll just need to sign that you got it." He held out the pen and notebook to her and she quickly signed and took the proffered missive from his hand.

"Thank you, Harold. Wait just a minute while I get my purse."

"No ma'am, I don't need a tip." He touched his cap and turned away, stepping quickly down the steps and swinging his leg over his bike. He glanced back once more and then rode away.

Molly had returned to the house and stood by the dining table watching him ride away before she turned to Dorothy. "Ma?"

"It's for our Lucy."

The relief that flooded Molly's face was quickly followed by sorrow and resignation, but for that one moment all she could think was "Thank God, thank God, it's not one of my boys."

The two of them sat at the kitchen table sipping tea with the offending envelope on the table between them until they heard Lucy's moving around upstairs. They went up together to deliver the news and to help in whatever way they could.

CHAPTER THIRTY-NINE

May 1944

Molly stepped out onto the screened-in porch. The rattle and roll of the old wringer washer had stopped, signaling that the washing part was done, and it was time to move on to the wringing and hanging.

She saw that Lucy and Tilda had spread out a blanket on the strips of what passed for grass between the weathered fence and the neat rows of vegetables. The smell of sun-baked baby oil spread on pale legs permeated the air. Lucy had been combing lemon juice through her hair in hopes the sun would brighten the color. Even though Tilda had offered to peroxide her curls for her, Lucy was resisting. Lemon juice just seemed so natural, and better somehow.

Seldom was there a day where two or more of the boarders were off, and they took advantage of it when they could. Sometimes they would go see a movie or go shopping, but most often they would sleep until noon, chat over a midday snack and just spend what Julia liked to call "normal" time. It couldn't really be described but it involved not talking and thinking about war and what you could not buy or do. There would be time later for writing letters to their own personal members of the military, or family back home. They would still need to prepare for the next ten or more days that they would be working

Today they would soak their fingertips in soapy water and trim them to look as professional as possible. The latest fad was to mix clear nail polish and a specific shade of pink called Windsor Rose, for Princess

Elizabeth. The resultant almost invisible shade seemed both subtle and sophisticated and couldn't be frowned upon by even the most judgmental of bosses.

Tilda's Nordic complexion struggled to attain even the faintest of summer color and Lucy bemoaned mightily her abundance of freckles. Someone had told her that mercolized wax would fade the annoying dots sprinkled across her nose, shoulders, and truth be known, every place else. She'd read that the magic elixir contained mercury and was dangerous, but she figured it was worth the risk if it worked.

Usually, a stack of movie magazines and newspapers had been obtained and were examined. It was a house rule that all issues of the LA papers containing columns from Hedda Hopper and Louella Parsons would be held onto until everyone had a chance to read them.

Molly's mind wandered as she cranked the wet clothes through the wringer and dumped them into the basket for hanging. The rise and fall of the girls' voices was a cheerful background to her thoughts. She often wondered where her boys were, what Keiko was doing, how her life would be different if Al had lived longer…. Today her thoughts had wandered back to when Diedre had been born.

Suddenly there was a shriek from the yard and all conversation stopped. When she turned to look at the girls she saw that Tilda had bolted to her feet holding a recent copy of the *LA Times.*

"What does she think she's doing? She can't just say those things!" Tilda's voice had risen as she spoke.

"It's nothing, you know she just says any old thing to stir up trouble. That's what we like about her, that she is such a …witch." Lucy's glance slid toward Molly before she changed the final word. Lucy also stood up.

"But this is different. This could ruin his career. It could ruin everything."

"Nobody really reads her, though…." Lucy lamely claimed.

"*Everybody* reads her. I have to call him right away. What is the date on this? The paper rattled in her hand as she searched for the date.

Molly barely had time to move aside as Tilda ran past her into the house, still clutching the newspaper.

"What's going on, Lucy?"

Lucy had followed Tilda up the steps and stopped beside Molly, both of them still gazing at the recently slammed screen door.

"It's Hedda Hopper…in her column. She…said some kind of awful-sounding things about Carlos."

"What kind of things, is he married or something?"

"Way worse, it sounds like she thinks he's a…fancy boy, or something. I don't really understand it, but it didn't sound nice at all the way she said it."

"Tilda must know that's not true,…I mean she's been seeing him for a while."

Lucy just shook her head and walked back down the steps to gather the remains of their quiet afternoon. The newspapers were blowing across the grass and a glass of lemonade had overturned onto the blanket they had shared.

Finishing the wringing of the clothes Molly picked up the heavy basket and hefted it down the steps to the clothesline where the bag of pins hung. She could hear Tilda's voice speaking urgently into the phone. "Well, when will he be home? I have to talk to him."

CHAPTER FORTY

May 1944

Carlos dove into the sparkling pool before the sun rose and struggled his way through the water. Swimming did not come naturally to him, but he felt that he should use the pool that came with the house. He needed to learn to swim strongly in case there ever was the need in one of his movies. In his childhood neighborhood a sprinkler set up on a muddy lot, or getting a wrench and opening the street's single fire hydrant, was the best way to cool off.

He needed to feel confident and strong to face the day ahead. He had a meeting at the studio at ten a.m. that he was not looking forward to. He'd been the perfect movie star as far as the studio was concerned. He did bond drives, he wasn't demanding, he kept up his physique and said all the right things in interviews, but one of the "dames de gossip" had made some insinuations that could be damaging. He'd already debunked the claims of cowardice (he was an Argentine citizen, after all), he'd dated the youngest and most beautiful of starlets, and he'd been generous with his money, but now, he needed a bold a plan to quell the gossips, and today the plan would be laid out before the worried studio head.

Robbie would be driving the immaculate Cadillac through the studio gates and his publicist, Bertram, would accompany him. "Carlos, you just let me do the talking today. I know what these people want. You've got everything set up with the girl, right?"

"Tilda, not 'the girl,'" Carlos objected.

"Okay then, Tilda. Couldn't you have found someone with a more melodic name?"

"No, I could not."

Bertram had done a photo shoot with Tilda the day before. He used her most wholesome and down-to-earth poses, even taking photos in her canteen uniform. "A princess would have been better, but an all-American waitress is the next best thing. The fans love a rags-to-riches story."

Carlos had just leaned his head back and closed his eyes. Bertram hadn't steered him wrong yet in his career, so he just hoped they knew what they were doing now.

In the driver's seat Robbie sat with a rigid back, surreptitiously glancing at them in the mirror. He saw that Carlos's jaw was clenched and that the jumpy Bertramwas more nervous than usual.

The officious secretary that sat sentinel outside Bedford Myers's office did not swoon when Carlos entered the way that the receptionist had. She'd had her fill of movie pretty boys and opted for the surety of money and luxury her boss could provide. "Mr. Myers is waiting for you, Mr. Salida. Please go right in."

"Thank you, Sylvia." Carlos flashed her his warmest smile. Remembering people's names had always stood him in good stead.

Inside the luxurious office, the windows looking out over the studio he had built, Bedford Myers sat behind his huge desk. He stood and extended his hand when Carlos entered. At least that was a good sign. He wanted to work this out. "Carlos, please sit down. You, too, Bertram. Good to see you both."

Once they were all seated Bedford sat back in his seat, steepling his hands before him. "It looks like Hedda Hopper has you in her sights this week, Carlos."

"Yes, sir, it does. I can't think what might have set her off."

"I am sure it is just her ravenous appetite for scandal and squalor, and it was only a matter of time until she focused on you. The question isn't why she did it, but how to shut her down immediately. Bertram tells me that he has a plan."

The agent sat forward in his chair and pulled a file folder out of his briefcase. "I think you are going to be happy with this, Bedford…I mean Mr. Myers." Bertram had noted the studio head's reaction to being called by his first name by a lowly publicist. "Carlos has been very cagey about it, but he is actually engaged to be married."

"Married, really? He has been quiet about it."

"Well, initially he didn't want to upset his fans who love it that he is still single. But now seems the perfect time to announce his intentions to the world."

Myers was silent for a few seconds, considering. "That does seem very convenient. Is it some young starlet, or someone he's been linked with before?"

Bertram almost rubbed his little hands together. "Better, it is a beautiful young *waitress* he met here in the studio canteen."

"Carlos eats in the canteen?"

"They didn't exactly meet there, but she does work there. Of course she's an aspiring actress, from New York City, with off-Broadway credits. She sings and dances, as well, and she's gorgeous." Bertram stood up and placed the file folder on Myers' desk.

"I'm sure those are qualities every man looks for in a wife." Myers pulled the folder closer, although his expression was a bit skeptical. "Sounds like someone from Central Casting."

Bertram laughed nervously. "No, not at all. Just look at the pictures."

Myers opened the folder and for several moments the only sound in the room was the shuffling of the photographs. "Okay, I think I can add to your plan. Louella owes me a favor or two, although I think I can make this look like I'm doing her a favor."

Carlos had noticed that the deep furrows in Myers's forehead had softened a bit as he'd considered Tilda as a solution to their problem. He resented the feeling that Tilda was being perused like a prize heifer but was still grateful that Myers seemed to buy the idea.

Myers slid the folder back toward Bertram. "You two go get

yourselves a cup of coffee, preferably at the canteen. I have a couple of calls to make. Meet me back here in an hour."

It had been a slow morning for Tilda, but she was preparing for the usual lunch rush. Throngs of princesses, knights, cowboys, bus conductors, gangsters, and soldiers (American, German, and Japanese) would soon descend, ravenous for tuna sandwiches, hamburgers, frankfurters, and pie. She hummed along to "Let's have another cup of coffee, and let's have another piece of pie," as she worked to make sure the coffeepots were fresh, and all was ready to go.

She almost dropped the fresh pot of java when she turned and saw Carlos and that little weasel, Bertram, come through the door. She had never seen Carlos here before, although Bertram had been there just yesterday with a photographer. Suddenly she realized she didn't know quite how to behave toward them. Should she act like she'd never seen them before? Should she go over and say hello? Should she throw her arms around Carlos's neck and give him a huge smooch?

Fortunately, she didn't have to decide as the two men walked directly up to her at the counter and took stools in front of where she stood. "Good morning, Mr. Salida, Mr. Spencer."

Bertram didn't speak, but Carlos reached for her hand so that she had to set the coffee pot down on the counter. Taking her hand in his he bent over it and gave it a kiss. "Ah, Tilda. How are you today?"

The room had gone quiet when Carlos entered. Tilda could feel every eye in the place on the two of them. She blushed, she hoped "prettily," and pulled her hand back. "I am fine. How can I help you?"

Carlos smiled and looked past her to the day's menu board. "What is good?"

Tilda glanced behind her. "Well, the tuna salad is fresh." Her voice dropped and she leaned forward. "I'd take a pass on the salmon croquettes."

"I will have coffee and a piece of that apple pie. How about you, Bertram?"

"Sure, coffee and pie sound good for me, too."

While they ate, the small room became crowded but remained fairly quiet. As each boisterous group entered, they were quickly silenced by those already watching the tableau playing out at the counter. A complex array of head nods, chin lifts, shoulder shrugs, and raised eyebrows directed attention to Carlos, and then to Tilda. Bertram quickly faded into the background but may not have minded as he was accustomed to it.

"Thank you, Tilda." Carlos pushed back his empty plate and mug and stood. He took a fiver from his pocket and held it out to her. When she reached out he grabbed her hand and pulled her toward him.

"Carlos, everyone is watching us."

"Yes, and it is just the beginning. I will call you later." With that he left the bill in her hand. "Keep the change," and he winked.

In his office, Myers hung up the phone and sat back with a satisfied sigh and a grin. He considered it one of his greatest talents that he could take a pretty good movie and make it better, and this problem with Carlos was just like a movie awaiting his magical touch. He couldn't wait for the two men to return so that he could unfold his idea.

CHAPTER FORTY-ONE

May 1944

Tilda reminded herself that she was playing the biggest part in her career, so far. Robbie had driven her and Carlos to some of the finer shops in Los Angeles, making sure to be seen by anyone who might make a difference. After great deliberation he had bought her a lovely, drapey dress of glistening satin that bared her shoulders and much of her bosom. It flowed down to mid-calf and swirled gracefully obove the strappy shoes bought to go with it. Of course, they'd also purchased the matching beaded bolero jacket.

She had been dropped off for her appointment to have her hair and makeup done while Carlos and Robbie ran errands. They had returned to his home in the hills and she'd unpackaged the purchases and repackaged herself. It had very much felt like being in a play and she gave in to the part fully. This might be her first great performance and the most important one, but it was just the first of many, both personal and professional. Seeing her artfully made-up face and shining hair in the mirror had added to the feeling of unreality that had surrounded the entire day.

In the car on the way to their eight p.m. reservation at the Brown Derby, Carlos had pulled a flat, rectangular box from his inside coat pocket. "One final thing to make the ensemble complete." And he had carefully opened the box.

Inside was a simple but sparkling necklace and matching earrings. "I can't accept a gift like that from you, Carlos. What would people think?"

"They would think that you are getting a lovely gift from your fiancé, that is all. Here, let me help you with the necklace." She turned her back to him and the brush of his warm hands on her neck felt exciting and intimate, although she doubted he felt the same way. She couldn't resist sliding her glance toward Robbie, sitting stoically behind the steering wheel. He did not move but she knew that he was watching them in the rearview mirror.

When they entered the restaurant the maître d' spotted them immediately and swept toward them with his welcoming arms held wide. "Ah, Monsieur Salida, welcome to the Brown Derby. Miss Parsons has just been seated and is expecting you." With a flourish he hoisted two of the gigantic menus and led the way to the most visible and central table in the restaurant, where sat Louella Parsons herself.

Miss Parsons held out her beringed hand to Carlos and he bent low to kiss it. "Dearest Louella, it is lovely to see you." You could tell she knew that every eye in the room was on them and she ate it up with a spoon. "Please, let me introduce you to my lovely fiancée, Tilda Morrison. Of course, you are the very first person to know of our engagement. Not even Tilda's own parents have heard yet, nor my own family in Argentina."

Louella, eyes sparkling, motioned to the chair on her right. "Dear Tilda, you must sit here next to me, and Carlos on my other side. I just cannot resist being surrounded by young love."

Louella made quite the show of admiring the glittering diamond ring that Tilda had removed from its hidden box in her dresser and placed on her ring finger before leaving the house.

Carlos ordered champagne and the photographer who just happened to have accompanied Louella snapped pictures of them all having a lovely time.

Of course, not a single moment of this evening had gone unplanned and at exactly 8:55 p.m. Hedda Hopper and her entourage entered the restaurant to be seated at the table she invariably occupied every

Wednesday evening. The fact that it was mere feet from where Louella's jolly little party sat may have been a coincidence, but probably not.

To give her credit, not once did Hedda's smiling visage dim, and while she couldn't miss the celebratory tableau before her, she did not gawk but listened carefully to all that was said.

Once Miss Hopper's story of Carlos's questionable sexual preferences had hit her column it had been only hours before he'd been summoned to the studio and the plan had been laid to assure that his engagement to the lovely commissary waitress from New York City was the big headline in Louella's next column. She'd already received a brief of the most romantic and interesting bits about Tilda, daughter of a cab driver, employee at the Automat, aspiring actress with Broadway credits. Well, maybe off-Broadway bit parts, but Broadway, nonetheless. It had all the markings of a rags to riches story.

CHAPTER FORTY-TWO

June 1944

Things had been going well with Delia there. She helped with breakfast and dinner, but during the day, when most of the lodgers were gone she searched for work. Not many jobs were close by, so she spent many hours standing at bus stops and riding buses.

The nearest place had been the Lockheed plant in Burbank, where she was hired on. From the bus stop by Union Airport the plant appeared to be covered with an awning that stretched across the entire factory. The awning was constructed from chicken wire, netting, and canvas. But, from the air, it was different. It was said that a War Department general had been flown over the plant at 5,000 feet and only seen suburbs with trees. Delia was proudly informed that artists and set designers from all the major studios had helped build the elaborate ruse.

Delia looked around as she sat down to wait for her bus. At the other end of the bench, she spied a young colored woman wearing a uniform. It wasn't an outfit that Delia recognized. When the woman looked toward her she quickly glanced away. She didn't want to be caught gawking, but her curiosity overcame her shyness. "Excuse me, do you mind if I sit here?"

The young woman turned to her. "Of course not."

As she sat back, Delia spoke again. "Can I ask you what kind of uniform you're wearing?"

"I'm a Nurse Cadet," the woman answered proudly.

"A Nurse Cadet? I've never heard of that."

"We're kind of new. Eleanor Roosevelt came up with the plan because so many of the nurses went and joined the military to help with the war. We are getting trained to take their places in the hospitals at home."

Delia wasn't quite sure how to ask her next question. "They let us, I mean colored women, into the Nurse Cadets?"

The other woman blushed. "Well, there aren't a lot of us, and not all of the training hospitals do, but the one here in Burbank does." The woman looked down the street. "My bus is coming, but I have a brochure you can have." She reached into her purse and pulled out the paper. "You just need to go to the hospital and get an application. You've graduated from high school, right?"

"Yes, yes I graduated. Is that a requirement?"

"You'll be most of the way there then. I have to go, but good luck. Maybe I will see you in class." The girl jumped to her feet and quickly boarded her bus.

Delia eagerly read the brochure. The program provided three years of nurse training, including room, board, and uniforms. Eleanor Roosevelt had insisted that the applicants could not be discriminated against because of race, color, or creed. She stopped at the hospital to pick up an application on her way home.

After dinner Delia and Molly sat at the kitchen table, under the single bulb, and filled out the application. Once it could be sent to the hospital it was just a matter of waiting for an answer.

Molly opened the screen door as the postman approached the steps. "Good morning, Mr. Gillis. How are you today?"

"I am just fine, Mrs. Moseby, just fine. Great weather we're having." He had already pulled the letters for her household from his bags and today there was quite a handful. Of course, all the boarders got their mail here, and letters came for her from time to time. She sorted through the stack of letters as Mr. Gillis walked away.

Her heart jumped into her throat. There was a letter here for Delia and it was not postmarked Alabama as her family letters were. No, this one was local, and official, with a letterhead envelope.

She took her mail and that letter with her, leaving the other items on the table by the door for the girls to pick up as they came home.

Molly strode into the kitchen where her mother-in-law sat nursing her last cup of tea and smoking her morning cigarette. Dorothy had not been able to fully quit smoking, but she allocated two cigarettes a day to after breakfast and after dinner. Actually, there was a third one she thought Molly didn't know about. It was generally smoked out behind the shed and put out in a flowerpot filled with sand.

"Dorothy, there's a letter from the hospital here for Delia."

"Well, are you going to open it?"

"Of course not, it's addressed to Delia." Molly hoped she sounded incensed but failed.

"We could…you know." Dorothy looked pointedly at the hot teakettle on the stove.

"Yes, we could, but we're not going to. This is Delia's news, good or bad. We'll let her tell us. Anyway, you'll be happy, there is a letter here for you, and one for me. Ian must have started feeling homesick."

Dorothy just shrugged and took another pull at the cigarette, the ash balanced precariously over her teacup.

Molly poured more hot water over her already depleted tea bag and sat down at the table. Both women opened their letters and read them more than once. Ian wasn't much of a writer, so the letters were short. Bobby never wrote at all. They were careful in what they wrote, but once in a while a letter would arrive with heavy black marks obscuring much of the content. It didn't really matter who wrote to whom, as the rare letters would be shared back and forth between the two women and discussed at great length to try to determine how their boy was doing. Often Dorothy would be moved to bake a batch of hermit cookies after receiving a letter. Once, Ian had mentioned missing them and she felt she needed to keep the cookie jar full, just in case. She had tried shipping a batch of cookies to her grandson but it had taken so long to get there that every cookie was broken to pieces and stale; although he'd written back to tell her that he and his friends had eaten every single crumb.

When they had traded letters and determined that Ian sounded like he–was doing okay, wherever he was, Molly propped Delia's letter up against the salt and pepper shakers on the oilcloth covered tabletop and cleared away the breakfast dishes.

Delia was working night shifts so she slept during the day. Molly thought to wake her, but didn't want to, although she did bang around a bit when she went out onto the back porch and started the washing machine a bit early in hopes of rousing Delia. Still, the sleeping woman was exhausted and deserved her rest.

Finally, midafternoon, Delia made her way into the kitchen. Molly pounced immediately, "You have a letter, Delia…from the hospital." She waved her hand in the direction of the table where the letter still sat propped up, waiting for her.

Delia stopped where she stood and stared across the room at the official-looking envelope.

"Well, aren't you going to open it?"

Delia walked closer to the table but didn't reach out for the letter. Molly grabbed it up and handed it to her. "Delia, you need to open it. Dorothy and I have been waiting all day." Molly laughed nervously.

Still, Delia just looked down at the letter and held it gingerly, as though it might break, or disappear if she moved too quickly. "I think I maybe need to open it by myself. What if it is bad news? What if they don't want me?"

This had occurred to Molly, but she shrugged it off. "Of course they'll want you."

"I think I need to take it outside." With that, Delia turned and walked out the back door into the yard.

Molly could see her from the window. The young woman stood for a long moment staring down at the envelope in her hands and then she carefully opened it. It was a single sheet of paper and when she had perused it, she raised her head and stared out across the tidy Victory Garden and the revolving clothesline. She stood there for some time. It was all Molly could do to not run out the door and rip the paper from her hands.

Finally, she turned and walked back into the kitchen. "They want me.... I am going to be a nurse."

Molly threw her arms around Delia and shouted out, "Dorothy, she got in, she's going to nursing school."

Molly had been ready to burst for the past two days. She wanted to celebrate with everyone. The letter had come, but Delia had left for work before the other tenants got home. Finally, Delia had a night off from Lockheed and would be here for dinner. As she slept, Molly pulled out the ingredients to make some brownies with items she already had in her pantry. Using corn syrup and a bit of brown sugar with the shortening she had on hand she slid the pan into the oven early so the chocolate treats would have plenty of time to cool before dinner.

It was Sunday; all the boarders slept in. Dorothy had gone to Mass and then to lunch with friends. The house was quiet.

Molly had frozen leftovers from a meatloaf, a small pot roast, and some bacon ends to chop up and make a cottage pie, topped with mashed potatoes, and rich with gravy. The garden and the last of the previous year's canning would provide the vegetables, and she pulled together some biscuits from the recipe Delia had given her. They would be having a feast to celebrate Delia's news.

There were not many events to celebrate these days. Of course, a day without a telegram or terrible news in the paper was a celebration of sorts, but the kind of news that warmed your heart and made wartime less tedious was hard to come by.

Dorothy had pulled one of her mother's lace tablecloths from the trunk in the attic and had washed and freshened it in the sunshine. There would be flowers from Keiko's Garden, and music in the background. Molly had brought out her Kodak Brownie camera and had managed to obtain a roll of film for it. Of course, it would not be developed until the roll was complete, and you didn't just take pictures of any old thing. Film and processing were expensive. Still this dinner and this announcement would be captured with that same camera that had taken pictures of her boys when they were young, and of Al, when he was a laughing young man. Even of Dorothy, smiling stiffly into the little box.

When Molly had gone upstairs to get the camera from its special place on the high shelf in the linen cupboard, she'd taken a few minutes to look through some of the albums and then taken quite a few minutes more to sob over things that were precious and past. You could recall the old memories, but you had to keep an eye out for new memories, or you just felt that everything was over for you. Her boys would never be children again, Aloysius would never laugh again, and neither she nor Dorothy would ever be young again.

Delia would be leaving in a few days to take up residence with the other Nurse Cadets. They had grown used to her easy laugh and helpful nature, but Molly was glad for her. Glad for her mother back in Alabama who would soon receive a carefully written letter telling her of Delia's good fortune. Delia claimed her mother would not even believe it and would insist that someone was playing a mean-spirited joke on her daughter.

One by one the women wandered down the stairs. Sunday was a day for lazy baths, washing your hair, painting your nails, and reading magazines. Even those who had gone out on Saturday with their friends, or beaus, would be home for dinner and preparing for a long and busy week. Tilda came down smelling of peroxide from touching up her slightly darker roots, and Lucy would lie in the sun redolent of lemon juice to brighten her hair. Julia would sit under the arbor and paint her toenails as she listened to the gossip from her friends. Dorothy would still smell subtly of incense when she returned from Mass. Sometimes Molly felt guilty for not attending church, but she got some solace from the prayers and candles her mother-in-law dedicated to those she loved both past and present. Molly sometimes wondered if Dorothy said prayers for her, as well. She hoped so.

CHAPTER FORTY-THREE

June 1944

Tilda, Carlos, and the Studio had agreed that it would look best if Tilda continued her current home and work life until the wedding, so things continued in their normal way.

Tilda left for work before dawn in order to do the breakfast and lunch shift at the commissary. By four p.m. she was home and usually her first call, after the urgent dash to the bathroom, was the kitchen. Molly, and most everyone else in the house was jealous that Tilda seemed to be constantly eating and never gained an ounce. She pretty much ate all day at work, There was breakfast between customers, sandwiches sitting outside the back door watching the movie stars and bit players walking by. She also had cookies and glasses of foamy milk later in the afternoon. She told everyone that she took the low-paying job because the food was included. She could have made more money at Lockheed but she ate her body weight in food each week for free.

Still, when she got home from work her second most urgent concern was finding a snack to hold her until dinner, or supper as her fellow boarders called it.

Today she entered the kitchen just as Molly and Dorothy were discussing the task of turning the leftovers into something resembling a pie.

"I have just never figured out how to make pie crust flaky. Mine usually resembles cardboard by the time it is done. It looks all right but you can hardly chew through it." Molly grumbled.

Dorothy, ensconced at the table with a cup of tea, chimed in, "Amen to that," ignoring the sharp glance Molly sent her way. "Why don't you just plop some mashed potatoes on the top of it and make it a shepherd's pie," she suggested.

Tilda glanced at the meager ingredients gathered on the counter; flour, shortening, salt…

"Use ice water and add some vinegar to it," she said.

"Vinegar? What do you know about pie crusts?" Molly objected.

Tilda stopped her rummage through the ice box. "I made about a thousand of them working at Horn and Hardart."

"What's Horn and Hardart?" Delia asked.

"You know, the Automat." Tilda gestured toward Molly with a small dish. "Is anybody going to eat this?"

"I don't even know what it is. Like I always say, if you can find it you can eat it. If you know so much about pie crust, why don't you make it, then?"

Tilda shrugged as she pulled a spoon from the dish drainer. "Sure, I can do that."

She spooned the contents of the mystery bowl into her mouth in two big bites and moved to the counter, depositing the bowl and spoon in the sink.

"I'm gonna need two knives, some ice chips, and about a soup spoon of white vinegar."

Molly moved to get the extra items and then stepped back as Tilda scooped flour and shortening into the waiting bowl and threw in a good pinch of salt.

She used the knives to cut through the shortening and flour mixture again and again until it looked like crumbs about the size of small peas. Then she took the ice chips and poured water and the vinegar into the glass. Working fast, she sprinkled the vinegar mixture into the flour, tossing it all with her fingers until it started coming together into a ball. The whole procedure took about five minutes.

"Now, just wrap it up in some waxed paper and put it in the chiller for a little while. It will be ready to go by the time you chop up the filling."

Tilda turned to the sink and rinsed off her sticky fingers. "I'll be back downstairs to roll out the dough after I change out of this stinky uniform and rinse it out."

Everyone agreed that supper had been a great success, but Molly was still confused as to why Tilda, who had never mentioned being able to cook a thing, knew how to produce a great crust in the blink of an eye.

"Where was you said you worked in New York?"

"At the Horn and Hardart, at the Automat."

"What is an automat?" Delia asked.

"It's an automat, I don't know. Like a wall of glass windows with food inside and you put your nickel in and take your food."

"I've never heard of such a thing," Molly declared and everyone around the table nodded in agreement.

Dorothy snorted. "That doesn't make a bit of sense."

"They have them all over New York City, and I think in Philadelphia."

She spent the rest of the meal trying her best to describe an automat. The closest she could come to helping them understand was talking about cafeterias.

Most everyone had heard of or eaten at a cafeteria. Tilda explained that she'd started out at H&H as the change girl, turning people's dollars and quarters into little piles of nickels that could be used to purchase food from the bank of windows.

She'd liked it better when she got moved behind the wall of windows and spent her time cutting pies and making sandwiches to refill the spaces as people selected their food.

"When I was a kid my mom would take me there when we went shopping in Manhattan. We'd take the subway into Manhattan and when we were done she'd give me a handful of nickels and I could choose my own food. So, when I got a chance to work there, I jumped at it. There were so many good memories."

When she had finished Delia looked at her seriously and asked, "What is a subway?"

After dinner Tilda had gone upstairs to write some letters. Talking about her early trips to Manhattan had brought back a lot of good memories from her childhood.

But mostly she started thinking about how war had changed their lives. It was better than the Depression had been. The sad men selling apples on the street corners; buy a box for a couple of bucks at dawn and sell them, at five cents per apple all day on some hard-won street corner, and you might make some money, if you were lucky. Or your family might eat apples for dinner. Long lines of job seekers outside the soup kitchens had disappeared but now the streets were busy but somber. There was energy, but it all went toward just trying to get through whatever tragic possibility hung over your head. The threat of your husband or father or son being killed, the fear that the "good guys" might not win the war. The ever-present awareness that the world was changing, and you had little control over what those changes would be.

CHAPTER FORTY-FOUR

June 1944

Tilda had been awake before dawn, really most of the night. When the sun finally began its ascent she leapt from the bed. "Julia, Julia, wake up. We have to start getting ready."

Julia started. "Tilda, please just give me a minute. I can't even focus until I've had coffee." She threw the blankets off and sat up. "What time is it anyway?"

"It's after six, we need to be there by nine o'clock."

Julia stood up and shuffled out the bedroom door.

Tilda could hear her mumbling under her breath. "What?"

"Nothing." Julia just waved her hand in the air.

Downstairs things were already stirring. The coffeepot was perking on the stove and Molly was just pulling some muffins from the oven. "Good morning, all set for the exciting day ahead?"

Julia rolled her eyes and pulled a coffee mug from a hook under the cabinet. "I need coffee more than I need excitement." Generally speaking, Julia believed excitement was overrated. "Is everyone else up?"

"I think so, although I haven't seen Tilda or Lucy yet."

"Oh, don't worry about that, I'm sure she's right behind me."

As if on cue, Tilda swept into the kitchen. "My gosh, something smells wonderful, but I'm sure I can't eat a thing."

Julia and Molly glanced at each other. They'd never known Tilda to not be able to eat.

"Robbie and Dusty are going to pick us all up about eight-thirty."

It had been decided that the wedding party would all make their dressing preparations at Carlos's home. If they got out early enough they could avoid the cadre of journalists and photographers anxious to document the squalor that Tilda was leaving to marry her Prince Charming and be swept away to the castle on the hill.

Both Dorothy and Molly had been miffed by some of the articles that made it sound like Tilda was escaping a life of dire poverty.

Molly had been especially humiliated by the photo of Dorothy in her chenille robe and bedroom slippers turning the hose on a cluster of tatty journalists gathered in the driveway. Dorothy was not sorry she'd done it, but she wished she'd thought of taking the curlers out of her hair before venturing outside that morning.

"Dusty's here, Dusty's here," shouted Tilda from her post at the parlor window. "Hurry…"

Only Tilda had been to Carlos's house before this. It took a few minutes for the others to acclimate to the size and luxury of it. Before they could wander off in different directions, Carlos stepped in. "Ladies, please, just follow me. I will give you a quick tour of the downstairs and then you may all proceed upstairs to get ready."

This wedding would take place beside the sparkling pool. His mother and brother could not attend, but he had promised to stage a second Catholic Church wedding across the border to calm his mother's concern that he wasn't really going to be married if he'd not been blessed by a priest.

An elaborate reception was planned in Manhattan to be attended by the New York elite and Tilda's family and friends.

Hairdressers and makeup artists from the studio stood at the ready to turn them all into appropriate bridal attendants. Lucy and Julia were bridesmaids; Dusty and Carlos's driver, Robbie, would stand up for him. The other bridesmaids and groomsmen came directly from Central Casting for the sole purpose of adding to the grandeur of the event.

The studio had also sent out the invitations and the guests were meant to impress. Carlos didn't know most of them, but everyone knew who they were.

Hedda Hopper and Louella Parsons were there, seated on opposite sides of the room but equidistant from the bridal table.

The vows were spoken, the toasts were made, the doves released, and the champagne flowed. The press was seated separately from the rest of the guests but had no reason to complain. Their meals were as elaborate and their libations as generous as anyone's. Their goodwill and fawning stories were guaranteed. The home was not so elaborate as to have a ballroom, but a string quartet played in the background as the sun sank on the horizon and the lights came up on the party.

Bedford Myers, the studio head, was assured that the event was an unqualified success by the fact that people did not drift off early and, in some cases had to be escorted off the property. As the sky darkened the limousines and taxicabs trundled down the hill bearing happily fed and inebriated guests.

On cue, a crew of minions descended and dismantled the elaborate set, hauling all signs of the celebrations away. When all was quiet, Carlos and Tilda went up the stairs to their room bearing a bottle of champagne and two glasses.

"You look beautiful." Carlos looked across the room as he poured two glasses of bubbly.

"As do you." Tilda smiled.

Even though her head was already spinning, she accepted the glass of champagne.

"To a perfect wedding day." Carlos raised his glass and Tilda raised hers as well. "I am going to give you a perfect life. Everything you ever wanted. I am so grateful to you, *cara mia.*"

"I would do anything for you, Carlos. You know that."

"Yes, I do, but that doesn't mean I don't appreciate you." Carlos set his glass down on the dresser and took her in his arms. "I hope you will be happy living here."

She laid her head against his shoulder and closed her eyes. Who wouldn't be happy living here? Within weeks she would begin making her first film with the studio. Soon she would go back east and bring her handsome and successful husband to meet all her family. She would have everything she'd ever wanted; she had but to ask.

"Well, then I will say good night. You must be exhausted."

"You must be, too."

"Yes, I do need to get some sleep."

He kissed her on the forehead and walked out of the room, closing the door firmly behind himself.

Tilda looked around the room. It looked just like a set from a Fred Astaire movie. Shamelessly luxurious. She wondered if it had been decorated by the set designers from the studio. Certainly, nobody had asked her opinion about any of it. She supposed she could change it, if she liked. But why would she? A lot of time and effort had gone into this fairytale and she was sure she'd have her happily ever after.

She slipped out of the wedding dress and draped it carefully across the settee. She opened the closet and removed one of several nightgowns from its padded hanger and slipped it over her head before she swathed herself in a floor length negligee. The costume department had certainly done a fine job.

There were several movie scripts waiting for her review on the bedside table and she turned the lamp on.

Finally, she refilled her champagne glass and stepped to the window. Pulling back the shade she caught the shadow of someone crossing the driveway toward the garage. It was Carlos. He had removed his coat and he carried a bottle of champagne and two glasses.

He did not look back but proceeded up the stairs leading to the chauffeur's quarters above the garage. A light fell across him from the door when it opened and then went out.

She stood sipping from her glass and watching the slightest of shadows moving in the window, until the light went out and then she turned away.

She filled the glass, once more, before turning back the silky counterpane and climbing into the vast bed.

CHAPTER FORTY-FIVE

July 1944

Dorothy had just settled herself in the rocking chair in the parlor with her crocheting and a hot cup of tea on the spindle-legged table beside her. She leaned forward to plump the pillow behind her a bit and glanced with satisfaction around the room.

The furniture was the same furniture she'd had in her own parlor, carefully tended and mended, polished and adorned on almost every surface with Irish lace doilies and antimacassars. A small, tiered table in front of the window held her carefully tended collection of African violets. She couldn't grow a tomato to save her life, but she had a magic way with violets, and they rewarded her for her efforts. The indirect light and warm temperatures in the front window helped a lot but she was convinced that mulching with crushed eggshells and coffee grounds made all the difference. Since Molly had been making coffee mixed with chicory, passing it off as a fancy New Orleans blend, instead of a way to stretch the precious brew as far as possible, the violets were even more lush. Also, Dorothy's secret brew of molasses, fish emulsion, and lemon juice really helped. It sat ugly and smelly in the canning jar behind the drapes. More than once, she'd caught Molly trying to toss it away and she had taken to hiding it. Of course, she *never* got the leaves wet!

The house was quiet. Molly had taken her stack of ration coupons, change-purse, and shopping trolley down to the shops, and Julia was off to work. Only Lucy was in the house and she lay upstairs like a huge egg waiting to hatch.

Dorothy rocked rhythmically as she worked away on the lacy baby blanket. It had been a chore to keep Lucy from seeing what she was working on, but so far it would still be a surprise. As she rocked, she was transported back to a time and place where she had made the same blanket when she was waiting for Aloysius to be born. The furniture had been the same but the hands wielding the fine thread then were young and plump, not the gnarled claws she saw when she looked into her lap now.

She had heard a creak on the stairs and halted her work for a moment, ready to whip the blanket off her lap and into her bag if needed. No more sound. She must have imagined it.

Behind her she heard an anguished groan and turning, spotted Lucy bent over in the doorway clutching her huge belly.

"I think I need help.... I think something's wrong," the girl gasped. Her eyes were huge and frightened in the face rounded by pregnancy and water weight.

Dorothy rolled her eyes. "I'm sure it's nothing. You're not due for a couple of weeks, are you? First babies are usually late." She had thrust the blanket into her crochet bag and stood up. As she did, Lucy doubled up again and groaned.

"There's water everywhere on the bed and it hurts." She stood upright again as the pang passed.

Dorothy still thought Lucy was making something out of nothing, but she cast back through her mind trying to remember what little she knew about babies being born. Didn't first babies take forever; hours and hours, or sometimes days? She'd labored with Al for forty-eight hours before he had slid screaming out into the world. She remembered thinking that she should be the one doing the screaming rather than him, and she would have if she'd known what a trial he would turn out to be.

Dorothy realized that she didn't even know what the plan was for having this baby. "Are you supposed to call the doctor, or go to the hospital, or something?" She realized her voice had been rising and the final words squeaked out weakly.

"We call Dr. Brody. The number is by the phone...." Lucy waved her hand in the direction of the kitchen and bent over again, staggered toward the sofa. Horrified, Dorothy jumped to her feet. "Not there, not there..." She slipped her arm around Lucy's shoulders and steered her toward the dining room. "Let's get you upstairs and call the Doc."

As they reached the bottom of the staircase Lucy let out a howl and slid down to sit on the bottom step. "I can't, I can't walk up the stairs. I can't even stand up. Do something...help me!"

Dorothy looked around the room frantically, and finally swept the snowy white, hand-embroidered tablecloth from the dining table, spreading it out at the base of the stairs.

"Here, lie down here while I make the phone call." Lucy's contraction had ended and she was able to drop to her hands and knees and roll onto the cloth.

As Dorothy turned to run to the phone Lucy balled up in pain.

"We're fine, you're fine. I don't know if the birth pains are supposed to be coming so fast." She patted Lucy on the back.

In the kitchen Dorothy rifled through the stack of papers with numbers on them next to the phone and picked up the receiver, her hand shaking so hard she could hardly dial the operator.

A bored, nasal voice responded. "This is the operator; how may I direct your call?"

"I need Dr. Brody in Burbank, I need his office right away....This damnfool girl is having her baby right here on my mother's embroidered tablecloth."

Dorothy was amazed by the lack of urgency in the tinny voice emanating from the phone. "Just one moment and I will connect you with Dr. Brody's office."

Obviously this woman had never had a crazy girl having a baby at the base of the stairs.

The phone only rang a couple of times, but it seemed like it was forever. Of course, Dr. Brody was out, but his nurse would contact him at the hospital and ask him what they should do.

Lucy let out another howl from the dining room as Dorothy racked her brain to remember their phone number to leave for the doctor.

Hanging up the phone she wiped her sweaty palms on her skirt. She had no idea what to do, so she grabbed the still hot teakettle from the stove and refilled it. She'd heard something about boiling water for babies but had no idea of the purpose. She was definitely going to need a cup of tea when this was over, or something stronger.

The sobs and cries from the dining room had increased. But there was nothing to do but go back in there and face this new challenge. Didn't life ever get over being challenging? Sixty-five years old, and it had never gotten easier. She guessed not, and shrugged, straightening her spine and marching back to Lucy's side.

"I think it's coming, help me."

Dorothy lowered herself carefully to her knees. "Roll over on your back, honey. Let me see if I can figure out what's happening." She did her best to sound confident but was still amazed when Lucy obeyed her and reached out and grabbed her hand.

"You've had babies, you and Molly."

"Yes, dearie, we've both had babies." She didn't add that she had hardly been conscious when Al was born and had sat in the waiting room while Molly had her babies.

"Put your knees up and let's get this dress out of the way." Dorothy pulled the soggy hem of the dress up onto Lucy's distended stomach.

She hesitated briefly before slipping the panties down over the girl's knees. She'd never given it much thought, but realized she'd never seen a naked woman from this angle before.

The belly moved and hardened in front of her eyes as another contraction hit, and she could see that the crown of the baby's head was forcing its way between the legs.

The contraction stopped and the top of the curly head retracted. Was that supposed to happen?

"I can see the baby, I can see its head! You are doing fine Lucy; you were made to have babies."

Dorothy took no offense at the look Lucy cast at her. The girl said nothing and Dorothy could see that another contraction was starting as the belly tightened and heaved.

For a moment Dorothy thought someone else was screaming, but realized it was the teakettle on the stove, just as the phone began to ring.

"You wait here, I'll be right back." She struggled to rise to her feet. Getting up and down like this was something she hadn't done in a while and wasn't looking forward to doing in the future.

In the kitchen she grabbed the phone before the caller could hang up, leaving the kettle whistling. "Hold on just a moment, let me turn the damned stove off," she shouted into the phone.

"Hello…hello," a voice squawked as she slipped the kettle off the burner and returned to pick up the dangling receiver.

"Hello, who's there," she barked.

"This is Dr. Brody. I got a message that Mrs. Scoggins was in labor."

"Oh, yes, she is…. The baby is coming and I'm here alone with her,…Can't you come right away?"

"I can't fly, and it will take me at least fifteen minutes to get there from the hospital. Tell me what is going on and I will tell you what you can do until I get there."

"There's water everywhere, and I can see the stomach heaving up and I can see the top of the head. What can I do?"

There was a moment of silence on the other end of the line, then, "Madam, at this point I think all you can do is catch that baby."

Dorothy struggled to hear the doctor over Lucy's cries and her own fear. "Get some clean cloths and something to wrap the baby in. After the baby comes there will be a few more contractions before the placenta is birthed. Don't cut the cord, I'll do that when I get there. Just make sure the baby is breathing. If you have a bulb syringe in the house suck any mucus out of the nose and mouth, and if the baby doesn't start crying give it a little smack on the butt to make it cry."

"Okay, cloths, syringe…don't cut the cord."

"Yes, just wrap everyone up. Let the mama hold the baby against her to keep it warm."

"Okay…" Another wail from the dining room had Dorothy ready to hang up the phone.

"The baby is going to look kind of blue at first, and there will be some mess, but everything sounds like it is going like it is supposed to. I'll be there as soon as I can. Oh, and leave the front door open so I can get in."

Dorothy didn't even say good-bye as she hung up the phone. She opened the kitchen drawer and pulled out a stack of freshly laundered dishtowels.

She found Lucy half sitting up, face screwed up and pushing with all her might. She had grabbed her knees to support herself and Dorothy could see the dome of the baby's head before the contraction slowed and the dark halo of curls disappeared again.

"Is the doctor coming?" Lucy panted.

"Yes, he's coming, but I think this baby may be getting here before the doctor does."

Lucy's expression changed from shocked panic to intense concentration as another contraction hit and she pulled herself into a sitting position holding her knees. Her eyes were tightly shut and her whole body strained with the effort.

Dorothy could see the crown of the head emerging again, sliding further down the birth canal. She remembered hearing once that the baby should be helped to turn so that the shoulders could slide through the vagina more easily. She took a deep breath and reached out before the baby could slip away again.

Her hands felt the warm wetness of the head and she slid her hands down onto the babe's shoulders, turning it tenderly. She released it when she felt the body begin to recede again as the contraction stopped and Lucy dropped exhausted onto her back.

"I think you're almost there, honey. You are doing great!"

Lucy smiled wanly before her eyes grew huge with the onset of the next pang. "It's coming, it's coming now," she blurted and lurched forward pushing with all her might.

This time, the head emerged steadily until the shoulders popped through the opening and the wet bundle slid out with a gush of wetness into Dorothy's waiting hands.

Dorothy gasped and tightened her grip on the slippery mass, afraid she would drop it as Lucy lay back on the floor.

Dorothy quickly grabbed up one of the dishtowels she'd brought from the kitchen and wrapped it around the wriggling baby. At first she feared something was amiss. The baby's skin looked mottled and bluish, but as the cool air hit its warm skin, it gasped and sucked in a huge breath before letting out a hearty wail. A blush of pink bloomed across its body as the cries intensified.

Grabbing another dishtowel, Dorothy wiped the child's face and wrapped it more tightly.

Lucy struggled to support herself on her elbows. "Is it a boy or a girl?"

"I forgot to look! It's a boy! It's a beautiful, perfect baby boy!" she whispered as she re-wrapped the towel around him.

"A boy…a little boy. Oh my gosh." Lucy lay back again and reached her arms out to Dorothy.

"The doctor said to hold the baby close to you to keep him warm. Stay here, I'm going to get a blanket for you. I'll be right back."

Dorothy looked up the long flight of stairs and decided to charge into her downstairs room looking for a cover. Running up and down those stairs was just going to be too much right now.

In her room she grabbed the first thing she saw, which just happened to be the heirloom quilt that lay folded across the foot of her bed. While she was there, she grabbed the throw pillow off the chair.

At the base of the stairs, she tucked the pillow under Lucy's head and carefully placed the blanket over Lucy and the babe. Now that it was all over but the shouting, it seemed indecent to leave Lucy all exposed like she was.

Dorothy sat down at the bottom of the stairway and breathed deeply. Before her, where there had been one, now there were two. She was too much in awe to be overcome by what the three of them had just accomplished.

A light knock at the front door signaled the doctor's arrival. He announced himself as he pushed the screen door open. "It's me, Dr. Brody."

"We're in here," Dorothy called. "Come through the parlor."

Dr. Brody stopped at the dining room door and assessed the situation. "Looks like you didn't really need me but let me take a look and make sure that everything is okay."

As he knelt in front of Lucy he looked up at Dorothy. "Could you get a warm, wet cloth so we can bathe off the baby, and some old newspapers? Oh, and a pot of tea would be great."

Dorothy returned to the kitchen, mumbling under her breath until she realized that the doc was just trying to get her out of the way doing something useful while he did what he needed to do.

By the time she returned with a tray holding a teapot, three cups, and a couple of warm, wet dishtowels, with a stack of newspapers under her arm, Lucy had rolled over onto her side and was cradling the baby in her arms while the doctor put away his stethoscope.

"Would you take the baby and clean him up a bit, Mrs. … I don't think we've met."

"I'm Dorothy Moseby."

"I'd shake your hand, but I think I will wait until I can clean up."

Dorothy had already reached out to take the baby from Lucy and she sat on one of the dining room chairs and settled the little boy onto her lap, gently wiping him off with the warm cloth. "Just look at him," she cooed. "All the fingers and all the toes…and that hair…"

Dr. Brody used the newspapers to wrap the placenta and Lucy used one of the warm cloths that Dorothy had brought to gently bathe herself. She was exhausted and exhilarated at the same time, and it was just a few minutes before she reclaimed "Baby Jack" as she was already calling him.

Molly wrangled the grocery trolley off the bus and dragged it the two blocks to the house, going around to the back door into the kitchen.

The washing machine was chugging and rattling away on the screened porch. It was too early for the boarders to be home, and unusual for Dorothy to be doing laundry on a Wednesday afternoon.

Thump, thump… she backed up the steps hefting the loaded cart up each of the six steps and rolled it into the kitchen. All was quiet as she began unloading the staples, and the few treasures she'd found on her trek to the markets and shops in search of what might still be available. Many of the stores got their deliveries on Tuesday afternoons and Wednesday mornings, and the fact that she didn't have to go out to work meant she could be there early for whatever might be for sale that week.

Her shopping list was more like an "if" list. If she could find the items she hoped for, and if she could afford them, and if she had enough of the right ration coupons, she could plan her meals ahead. Much of the time the meals for the week depended on the lucky finds that were not on her list. She knew what was coming up in her garden, and she knew she had eggs from her chickens, and she knew what she had stashed away from earlier weeks, but the rest was a mystery.

She turned to the stove to fill up the teakettle and found it full and still fairly warm. She turned on the gas beneath it and unpacked her cart. It didn't take long. She could only haul so much stuff home on two buses and a streetcar.

She snagged the kettle off the stove just as it started to whistle. The house was quiet and she suspected that Dorothy and Lucy were blissfully napping the afternoon away.

She spooned two heaping spoons of sugar into her hot mug of tea, with almost no guilt. She deserved it. Walking into the dining room she noticed that the tablecloth had been removed from the table and then she heard the quiet creak of Dorothy's rocking chair in the parlor.

"Hey, I thought you might be taking a nap."

"Not today, my bed is already in use."

"In use?"

"Go take a look."

Molly set her mug down on the table by the rocker, noting that the bottle of whiskey usually kept in the far back of the cupboard under the kitchen sink sat on the table, as well.

She walked back to the door of Dorothy's bedroom where the door stood ajar and pushed it open a little further until she could see the bed. The first shock was that Lucy lay there under the counterpane, but the second surprise was when she realized that Lucy slept curled around a bundle of dishtowels, swaddling a sleeping baby.

"What happened here? She's had the baby!"

"Yes, I know. Sit down on the sofa and I'll tell you all about it.... First hold out your mug."

Dorothy pulled the stopper from the dusty whiskey bottle and poured a generous slug of it into Molly's tea before topping off her own cup, the color of whose contents suggested rather more whiskey than tea.

Molly sat, and in hushed tones, tinged with awe, Dorothy told the story that would entertain her friends for months to come.

CHAPTER FORTY-SIX

July 1944

A bead of sweat slid down Molly's forehead and into her eye as she raised her wrist to wipe it away. It was one of the curses of Mother Nature that the fruits and vegetables that most needed the steamy side of canning all came ripe and ready during the hottest months of the year. Today she had washed and sterilized the various jars that had been saved from last year's operation. They sat draining on dishcloths spread along the counter. You could reuse the jars and the rings, but finding the new lids that were required had been a challenge. She'd been on the lookout for them at the hardware store since the first of the year, and finally she had accumulated enough for all the jars.

Her own yard harbored a peach tree that was loaded with fruit this year. Keiko's yard had plums, and another neighbor down the street had been happy to trade a glut of tomatoes for a dozen eggs and the promise of more over the next month. Plus, she'd be expected to share the bounty of today's labors.

Probably her biggest challenge was to obtain enough sugar to preserve the fruit. Vegetables didn't require any, but you couldn't can fruit without sugar. You could use thickener and you could buy packets of pectin to help things set up, but you couldn't just leave out the sugar. She'd heard that one of the national radio newscasters had said, "Roses are red, violets are blue, sugar is sweet… Remember?" and that's how she felt about it. Thankfully, the government increased the per-person sugar allotment during harvest time to help with canning.

The kitchen had become what Molly imagined a steam bath was like before she lifted the final jar from the boiling water and set it to cool on the counter.

She made herself a cup of tea and moved out into the yard to settle in the shade. There was a slight breeze, and she closed her eyes as it played across her damp skin. Before long she heard the satisfying pop of each jar sealing, one by one.

She heard some activity in the kitchen behind her and realized that Dorothy had roused from her nap and she could hear the clink of a teacup, then the screen door swinging open as the older woman came out into the yard. "I don't know how you work in that heat, Molly. Why don't you wait until evening to do your canning?"

"Because, when the sun goes down and it gets cool I just can't feel motivated to do my housework. Old habits, I guess."

Dorothy groaned slightly as she settled into the other old kitchen chair beneath the apple tree. "Next thing you'll have to be doing applesauce and pie filling. It never seems to end."

"At least we have food to preserve. We both remember times when that wasn't the case."

"That's true, though I have to hand it to you. I never saw a body in my life that could go into an empty cupboard and make a dinner like you can."

"Yes, sometimes I even surprised myself. I'm convinced half the food families eat was conjured up by mothers trying to figure out how to feed a family with something like two potatoes, some milk, an onion, and a few bacon ends."

They sat companionably for some time before Dorothy spoke again. "I've been thinking that maybe I should get a little job."

Molly opened her eyes and sat up. "A job? What kind of a job?"

"I don't know. It's just every place I go I see signs for folks needing some help to keep things running. It makes me feel guilty that I'me not doing anything."

It had never occurred to Molly that Dorothy might be feeling useless. "Well, it would have to be close to home unless you want to spend a lot of time on buses."

"I was thinking of trying at the drug store. I could probably handle the cash register there."

Molly thought that the fact that Ned Nieman, the druggist, had lost his wife a few months ago might weigh into that choice, but only said, "That sounds like the perfect place."

CHAPTER FORTY-SEVEN

August 1944

Molly sat at the kitchen table sipping her tea and making a list of errands. Since Tilda had moved out she would be looking for a new boarder.

On the top of the list was the planning of a baby shower for Lucy and Little Jack. New babies only needed food, warmth, and love, so the infant had not wanted for anything, but it was time to put the sadness of Jack's death and the excitement of Tilda's wedding aside and take care of some business.

Dorothy was reconciled to having Lucy stay with them, indefinitely, and she didn't mind too much. It had been a generation since anyone had taken her advice about babies. Maybe no one ever had; her relationship with Molly during her pregnancies had not been the kind where advice was appreciated.

Neither Dorothy nor Molly had daughters; they found themselves hovering over Lucy. They encouraged naps and walks in the fresh air, cooked special tidbits to tempt her appetite, and happily took the baby into their arms so she could get things done.

Lucy had nothing for the baby. She had no family nearby, and Molly suspected that she hadn't written to her father to tell him the happy news. It was a difficult announcement since she hadn't gotten around to telling him that she and Jack had married.

So, an appropriate Sunday had been chosen for the event. It would be combined with a special luncheon, including a cake, and silly games. Eggs, butter, and sugar had been carefully reserved for baking. Those items were tightly rationed and baking a real, pre-war cake required the sacrifice of sugar in their tea and coffee, with oatmeal for breakfast and the dreaded yellow dyed shortening spread on their bread. Nobody had complained. There was debate over supper about what kind of cake was best. Much planning went into the buying or making of gifts. Dorothy had been working for some weeks on crocheting a blanket like the one she had made before her son was born. Molly had ventured into the attic, repository of all her memories, and clearing a space in the center of the floor, had slid the bassinet used for her own sons into the light. It had been covered with a sheet for twenty years and it was not so much dirty as it was dull. She dusted it off carefully, running her hands along edges and feeling for flaws or cracks. The faded pad in the bottom would need to be replaced, and she thought she might give it a new coat of paint. Funny, she didn't even know if paint was rationed. She hadn't given any thought to paint anything in the house since before the war.

Well, she'd just have to find out how you could get some paint. White, she thought. It was blue now. Rather a sad, faded blue, but blue, nonetheless. It needed to be spiffed up for Baby Jack, so she would have to give it a natty new coat of white paint.

Julia had originally leaned toward giving a silver cup with two handles, although it wasn't something the baby would be using right away. It was something he could keep and pass along to his own children. But, finally, she had decided on a dozen gauzy white diapers. The practical side of her that had done without the necessities through the Depression just couldn't bring her to spend money on something so impractical as the cup.

Tilda had absolutely no idea what sort of things babies might need when coming into the world. She had seen babies and they seemed usually to be bundled up in blankets and wearing caps or little bonnets. There were sometimes little footie things on their feet. They needed bottles supposedly, and bibs, she'd once seen little bibs on a rack in the store. In Woolworth's she had found a section of embroidery supplies that stocked cunning little flannel gowns imprinted with a pattern of tiny flowers and, on a whim had bought two of those, a packet of needles and a package of multi-colored "floss," whatever that meant. Her only reference to the word was that her granny from England had always called cotton candy, candy floss.

Tilda and Dorothy had never gotten on. Tilda thought Dorothy a cranky old harridan and Dorothy thought Tilda a bleached blond floozy. But, putting those differences aside, they had found an uneasy truce when Tilda had taken her cache of purchases to Dorothy and asked for her help. It had been a long time since Dorothy had practiced her French knots or chain stitch but seeing the little gowns her fingers itched to pick up the needle and begin. Of course, she wasn't going to do it for Tilda, but she could teach the girl a good old-fashioned skill. The two of them had discovered they both had sly wits and a sharp eye for people's failings. The hours they spent together over cups of strong tea passed surprisingly quickly. They had hurried to finish them before Tilda had moved out and the gift sat, wrapped in tissue paper, at the bottom of Dorothy's dresser.

CHAPTER FORTY-EIGHT

September 1944

Dorothy attended Mass each Sunday at St. Benedict's but Sunday mornings were often the only time their boarders could sleep in, so they only rose for the Sunday dinner served at noon each week. Lucy had grown up Protestant and Tilda's background was a strange amalgam of Jewish and Episcopalian. Julia, on the other hand. was a product of a fundamentalist sect that thought Rome was the Beast in the Book of Revelations.

This Sunday was special. Lucy opted to rise early to attend the Mass even though she had only entered a Catholic church once before. Julia rolled over and pulled a pillow over her head. One thing her years of Bible study had taught her was disdain for all religions.

Molly had managed to trade some of her garden produce, a rare commodity in the stores, for a rather scrawny hen a neighbor wanted to get rid of. There was not a lot of meat on the old bird, but she hadn't cost any ration coupons and was left simmering away on the stove with carrots and onions for company. Molly would pluck the meager meat from the bones and make a gravy with the stock for chicken a la king to be served over buttermilk biscuits. The cake sat proudly on the cake plate exhumed from the back of the cabinet for the event, a two-layer circle of chocolate piled high with seven-minute frosting. The yolks from the two egg whites in the frosting would be used to enrich the chicken dish. It was Julia who would rise before they returned and use the last of the season's tomatoes to fry up some of her mama's fried green tomatoes to accompany the meal.

The slanted light from the autumn sun shone through the stained glass windows splattering colors across the stone floor of St. Benedict's. Lucy struggled to her feet, to her knees, and back to her seat with the other worshippers more from courtesy than anything else. She had a dim memory of attending the wedding of an apostate cousin back home as a child, but the only real impression it had left was of a vast cavernous room echoing with organ music. Between the rising, kneeling, and sitting she could gaze about her and take in the grandeur.

St. Benedict's wasn't much of a church and the congregation was robust but poor. Its parish bounds included neighborhoods of Irish and Italian worshipers and extended to include the Mexican neighborhood beyond the Southern Pacific rail line, already the demarcation between "us" and "them." Still, compared with the little white Baptist Church at home, it seemed holier somehow with its soaring ceiling and stone floor.

The congregation was composed mostly of women of all ages and children. A few elderly men and pimply boys dotted the pews, but it was obvious that most everyone here was waiting and praying for the return of a loved one from the battlefields. Lucy didn't think of Jack often. She'd received the news that Jack's ship had sunk in the South Pacific not long after she'd had to finally accept that their brief honeymoon had resulted in a little human. She had written him a carefully worded letter on special paper that would allow the Navy to photograph the letter along with thousands of others, send them across the sea, develop the film, and deliver the output. So, eventually, Jack would find out he was going to be a father. Except that he never did and never would.

The day she married Jack he had called his mother from the drugstore in town to tell her he was married, and he had given Lucy his mother's address before he shipped out. Lucy didn't realize for several days after she heard of Jack's death that his mother might not have been notified since she, as his wife, was the "next of kin." She agonized for days over the writing to his mother to tell her both that he had been killed and that she was going to have his baby. She received a few letters from his mother with pictures of his sister, and younger brothers. She wondered if his mother wished that he had been content to stay home and be the head of his household. She never said anything about that and her letters were full of memories of his childhood and advice for expectant mothers.

She tried to focus on the baby, her baby, her baby with Jack.

She suddenly became very hot in the church. As huge as it was, it felt closed in. She rose and carefully made her way down the aisle…She left Dorothy cuddling the baby.

Outside the sun was shining, as it always seemed to be in California. Back home the leaves would have started to fall and folks would be preparing for winter weather. Here the evenings had cooled and the days were shorter, but there was no sign of rain. She would miss snow this year. She'd given a lot of thought to where she would go after the baby came. She wouldn't go home. There was no room for her in her father's new family. She couldn't stay here with Molly forever, though she knew her babe would be loved to death by everyone in the house, even Dorothy.

Lucy had left home for an adventure, and now her adventure would be over. She was a mother. A single mother. A mother who would have to get a job and leave her baby in someone else's care. Her mother had always been there for her. She'd worked beside her mother in the garden and in the kitchen. She'd learned to cook, and sew, and make things nice so that she could have a family of her own someday. She missed her mother now. She missed her more than she had even after she first died. What would her mother tell her to do? Would she brush her hair like she used to do before bed? Would she have good advice and tell her stories of when her babies were young?

Lucy sat down on a low stone bench under a shade tree and her eyes stung with tears. "Dang, all I do is cry, anymore," she muttered. This was a happy day, a beautiful and peaceful day in a world full of war. She was lucky. She was young and healthy and nobody was dropping bombs on her. She was safe. Safe. *Safe.* How many people in this war were not ever really safe? They had babies and lost mothers and husbands and homes, too. She should be happy. There, that felt a little better. Lucy was pretty good at giving herself little pep talks. She was looking forward to her lunch, especially the cake, and then, as was her recent habit, she would take a little nap upstairs in the bedroom she shared with her baby.

On the walk home Lucy chatted happily and Molly seemed glad to see it. She'd been quiet this morning and it made them all feel better to have the usual perky Lucy back.

Lunch was lovely and Lucy cooed and murmured over the little wrapped gifts and most of all over the bassinet. Up until now, Baby Jack had been sleeping in a dresser drawer carefully lined with soft bedding so she could keep him safe and close.

She had finished her second piece of cake and was nodding in the rocking chair in the parlor while the others cleared up the kitchen when she thought she heard a light knock on the screen door. She couldn't see who was there from where she sat and knew that the chattering group in the other room had not heard the knock. She rose from the chair and walked to the door. An older woman and a younger one stood there with suitcases at their feet. She thought they must be boarders looking for rooms. She unlatched and opened the screen door. The women looked familiar to her but she couldn't think why.

"You must be Lucy," the older woman said.

"Yes, I'm Lucy."

"I'm Grace Scoggins, and this is Sissy, actually Shirley." She gestured toward the younger woman.

"Scoggins, that's my name, too." Lucy was still a little drowsy.

"Yes, we know. I am Jack's mother, and this is his sister."

That was why they looked familiar. She could see it now. Jack's dark eyes, his dimples, his bright smile.

"Oh my, oh my…" Lucy's hand flew to her face and she burst into tears. Molly had just come laughing in from the kitchen followed by the others. When she saw Lucy crying at the door her heart lurched. She couldn't see who stood on the porch, but her first thought was it might be a telegram. She hesitated for a moment, afraid to see what was happening, but Lucy staggered and Molly rushed forward to support her. Thankfully, it was not the local boy who delivered the telegrams. "Lucy, what's wrong?" She gave the women a suspicious look.

"No…nothing's wrong. It's Jack's mother."

CHAPTER FORTY-NINE

September 1944

Given her druthers, Julia would have stayed home tonight, but this was the first time Tilda would be singing with a band. The USO dance was in full swing. Dusty had driven to Burbank to pick her up, so there wouldn't be a long bus ride home, and she had to admit the band was great.

Dusty had just returned with a couple of glasses of indifferent punch that had already been amply spiked by one or more of the attendees. Tilda's rendition of "Boogie Woogie Bugle Boy" really had the room jumping. Tonight, the military had commandeered the ballroom of an old hotel of noble lineage and the French doors were open but heavily draped to keep the bright light from spilling out onto the still lush and slightly overgrown gardens beyond. Julia figured the gardener was "gone with the draft."

Julia wasn't really older than most of the people here, but somehow she felt ancient. She was tired of the war and ready for something to happen in her life other than work and rationing.

The heavily draped room had become stifling and Tilda had mellowed to her rendition of "I'll Be Seeing You." Julia noticed a young woman slip out through the drapes to get some fresh air and then her heart almost stopped. Another person had slipped out the door, as well. A bulky man in a uniform marked by a sleeve of service stripes caught her eye, and she felt like she couldn't breathe. She thought that it couldn't be him, but in her heart she knew it was.

"Do you want to try one of these slow dances with your gimpy escort?" Dusty volunteered, but she wasn't really listening. Without responding she walked away from him and began a circuit around the crowd toward the garden. As she moved she became more agitated and by the time she almost shoved the last person out of her way and disappeared through the drapes she was dripping with perspiration.

The cool evening air hit her damp arms and gave her a chill, though the shiver that shook her had nothing to do with the temperature. The gardens were dark, lit only by the full moon. A few people clustered near the doorways, smoking and laughing, but she did not see the woman or the man.

She walked across the lawn in the direction of a line of trees that ran along a creek. Only the babbling water broke the silence as she got closer to the trees until she heard a stifled yelp and turned in that direction.

She moved swiftly and quietly. She felt like Diana hunting her prey, although she came armed only with the conviction of her memories. When she came upon them, he had pinned the woman to a tree by the little creek and had one hand covering her mouth while the other roughly tried to shove her skirt up as she struggled against his superior size.

Julia started to scream at him, but her voice caught in her throat. She looked down at the rock-lined waterway and bending down picked up a large, smooth stone with both hands. It only took a few steps to reach the man, who was so engrossed in his attack that he never heard her coming. The woman's wild eyes fixed on her as she raised her arms high above her head and brought the stone down on the man's head.

The sailor dropped to his knees and then slid down to the ground. Julia hefted the heavy stone and brought it down on his head a second time, and then again. She would have continued but was stopped by the woman grabbing her arm. "Oh my God, you've killed him. Stop…stop." Coming to her senses, Julia looked at the rapidly expanding pool of blood and dropped the stone into the creek.

From the ballroom she heard the first drum solo of "Sing, Sing, Sing."

"What have you done? You've killed him," the woman repeated.

Julia put her arms around the shaking woman and leaned to whisper in her ear as a plan formed from the scattered images in her head.

"Shh, it's going to be all right. Just do what I tell you."

The woman stilled in her arms, listening.

"Straighten up your clothes and go back into the hotel at one of the far doors where there are no people. I saw you dancing earlier with that Marine. Find him again and drag him to the middle of the dance floor."

"But I can't just go in there and start dancing."

"Yes, you can. Nothing happened out here. You saw nobody, you were never here at all. Okay?" Julia held the woman away from her and held her eyes. "Okay?"

"Yes…okay. I wasn't here."

"Find the guy and go to the front of the bandstand and start dancing."

"But what are you going to do?"

"It doesn't matter what I do. Just dance like crazy. Everyone should be watching you by the end of this number. Whatever happens after that, you have got to be as surprised as everyone else. Understand?"

The woman nodded quickly. "Yes, I was never here." Then she turned and ran toward the far end of the building staying out of the open lawn and skirting the bushes. She stopped once and looked back toward the shadows, but Julia waved her on.

When the woman had slipped back into the ballroom Julia turned to the body on the ground. The stone in the creek had already been washed clean and she stooped to wash the blood off her hands, wiping them dry on her dark skirt. She stooped down and rifled the man's pockets, rolling his body from one side to another, being sure to remove anything of value. Then she walked over next to the wall and dug a hole in the soft earth. Once the items were buried and the ground smoothed to look undisturbed she stopped to listen to the music. The last drum solo's crescendo had reached its zenith as she washed her hands again and she stood and looked down at the man below her.

When the music finally stopped and the wild applause had tapered off, she began to scream. Once she started it seemed that she couldn't stop. The screams rose up from her core and continued long and loud. She screamed all the screams she'd been holding in for so long, and even when people came running across the lawn in her direction she continued to scream.

A few Military Police were in attendance and they were the first to try to determine what had happened. In the confusion they spoke with her. She told them that she had been hot and come out for some air. She'd heard a scuffle in the bushes and some shouting and when she investigated she saw a man stooping over a body. When she began to scream he ran away, headed for the street beyond the hotel. She gave them a fake name, and when they took off chasing the assailant, she went back into the ballroom. She saw Dusty among the people who had stayed inside and she walked up to him. "Dusty, I need you to take me away from here now."

"What's going on Julia? What's happening out there?"

"I'll tell you later, but I need to leave here now. I just need to talk to someone for a minute."

She found the woman, near the bandstand. She leaned in, to whisper in her ear. "I am leaving now."

"But they might arrest me and ask about you," she said.

"They are not going to do either of those things. You were never outside; you don't know me. Even if they do find me, I never saw you with that monster."

The young woman nodded as Julia walked away.

"Dusty, I am going to go to the ladies' room. You need to go wait in your car until I get there. We need to get out of here before the police come."

He nodded his assent and nonchalantly sidled his way toward the lobby and the parking lot beyond it.

Julia reached the battle wagon just as the police cars roared up to the building, sirens screaming. Dusty started the car and slowly made his way to the furthest exit, headlights out. Once he was out on the roadway he turned on his lights and drove on, not sure where he was supposed to be going, but anxious to get away from whatever Julia was running from.

CHAPTER FIFTY

September 1944

Julia sat rigid in the car seat; her hands clasped tightly in her lap. Even in the dark her face showed deathly pale as silent tears ran down her face.

Dusty swung the battle wagon onto the highway and drove south toward the beach house instead of taking her home in this condition. Molly would shoot him and ask questions later if he brought her in like this.

The dark highway unwound before them. Neither of them spoke, but Julia continued to cry quietly. He reached into his jacket pocket and pulled out the silky handkerchief he'd just bought and held it out to her. After a few seconds she reached out and took the offering. By the time he pulled up in front of the beach house the crying had stopped and he thought she might have fallen asleep. The house was dark and just beyond it the moonlight shone on the crests of the small waves lapping against the shore. He stared out at the sea for a moment, not quite sure what he should do next. It startled him when she spoke.

"Where are we?" Her voice was calm and sad.

"We're at my place. Don't be afraid. I just didn't want to take you home so upset."

"I'm never afraid of you, Dusty."

"That's good. Sometimes I thought you were."

"No."

Both of them sat silently, staring into the night for some time.

"Do you want to come in for a few minutes? Wash your face…?"

She nodded and opened the door of the car, stepping out onto the crushed shells and sand of the driveway.

The moon was full and they had no trouble finding their way to the door.

Once the door was closed Dusty turned on a lamp. Heavy blackout curtains obscured the view from the windows. Julia was listless as though everything had been drained from her. She looked around the room curiously. She remembered this place from when they first came to Los Angeles. A pair of reading glasses and a stack of books sat on the end table. One book lay open on the sofa next to a crocheted blanket she assumed came with the house.

Funny, she'd never thought of Dusty as a reader. She looked at him speculatively, wondering what he looked like wearing the glasses.

Once they were in the house Dusty wasn't sure what to do. He'd acted from concern when he'd taken her from the club, but there hadn't been an actual plan.

He went into the small kitchen and came back with two glasses and a half bottle of whiskey. He poured two fingers in each glass and held one out to her.

"I don't need that," she said and waved it away.

"We both need it." He proffered it again and she took it from him.

Julia walked to the window and slid the curtain back the smallest crack so that she could look out on the peaceful sea. She sipped her drink. The whiskey burned her throat on the way down.

Watching her, Dusty realized he'd always thought that there was something underneath her quiet reserve, a sadness and fear of being seen.

"I suppose I should explain." Julia turned toward Dusty.

"You don't have to explain anything to me. I'm going to turn the lights off and open the drapes so we can watch the water."

Julia didn't object so Dusty turned off the lamp and pulled the cord parting the drapes. The moon was bright. The waves lapping against the expanse of sand ran up in endless ruffles of white. Two overstuffed chairs sat turned partly toward the window and Dusty sank into one. After a moment Julia sat in the other and they both stared out the window lost in their own thoughts.

Julia set down her glass and leaned her head back against the cushion. She sat that way for so long that Dusty thought she might have fallen asleep.

"Sometimes it is easier to talk in the dark." Her voice was quiet and calm. "Doctors should try getting you to talk in the darkness. Maybe police, too."

When Dusty didn't say anything, Julia continued. "I found that dead man outside the hotel tonight. I met him once before but I don't know his name. He attacked me, raped me…and there was nothing I could do to stop him."

She fell into silence once more, her head still back, her eyes still closed.

"I was in the Navy, a WAVE, stationed at the hospital in Bethesda."

Dusty was surprised but did not react. He'd learned long ago with skittish horses to not make sudden movements or speak when it wasn't necessary.

"It was not great, but it seemed safe. Three meals a day and I felt like I was doing something, helping with the war, you know?" She opened her eyes and looked to him for an answer.

"Yes, I know. We all want to help if we can." Dusty picked up the whiskey bottle and poured himself another drink. He motioned the bottle toward her and she held out her glass.

"I bet you looked nice in the uniform."

She smiled. "I did. I felt proud of myself for the first time in my life."

The smile left her face. "I had a friend in New York City and she wanted me to come visit, see her apartment, show me the town. I took the train up and when I got to Grand Central Station I went out onto 42nd Street and flagged down a cab, just like they do in the movies. I was in my uniform, you have to wear your uniform, and I had her address written down on a paper in my purse."

Several minutes passed. Dusty could picture Julia in her uniform, excited to be in the city, giving the address to the strange man driving the cab. Why did we trust those strangers with our lives? What was it that made us think that a cabbie was safer than another stranger?

"I was overwhelmed by the city, it was all so confusing, and we seemed to drive for a long time, through busy streets and then through some neighborhoods with kids playing in the streets and people mowing lawns, then the houses got fewer and there were factory buildings. We had gone over some bridge and we didn't seem to be in a city at all.

"I asked the driver when we would get there and he said, 'almost there.' He turned onto a side street with a sort of barn or stable there and he stopped. That man, from the dance tonight, same uniform, walked out of the shadows and opened the door. I didn't know what was happening and I started to scream when he pulled me out of the cab. He laughed and said, 'There's nobody out here to hear you,' and slammed the door, waving the driver away. The driver just waved back and drove off. I kept screaming and struggled against him but he dragged me into the building, into the darkness, and he slapped me across the face. 'Shut up, whore."

"When he was finished he got off me, refastened his pants, dusted off his uniform and left me lying there. I wanted to just stay lying there but I was afraid he'd come back so I got up and tried to clean myself up. I went out to the street and walked until I found a busier street with a bus route. I took three buses to get back to Grand Central Station and I got on the train and went back to Bethesda. I never contacted my friend and I never told anyone what happened, until now."

Dusty wanted to ask why she didn't go to the police, why she didn't tell the Navy, why she didn't *do* something. But he knew the answer, so he kept his anger and arguments to himself.

"I couldn't work; I couldn't eat. I couldn't sleep. When I got down to a hundred pounds the Navy decided I must be sick and they discharged me. They gave me my pay and put me on a bus home, and that's how you found me in Dallas."

"What happened tonight? Why did you follow him outside?"

There was a long silence before she spoke again. "When I saw him tonight I was terrified, but angry, too. I saw him go out the door into the gardens, and I couldn't help but follow him. I didn't know what I was going to do, but I was just drawn to follow him."

"Did you see him when you got outside?"

"I didn't really see anyone and I started walking down the path, and then I saw someone dash out of the bushes and run toward the highway."

Again, there was a long pause. "I came to the creek and saw him lying next to it. I just started screaming."

Finally, she spoke again. "I'm sorry if I got you into trouble tonight."

"No trouble…"

"The police will probably come looking for us."

"I doubt that. In the first place, nobody at that club knows you, or saw you with him. What did you tell the military police?"

"I gave them a name, not my real name, and I described seeing the man running away. I didn't tell them I had seen the dead man before. I couldn't. How would I explain being there."

"Didn't they ask you what you were doing out in the dark?"

"No, after I said I saw someone running away they headed off in that direction. They said they'd talk to me more later."

"That must be when you came to find me."

"Yes…I couldn't answer any more questions."

The darkness and the quiet closed around them. Dusty's head had begun to swim from the whiskey and then he woke with a start sometime later. Julia still sat staring out the window.

CHAPTER FIFTY-ONE

October 1944

Julia sat quietly on the bench in the train station, her two bags at her feet. Here she was, running away again. It seemed like she'd been running from something or other her whole life. Would she ever just find a place to be?

The train to San Francisco would be leaving in about an hour and she clung tightly to her ticket. She was excited to be going to someplace new but felt guilty about the way she was leaving.

She'd sidled down the stairs with her suitcases and paused only long enough to leave a brief note and a few dollars on the kitchen table. Molly or Dorothy would find it when they woke up. She imagined that her disappearance would be the topic of much speculation in the boarding house until something more interesting happened.

The cab she had called waited for her on the street and she didn't look back at the house as they pulled away from the curb.

Her friends had scattered: Jack was dead, Lucy and the baby were with Jack's family in Arkansas, Tilda had moved to the mansion high in the canyon, and Dusty had found his way to contribute to the war.

"The train to San Francisco is now boarding. Please proceed to your assigned track." The loudspeaker echoed through the cavernous building.

Julia stood and picked up her bags. She'd been surprised to have to buy a second suitcase but had accumulated more possessions than she'd had when she came to Los Angeles. She'd have to cull through them before long. It served her well to travel light.

She took a seat on the left side of the train car so that she could see the ocean and placed her bags in the overhead compartment.

When they pulled away from the station she closed her eyes. The sway and rattle of the train lulled her into a trance-like sleep full of images and memories. She smiled to herself.

"Excuse me, ma'am, is this seat taken?"

Julia looked up into a man's smiling face. "Dusty…what are you doing here?"

"Looks like we're both doing the same thing, heading for San Francisco. Mind if I sit down?"

"No…I mean, of course not. Sit down, please."

The tall man took the seat across from her. "It's taken me about an hour to decide whether I should speak to you."

"Are you following me, Dusty?"

"See, now? That's why I wasn't going to speak to you. I thought you might think I was following you."

"Are you?"

"No, ma'am, we just happen to both be on the same train. Kind of like we were just both on our way to Los Angeles, last year. Must be destiny." Dusty laughed.

Julia smiled, not really sure if she believed him. "It is quite a coincidence."

"Well, I'm on my way to meet with Henry Kaiser, so not too unexpected. Where are you headed?"

"Oh, I'm just going to see a friend for a few days."

Dusty leaned toward her. "Is this trip really necessary? You don't want to be upsetting Uncle Sam."

"Well, it's not an important trip, like yours, but it is necessary to me." Julia didn't exactly say "It's none of your business," but it was implied by her tone.

Not taking offense Dusty took off his hat and set it on the seat next to him, leaned back and closed his eyes.

The train stopped briefly in Santa Barbara. The city sat like a jewel on the edge of the sea and Julia wondered, for a moment, if she should just get off here.

"Nice little town." Dusty's voice interrupted her reverie.

"Yes, it's very pretty. Have you have been here, before?"

"No, I've never been to San Francisco, either. I am looking forward to it. Have you been there?"

"No, I've never been there. Does Mr. Kaiser have offices there?"

"He has a big shipyard east of the city. I hear they are building ships faster than the Japs can sink them."

"Well, I guess that's a good thing. Are you going to build ships with him?"

"No, I don't know anything about ships; never even been on a boat. We'll be working together to build houses for all the GI's when they come home from the war."

"If they ever come home." Julia sounded wistful.

"Oh, they'll be coming home before long, or most of them, and they are going to need homes for those families they are dreaming of making."

"I suppose so. Having a family and a nice home is the dream, isn't it?"

"Yes, ma'am, Mr. Kaiser and I think so, anyways."

Several minutes passed before Dusty spoke again. "I'm going to go looking for something to eat. I think there's a dining car on this train. Would you care to come along?"

"I don't think so, Dusty. But, if you find a stray sandwich along the way, I wouldn't mind that. I'm not picky."

"Okay, then, a sandwich it is."

When Dusty had gone in search of a meal, Julia closed her eyes again and wondered where her next adventure would take her.

She had fallen asleep when Dusty returned with a bottle of Coke, a cheese sandwich, and a cookie. He placed the food carefully on the seat next to her and then wandered off to check out the rest of the train.

It was growing dark outside when Julia woke up and she sat for some minutes gazing at the moonlight shining on the ocean. She imagined that there were small towns and residences along the way, but the West Coast was still under blackout orders and little could be seen of the seaside population.

Spying the food sitting beside her, she realized she was famished and quickly downed the meal.

As the train came closer to the city of San Francisco, there were more buildings and homes, but they, too, were dark after the sun set. Even the "city on the hills" was dim.

As the train pulled into the station Dusty returned for his bag and helped her with hers.

"There you go, Julia," he said as he set her bags down on the platform. "Do you want to share a cab? I'm headed for the Fairmont, but I could drop you wherever you need to go."

"No thanks, Dusty. Actually, my friend will be meeting me but she must be running late. I'll just wait here for her."

"All right, then I'll be going." Dusty started away toward the cabstand but turned back. "Hey, would you like to have dinner with me tomorrow night? Your friend is welcome, too."

There was a long pause before Julia responded. "That would be lovely, Dusty. Can we just meet you someplace?"

"I'm staying at the Fairmont and I'm sure they have a good restaurant. I will meet the two of you there at six o'clock."

"Great. I'll see you then." Julia smiled brightly as Dusty turned and walked away. When she was sure he was gone she proceeded to the cabstand.

"Where to, lady?"

Julia was delighted that the cabbie was a woman. Her history of cab rides was not great. "Here's the address."

Dusty had made a reservation for three in the Venetian Room at six o'clock before he left for his meeting and returned to the hotel just in time. The meeting had been successful and he was thinking he might even spring for a bottle of champagne to celebrate.

"May I help you?" The maître d' was better dressed than most of the guests.

"Yes, I am Mr. Rhodes. I have a reservation for six o'clock."

"Ah, yes, Mr. Rhodes. I believe we have a message for you." The maître d' reached into a cubbyhole in the podium and withdrew a folded paper. "Here it is."

Dusty opened the note.

Dusty,

I am sorry but I will not be able to make dinner this evening. I hope your business meetings are successful.

Much love, Julia.

He folded the paper back up and slipped it into his pocket. "It looks like my date is standing me up. I won't need the reservation, after all." Then he turned and walked away before the other man could respond.

Outside the Fairmont Dusty gazed across the Pacific Union Club grounds to Grace Cathedral and then out toward the bay, obscured in the darkness. Henry Kaiser was a member of the distinguished Club and had invited him to dinner there, but Dusty had thought he had a date.

Julia had said she was just visiting San Francisco, but it struck him that he might never see her again. San Francisco was a big city and he had no idea where she was. The air from the water was chilling and he finally turned back to the hotel.

In another hotel in the city Julia stood at the window of her room and looked down on the busy street. She liked the feel of San Francisco; so different from anyplace she'd ever been.

She had found release from one secret, but now had another, worse one, to protect. She'd shared one with Dusty but could never share the other with anyone.

The radio in her room announced the call letters of KFRC and announced, "Here's a little number from our favorite British chanteuse, Vera Lynn. "We'll Meet Again.""

Julia walked to the radio and switched it off. For just a moment she regretted leaving Dusty hanging, but she knew he wasn't her future and thought he should be glad that she wasn't his.

She picked up her purse, the room key, and today's newspaper. "MCARTHUR RETURNS TO THE PHILIPPINES" blared the headline.

The restaurant in the hotel was not great, but she'd spotted a little café down the block. She would spend her time over dinner searching the ads for a job and a room for rent. She thought idly that it was a shame that when you ran off to someplace new you always had to take yourself with you.

END NOTE

More than 70 million people died in the war we know as World War II, 400,000 of them were Americans. All of our families were affected and changed forever. I wish that I had talked less and listened more to those family members who experienced what we can only imagine.

Use the QR Code below to enjoy British singer Vera Lynn singing "We'll Meet Again" for the Royal Air Force in 1943.